"Did you learn your mating from the beasts, then, princeling?"

Liam was trying to keep his breath still. Orla knew better. His body gleamed with sweat. He was no more in control than she.

"You will accept me as I wish," he grated, reaching out.

Orla whirled away.

"Didn't I tell you and all your friends already? I am the daughter of the queen. Not a hot fairy's passing recreation. Meet me face-to-face or not at all, lordling."

He glared at her as if she were the enemy. Her hands were clenched to keep from reaching for him. *Answer, damn you,* she wanted to cry. *Finish this.*

Books by Kathleen Korbel

Silhouette Nocturne

Dangerous Temptation #2
Dark Seduction #34
Deadly Redemption #47

*Daughters of Myth

KATHLEEN KORBEL

lives in St. Louis with her husband and two children. She devotes her time to enjoying her family, writing, avoiding anyone who tries to explain the intricacies of the computer and searching for the fabled housecleaning fairies. She's had her best luck with her writing—for which she's won numerous awards—and with her family, without whom she couldn't have managed any of the rest. Over the years, she's garnered a *Romantic Times BOOKreviews* award for Best New Category Author of 1987, the 1990 Romance Writers of America RITA® Award for Best Romantic Suspense, and the 1990 and 1992 RITA® awards for Best Long Category Romance. She still hasn't given up on those fairies, though.

KATHLEEN KORBEL

~~~

DEADLY REDEMPTION

Silhouette Books

nocturne™

SILHOUETTE BOOKS

®

ISBN-13: 978-0-373-61794-4
ISBN-10:   0-373-61794-1

DEADLY REDEMPTION

www.silhouettenocturne.com

Printed in U.S.A.

Dear Reader,

Patricia Veryan made me do it. Ever since I read her brilliant *The Dedicated Villain*, I fell in love with the idea of redeeming the villain. It's a delicate balance, to be sure, for the villain must be someone worth saving. I believe that Orla, the third of Mab's daughters, is plenty worth saving. Her only mistake is that she is too much like her mother—and too impatient for a throne she feels she deserves. But her mother is more than happy to teach her a much-needed lesson by making Orla a hostage bride to the warring fairy clan, the Tuatha de Dannen.

Another of my favorite story lines is the marriage of convenience. I love putting two people in a confined emotional space—especially two proud, strong-willed people—and letting them duke it out. For poor Orla, I've added the spice of having her be a warrior princess from a matriarchal clan who suddenly finds herself nothing more than a second-class citizen in a patriarchal world. Even worse, Orla has had all her special powers revoked. She really has no idea who she is or how to go on. The fun for me was seeing just how she does. I hope it's just as much fun for you.

Slainte,

Kathleen

To Kieran.
I hope you like my picture of you.

Prologue

The queen was courting disaster. And she was using her daughter as bait.

"Please, lady," the boy begged as he stood before her in the rising wind of another storm. "Reconsider this action."

The queen stood tall on the Plain of Gates, where battle had only recently raged. She turned and looked high up Knocknarea Mountain to where her predecessor's cairn was silhouetted against the racing clouds.

"Tell me again, child," she said, her voice liquid in the turbulent air. "What is your position in this clan?"

The boy rolled his eyes. He wasn't one to play the games that amused the queen. "I am your seer, lady. He who detects the patterns of past, present and future in the weave of time."

"Ah," she said with a small nod, still not facing him. "Then you are *not* queen."

He battled a sigh. "No. I advise only. And I advise you to hold your action. She is your daughter. The last who can take the throne when you go."

"Maybe," she said. "Maybe not. She grievously disappointed me, seer."

"It is ever the way of children and parents, my queen."

That got her to finally turn around, her ghostly blond hair lifting like a heavy banner in the wind. She offered the boy a wry smile. "You would know this with your centuries of experience?"

"I would know it from observing," he said, his dimple showing. "It's my job."

She considered him for a minute, then shook her head. "And mine is to discard your advice if I so deem."

He reached out a small hand, but did not touch her. Faint sunlight glinted off the burnished copper of his hair. "Don't discard this. You know what the *Dubhlainn Sidhe* are capable of. You cannot be so angry you would offer her up to them."

The queen's smile was not as delighted now. "Oh, I can, seer. I can. And I think I will."

Without another word, the queen simply strolled away and left the boy with his misgivings. He saw what she refused to: the nightmares to be visited on her youngest daughter, the isolation, the pain. Orla had been foolish, there was no question. But even her crime didn't warrant the punishment about to be meted out. No crime warranted that.

There was nothing the boy could do to stop it, though. Bowing his head with the weight of things no small boy should carry, he went in search of the queen's daughter.

Chapter 1

They found her on the mountain. It wasn't uncommon for Orla to visit it. After all, it was the burial site of her ancestress, the first Mab, greatest queen in the history of faerie. Here that lady's cairn rose fifty feet off the bald rock summit at the edge of the sea. Here the world she had ruled lay spread out before her like a vast emerald-and-sapphire blanket.

Orla loved the view. Ireland's curious patchwork green stretched across the gentle valleys, and mountains crowned with the cairns of other ancestors rose to claim much of the horizon. The ocean commanded the rest.

The sun was setting, raining silver upon the roiling pewter waves. A band of thick, dark clouds had begun to climb the distant mountains, and the wind was rising. Another storm was coming, and Orla would greet it from this place of greatest power and danger. She wished to challenge it at its most primal. She yearned to wash herself in it and cleanse away the sins that had brought her here.

Nothing could do that, though. The funeral pyres had been lit the night before. She would never be able to reclaim the voices silenced because of her impatience.

"Lady," a voice said from behind her.

She ignored it as long as she could. The wind had risen, and it battered at her face and clothing, cold fingers of accusation flaying her. Thunder rumbled and cracked, and lightning forked among the thunderheads that writhed over the northern horizon. She was so taken up in it that she'd failed to hear anyone approach.

"Your pardon, my princess," the voice spoke again, a voice she knew well, "but it is the queen."

Orla turned to see her personal guard, Declan, standing behind her. A tall, proud elven prince, Declan had been sworn to the queen's service and acquitted himself well in the recent battle with the *Dubhlainn Sidhe*. If Orla had been the fairy she'd been only days ago, she would have liked nothing better than to pull him down onto this bare, rocky earth and wear him out with a bit of gymnastic sex. Nothing scratched the itch of moral discomfort like the blank surprise in a man's eyes as she gifted him with his climax.

But nothing was the same as it had been only days ago.

"Ah, Declan," she said, looking back to where the last of the blue sky was being swallowed by the storm. "I don't suppose herself would be in a mood to wait, would she? I'm thinking this is going to be a storm worthy of tale-telling."

For a great, braw elf, Declan had an amusing reticence around lightning. "She didn't have the sound of a patient woman about her, lady," he said with a wary eye northward. "She sent the seer along with me. He waits below."

Orla nodded and pulled a strand of wind-whipped hair from her mouth. She wouldn't even have enough time for the rain. Ah, well, so be it. She owed her mother her attention.

"Have the pyres been cleared, then?" she asked, as if it made no difference.

"Aye, lady. The ashes of the honored dead have been collected for interment at Imbolc."

Burial in the earth in the dead of winter. It made Orla shiver. Given her druthers, sure wouldn't she rather be put down just as the new sun rose to promise the spring? Even if she weren't there with the ashes, but in the land of the west, as promised. The earth was just too cold and dark a place for any bit of a person to inhabit for long.

"Grand, Declan. Just grand." Finally despairing of the rain she'd so hoped for, Orla turned her feet down the mountain. "Well, then, we wouldn't want to keep the queen waiting now, would we?"

"Nay, lady." Even Declan knew better than to cause the queen any disturbance at all. "We wouldn't that."

Odd, Orla thought when she stepped into the imperial meadow that held the queen's throne, a great, gnarled oak that had bent itself to its primary purpose. Her mother didn't look impatient at all. She looked…smug.

Orla's steps faltered a bit at the realization. She stopped several feet from where Mab sat her oak throne in icy dignity, the throngs of faerie gathered around her. Fairies of all kinds populated the glen: trooping fairies in their somber gray; sprites tucked up in the leaves of the trees; brownies and flower fairies and gnomes, clustered like stands of wild iris in the soft grass.

Orla considered their number and found her steps slowing even further. It was time, then. Her mother was about to deliver her sentence. In all her fairy years, Orla had never known real fear. Not until recently, anyway. Not until she'd let her heart rule her head.

She felt fear now, sure. She trembled with it. If Mab thought she'd found a punishment greater than the taking of Orla's gifts from her, then it must be dire. It must be everything Orla deserved.

"Ah, then, you've been found, little girl," Mab greeted her in a fearsomely mild tone.

All among the ranks of faerie turned their faces toward Orla, and each face reflected her own fear. All knew the meaning when Mab's voice grew quiet.

Suddenly Orla missed her sisters, and who would have thought it? But if she had to have the truth on her, she had to admit that no matter her indiscretions, her sisters had always stood at her side. And it was her fault they didn't this day. Goddess, she hadn't even said a proper goodbye to them, either Nuala or Sorcha. And here she stood, alone for the first time in her life.

"I have, my queen," she said, and forced herself to walk closer. As surreptitiously as possible—for it never served to betray weakness to the queen—Orla drew a shaky breath and went down on a knee before the great queen of the *Tuatha de Dannan,* mightiest clan of the world of faerie. "I await your pleasure."

"My pleasure, Orla?" the queen echoed, tilting her elegant head to the side. "Do you indeed?"

Orla raised her head to face her mother. Groveling earned nothing but disdain from the great Mab, and Orla wouldn't abide her mother's disdain, even if it was all she had left of her. "I do, my queen."

"I have already taken from you your position as *leannan sidhe,* now, isn't that correct? You no longer hold the power to ensorcel mortal men. Is that punishment enough, do you think, for the crime of treason?"

It was obvious her mother didn't think so. *A mistake,* she wanted to cry and bury her face in her mother's lap. *It was a stupid mistake.* She should have known, though, that even for a good cause, a bad idea came back to haunt you. The good idea had been to make her mother see that the heir she'd picked was unsuitable. The bad act had been inviting the enemy into her world to help demonstrate that fact. Instead, he'd stolen the Coilin Stone.

Orla tried to stem her panic at the thought of how much she missed her power rings, for hadn't her mother already stripped her of them? Citrine and smoky quartz, the colors of mystery, of primal urge, of the magic that made mortal men her sexual slaves. The stones of the *leannan sidhe.*

Now her fingers were bare, and it shamed her. Now she looked to a man and no longer remembered how to bring him to his knees. It frightened her, for what else was there for her?

"It is not my opinion that matters, lady," she said. "I will pay whatever price you ask. It is my fault, and my punishment to bear."

The storm clouds fingered the near mountains and sent a wash of wind before them to lift the banner of Mab's moon-hued hair. Her pale, ivory skin seemed to glow from within, and her spring-green eyes smiled at her daughter without humor. Raising a languid hand, she motioned Orla to her feet.

"Sure, we're all glad you know that, little girl. I'm sure it would have made your sisters' exiles easier to have heard it before they left. It would have sent the dead more peacefully to their graves, now, wouldn't it?"

Orla refused to look away, even as she writhed inside at her mother's denunciation. "I imagine it would, lady. I'm afraid I was never given the chance to say so till now."

Orla thought for sure that Mab would punish her for her words. Capricious Mab did nothing more than smile. "Indeed. But we've all had a battle to clean up after, then, haven't we? And your sister Sorcha to be sent on her quest."

Orla nodded as regally as her mother. "Indeed."

"Seer," the queen called without breaking eye contact with her daughter. "Will you tell this daughter of mine what is at stake because of her small rebellion?"

Orla almost groaned. Sure, no one could twist the knife like her lady mother.

The boy Kieran stepped forward, an odd, grave frown on his bright face. "I caution you, lady—"

The queen swung on him. "Is it a new seer you're wishin' me to get, young Kieran?"

The boy gave her a resigned smile. "You cannot, my queen. It is our dual lot to share this time."

"Then I'd be obliged if you'd make it as easy as possible."

Orla watched the two of them share some private communication. In the end, though, the boy shrugged. She thought sure he muttered something under his breath about being glad to get back home. Leave it to her mother, then, to be given a seer who was as human as he was fairy. No other seer Orla knew of had to get back across the veil so he didn't miss basketball practice.

"There are three great stones," he intoned, his eyes closed, his copper hair gleaming like burnished metal in the watery light. "Donelle, ruler of them all, who lives in the Land of the West. Coilin the Virile, who balances the matriarchal *Tuatha* clan with his presence in their crown. And Dearann the Fruitful, she who gentles the patriarchal *Dubhlainn Sidhe*."

And what happened to the Lady Dearann? Orla intoned in her head, too tired of the story to give it the reverence it was due.

"But grievous to the heart of faerie," the little boy went on, as if answering, "Dearann was lost these many years past to the world of mortals."

"And who goes to find it?" the queen asked, as if Orla didn't know or feel guilty enough about it.

"The Royal Princess Sorcha."

"And what of the great Coilin Stone, seer?"

Kieran shot Orla a look, and she swore he looked as if he pitied her. She pulled herself to attention. She loathed pity.

"The *Tuatha* grew powerful with their Coilin Stone, leaving the *Dubhlainn Sidhe* resentful and dark for want of power or a female influence. In desperation, the *Dubhlainn Sidhe* have stolen the Coilin Stone."

"Ah," the queen said, as if hearing the story for the first time. "And what will happen if this great stone stays with the Faerie of the Dark Sword?"

Another look, another blast of pity. "All life will fail."

The queen said nothing. She simply lifted her hand to the great ancient oak in whose lowest branch she was poised. And as Orla knew they would, every eye followed to see what Orla hadn't yet. She gasped.

The leaves were falling.

The tree was dying.

Orla had never been one to wallow in the old lore. That had been her sister Sorcha's role. But Orla recognized this sign of disaster and, as her mother had wanted, was stricken by the sharp edge of grief.

"All life will fail," Mab repeated, in case anyone in the glen had missed the seer's meaning. "What must we do, seer?"

"My queen—"

"What has the queen declared?"

"The Dearann Stone must be recovered and given to the *Dubhlainn Sidhe*. The Coilin Stone must be returned to the *Tuatha* to restore balance."

"And in the meantime? To keep the *Dubhlainn* quiet?"

Kieran looked as if he were suffering actual physical pain. Orla held her breath. The only sound in the glen was the rumble of distant thunder over Maeve's Cairn.

"A gift, your majesty."

"A gift, is it?" she echoed. "And what kind of gift are you thinking?"

Kieran gave Orla such a look of pain that she knew, even before he said it. She braced herself all the same. "A daughter," he said, his voice hushed.

The glen erupted in noise. Wings battered the unsettled air. Voices tangled, inchoate cries of distress. Orla might not be the favorite of Mab's daughters, but she was a royal princess. To send her to the enemy…!

Orla met her mother's gaze. She trembled, and wondered if her mother knew. She hoped not. She refused to quail before this edict. Before the end of her world as she knew it.

The *Dubhlainn Sidhe* were monsters, destroyers of

dreams and dealers in darkness. They stole souls and ate hope. And her mother was delivering her up to them.

For just a moment Orla remembered the only *Dubhlainn Sidhe* she'd ever met. The one she'd let inside her mother's realm without anticipating his perfidy. He'd ridden a fire-eyed horse, black as death, galloping over the waves on the darkest of nights, his horse black, his attire black, his hair black, his eyes bottomless pools of night. A shiver ran through her at the memory.

He'd terrified her. He'd mesmerized her.

He'd betrayed her.

She wanted nothing to do with him or his people.

"What will you, my lady?" she asked her mother.

When her mother told her, she reeled back as if she'd been struck. "You want me to *what*?"

They found him on the mountain. Liam had gone there, as had been his custom since the day of the great battle, to pay honor to the valiant dead, to the memory of his friends, to the ghost of lost possibilities.

He went to assuage his guilt.

And now they had come for him, and they had a way for him to do just that.

"I am honored by your concern for me, my king," he said with a low bow to his uncle, Cathal, the king of the *Dubhlainn Sidhe,* when he reached him in the fairy glen. "How may I best serve you?"

His uncle was an austere man, for all that he was the lord of the *Dubhlainn Sidhe.* Tall and dignified, he wore colors that were muted, and a crown that was a simple circle of bronze. He had not worn the high crown since its great stone, the female force Dearann, had been lost years upon years before Liam's birth. There were rumors floating about that a search had been set under way to reclaim her. Liam didn't know about that. It wasn't his business. His business was to protect what the *Dubh-lainn Sidhe* had, not seek what they didn't.

Except once. Once he'd faced a temptation greater than any and succumbed to it. And by the high god, look where that had gotten them.

"Be seated here," the king offered, showing him the low, sleek chair alongside the great throne. Only those the king honored sat there, as he no longer had a queen.

Liam looked at the swooping line of the backless chair and felt a frisson of unease. The king wanted something of him, something important. Something Liam had a feeling he would not want to give. He wished they'd never found him atop his lonely perch in the rocky arms of Sliabh Corcra.

He eased his backside down onto the smooth, black bog oak, conscious of the fact that a warrior had no business in the queen's chair. He was afraid he would shatter the delicate thing.

"Rest easy," Cathal reassured him with a gentle smile. "That chair has withstood much more than your over-large frame."

It didn't make Liam feel appreciably better. "What is it you ask of me, my king?" he asked.

Again the king smiled, his ancient eyes wry and knowing. There were times when Liam thought the history of the world of faerie rested in those eyes. That and more, mysteries beyond the ken even of the fair folk. The king was as pale as Liam was dark, a sleek, silent being who ruled in whispers. He had been tested in the forges of war and carried their scars on his brow.

"I ask you to make a sacrifice, Liam the Protector. I

ask it in the name of your people, in the name of your family. I ask it for the chance of peace between two great clans."

Liam kept his silence, but he realized he'd curled his hands into fists in his lap. "You have only to say it, lord."

For a moment the king looked away, into the shadows that ruled the edges of the world of faerie. The glen was a quiet place, spilling over with green and water and the most fragile of flowers. Cupped within its boundaries, the land echoed with the music of rushing water, the flutter of birds, the soughing of the firs in the breeze.

It was a place of peace, a refuge from the world the *Dubhlainn Sidhe* must patrol. It was an illusion, just the same. The high crags of the Reeks were where the *Dubhlainn Sidhe* truly belonged, the desolate heights at the edge of emptiness. Or so thought Liam.

"The queen of the *Tuatha de Dannan* has contacted me about a truce," Cathal said in a soft voice that nevertheless carried terrible command.

"Why should we need a truce?" Liam asked. "We hold the power of their Coilin Stone."

He knew. He'd recovered it himself, a red-hot energy that filled a man with fight and fury. He'd carried it back to present it at this very throne, to make up for the eternal grief his clan had so long suffered from the loss of the Dearann Stone.

"She offers a sacrifice to us," Cathal said as if he hadn't heard. "A great sacrifice indeed, and I believe her offer to be both gracious and sincere."

"And my part in this sacrifice?"

The king looked at him, and Liam felt the command of the king to the very core of his fairy soul.

"You are the recipient."

* * *

They met at the border between their realms, a deep forest that existed only in the world of faerie. Mortals saw patchwork fields and fuchsia hedges, and wondered why they heard whispers at dusk. A vast contingent of the *Tuatha* approached the woods on soft gray horses, in the air, on the petals of the flowers that spread across the edges of the forest. Bright pennants flapped to declare each subclan, and the silver bells of fairy bridles caroled in the morning air. Orla rode at their head, clad in fairy gray, her crown a burden, her back as straight as a blade as she suffered the trip by horseback.

Horses, she thought impatiently. Couldn't we for once use the feet the goddess gave us? To be forever dependent on these arrogant beasts was more than a princess should have to tolerate.

Beneath her, the horse snorted with impatience.

Even worse, the bloody beast could hear her, even in silence. Intrusive, prideful creatures altogether. Well, she let hers hear her opinion of his species, because sure, wasn't it better than thinking about what really troubled her this day? What had brought her down the long distances to the gate into the world of the *Dubhlainn Sidhe.*

"You must begin as you mean to go on, my lady," Kieran said from his smaller mount alongside.

Orla didn't even bother to look over at him. "And what is that supposed to mean, seer?"

The little boy looked so solemn, so sincere. "You have much to deal with. You must take it on your terms."

"On my terms? Not my mother's? Not the king of the *Dubhlainn Sidhe?* Not my new *husband's?*"

Husband. Not even consort, which she would have

more easily accepted. Consorts came and went, depending on the wishes of each. The condition for this pact was marriage, though, and that meant that whatever came, she would be shackled to her *Dubhlainn Sidhe* husband until their ship sailed for the West.

Whatever came. She thought she would be ill.

Kieran answered as if he'd heard her. "If anyone can triumph, lady, it will be you."

"Don't bother with flattery, Kieran," she said, not taking her eyes from where the forest floor darkened to unnatural shadow. "This is no contest, and well you know it. It is punishment."

"Only if you see it that way."

She turned on him. "How else should I see it, then, seer? The queen has stripped me of my powers. I was *leannan sidhe.* I was the greatest, the most feared and coveted by mortal men for the skill of my seductions. But that is gone. And she has given me nothing in return. Not even new rings, new colors to reflect my soul."

"But that isn't who you are anymore."

And finally she spoke of what made her quake. "And who, then, am I, seer?"

The little boy faced forward. "That is for you to discover, my lady. It is time."

She caught her breath. Behind her, the horde came to a halt, setting the silver bridle bells ringing. At the head of the massive honor guard, Declan unfurled the great *Tuatha* banner, with its sickle moon aloft among the spreading branches of a great oak tree. Sprites fluttered into Orla's vision to take up position, and Kieran resettled in his saddle. With a hiss, a hundred swords were drawn from scabbards. The statement was made: *This is our princess. Disdain her at your peril.*

The *Dubhlainn Sidhe* materialized out of the shadows. A great army on black warhorses, with their own air fairies to attend them beating the air in among the heavy-branched trees, and half-seen flags curling in a sultry dance. Orla saw the black face of those flags and fought a shiver of dread. This was her future. A place without light or hope or grace. A nation represented by a dark sword on a darker flag. It was her penance for the rest of her long fairy life.

The two armies faced each other in absolute silence, even the great trees of the elven forest aware and waiting. Orla swore she could hear the collected heartbeats of her people and wondered if she would ever hear them again.

Enough! She was a princess royal, and this was her destiny. She might bring nothing to these people: no gift, no strength. But sure, they didn't have to know it. And the least she could offer her own clan was her dignity.

Begin as you mean to go on. Ah, well, she had no choice, then, did she? She edged her horse forward toward the invisible line that divided the two worlds. Her fairy heart battered at her chest, but none of them needed the knowing of it.

A husband from this grim group, was it? She couldn't see that there was any difference among them, all pale as night and grim-eyed as death. There was no one she would choose of her own will.

Then a single rider separated himself from the forces around him and approached. The breath hissed in Orla's throat.

No.

Not him. Goddess, you couldn't mean to visit such a sad farce on me.

"Greetings, wife," Liam the Protector greeted her, his own posture as rigid as the mountains that waited at his back.

He sat his horse like a prince, his black cloak lifting in the wind, his hair gleaming blue-black like a raven's feather, almost as black as his bottomless eyes. His posture was rigid, his cheek and nose and chin carved from the very granite beneath their horses' feet. The last time Orla had seen him had been in the teeth of a storm. It had been a moment when she'd found herself attracted, intrigued. But that had been before he'd stolen the Coilin Stone and sent them all to war.

And this was the fairy she was to take to her body for the rest of her days. How her mother must be smiling.

"Greetings, Lordling," she answered with perfect poise, as if the very sight of his hawklike face didn't set her pulse to hammering. Ah, goddess, but wasn't her punishment at least beautiful on the eyes? Couldn't she smell the power in him? "Have they decided the penance for our impulsiveness should be an eternity of wedded bliss?"

His answering smile was infinitesimal. "Evidently. You agree?"

"I am Mab's subject. I obey."

There was a tiny frown now. "But do you agree?"

Orla tilted her head. "Don't you see me sitting before you?"

Another dark fairy approached and swung from his mount on silver-shod feet. An old fairy, withered and white and just a bit stooped. His colors reflected the moon on the sea, and she knew she saw a priest. Clad in bright blue robes and crystal diadem, her own priestess, Areinh, dismounted, as well, to stand just before the other at the line that divided light from dark.

It was how Orla saw it. Night and day, the celestial white of the *Tuatha* and the midnight ebon of the *Dubh-lainn.* But not a night that was familiar to her, who so loved the moon and her children the stars. That night was magic and restful; it brought inspiration and mystery. This darkness was…empty. Threatening. Terrible.

Again she fought a shiver of despair. Did her mother now hate her so much? She hadn't even left her with weapons to protect herself.

"It is up to you," Kieran said in a whisper, as if that were some kind of answer.

"We begin," the *Dubhlainn* priest intoned in a sonorous voice, his hands raised, his head bowed.

"We begin," the priestess echoed, her own head up so that the cornstalk-yellow of her hair caught the edge of the sun and the goddess could see her eyes.

The ceremony took forever. First the two celebrants intoned the lineage of the couple, one after another. Then they called on Kieran to speak of the weaving of two mighty clans into one.

"In the days of our beginnings," he said, his high, piping voice like a bell in the still air, "the clans of the *Tuatha* and the *Dubhlainn* were as one. Two sides of the same whole, male and female, strength and gentleness, dark and light. The stones kept us and guided us, and to the great god and goddess we give thanks for their light. May this day set us back on the course of harmony."

Not in your lifetime, Orla thought grimly as she surveyed the faces of her new clan. *They greet this action with no more enthusiasm than I.* At best, they would ignore her. At worst…

Even she didn't have the imagination to contemplate the worst.

"So be it," Liam said without noticeable enthusiasm and swung down from his horse.

"So be it," Orla said, and did the same.

The two approached the dividing line, and the priest and priestess asked them to join hands. Orla felt a hot jolt up her arm at his touch and kept rigidly still so he couldn't know.

"From this day forward you cleave to your wife and meet her," the wizened old man intoned, eyes closed, "spirit to spirit, body to body, mind to mind, heart to heart. From this day she is of your clan, and you of hers. From this day she is yours to protect and provide for and bring peace to, till the day the ships sail. Do you so vow, Liam the Protector of the house of the Royal Princess Maeve and the Elven Prince Kilell?"

Orla could actually hear the fairy prince gnash his teeth. Once he said the words, there was no turning back.

"This I so vow," he said, his face expressionless, his gaze on his priest rather than his wife, his hand barely touching hers in ritual contact.

"From this day forward," the priestess Areinh intoned, her voice sweet as the wind, "you cleave to your husband and meet him, spirit to spirit, body to body, mind to mind, heart to heart. From this day he is of your clan and you of his. From this day he is yours to comfort and care for and bring peace to—"

"And protect," Orla inserted. "Do not forget protect."

She could hear the *Dubhlainn* suck in startled breaths, and it wasn't just the interruption of a sacred ritual.

"If you are of my clan also," she said to her husband, who was finally meeting her gaze, "you will accept this vow from me. The *Tuatha* do not stand aside if their men go into battle."

She could see eyes widen among the women in the shadows. She didn't care.

Liam glared at her. "No."

She nodded. "Fine. Then we all go home."

She could feel the fury radiate off him. She almost bowed before it, it was so fierce. But sure, he'd agreed to this farce as much as she and would lose face by stepping aside.

He turned to the priestess. "Say it," he grated out, and turned his face aside.

Orla could have sworn Areinh battled a smile. "And protect," she said, "until the ships sail. Do you so vow this, Orla, Princess Royal of the House of Mab and Ardai, Lord of Storms?"

Liam refused to face her. Orla refused to look away. "I so vow," she said in the same voice she used to call her troops to battle.

Both priest and priestess bowed their heads. "Then so be it in the sight of the great god Lugh and the goddess Danu."

It was over, then. Orla was committed to these people who resented her and this man who hated her. Ah, well, she'd said she would pay her penance, hadn't she?

She would walk away from her people now, leave everything that was familiar. Liam stepped away from her and held up a hand. One of his guard trotted up leading a black mare with high, arched neck and flared nostrils. Orla could already hear the beast's objections at having to carry a *Tuatha.* Lovely.

She took a step forward. The *Dubhlainn* priest stopped her.

"You will remove all that you were," he said, reaching for a long, mud-brown robe. "You will return the stones of whom you have been and the garments that identified you in your world."

Ah, here it was, then. The truth so soon, whether she was ready or not. But they didn't need to see her fear. She was a queen's daughter. She straightened and stared down at the official.

"I beg your pardon," she said, looking down at the old man as she would have a too-familiar lackey.

"You choose to become a *Dubhlainn Sidhe*," Liam said without heat. "You will leave all you are behind."

"I strip for no one, lordling," she snapped.

"Lady," Kieran murmured.

Orla whipped around on him. "This you knew?" she demanded.

His troubled young eyes met hers without flinching. "It is up to you," he said too softly for anyone else to hear.

And this was to be her first test. Goddess.

Nakedness was not the problem. Ah, sure, the world of faerie saw it as optional at the best of times. But in this place, it wasn't a choice. It was a statement. A way to show her how small her place would be in her new world. Could they hear her thoughts, after all, then? Could they smell her despair?

Well, they would see about that, then, wouldn't they?

Straightening until she thought her spine would snap, Orla turned. She glared at the man who was now her husband, lifted her intricate bronze crown from her brow and handed it to Areinh. Then, facing her new clan, she raised her hands and slowly, so no one could mistake her intent, spread her fingers.

A gasp went up from the *Dubhlainn Sidhe*. She had no stones to sacrifice. *What did it mean?* She could hear them think the words in their little minds. She ignored them. Her attention was for the man who was now her husband. She measured the widening of his eyes, the clenching of his jaw. And then slowly, in challenge rather than submission, she stepped out of her wedding robe and stood before him as naked as the day of her birth.

He took a slow, long look down her body, all the way to her toes. Then he ran his eyes back up her, as if they were his hands on her. She stood tall and silent and proud, and no matter the provocation, kept her flushes away and her eyes on him. She would not let him humiliate her before her people and her goddess.

"Fine," Liam said, reaching out a hand. "Now we consummate this."

"Here?" she heard Kieran gasp.

Liam nodded. "Here."

Chapter 2

Orla smiled. She had no idea whether Liam's clan understood, but every fairy in her own clan took a step back.

"We will consummate the marriage, aye," she said in her quietest, deadliest voice. "But we will do it as celebration. *Not*—" she met him eye-to-eye, so there was no question "—as a conquest. For there is no conquest here, Liam the Protector. Is there?"

"There is submission," he said, looking more irritable then mighty. "It is your obligation."

"I have fulfilled my obligation," she said, ramrod straight with pride. "You may have my cooperation, my felicitation, even my delectation. If you wish for submission, however, might I suggest ensorceling some poor mortal woman? Faith, it's not hard to do. As the last *leannan sidhe,* sure I could show you how—if you can't manage the task on your own."

The air fairly crackled with tension.

Ah, well, more than tension, Orla admitted. For all that she never would have chosen this punishment, sure, wasn't it a braw one that set her pulses racing and her skin prickling and anxious? Wasn't he every bit as compelling as he'd been that midnight they'd met by the ocean? Sure, she would be more than happy to welcome his touch. Just standing so close made her breasts tight with the wanting of him.

But as a wife. Not as a hostage, no matter what her mother might have offered.

She just hoped none of these fairies could hear the thundering of her heart.

If only she still had her own rings...

"I come freely, priest," she said to the wizened little man who stood silently next to her husband. "I have walked away from my world and stand now in yours. But I am a Princess of the Blood and wife to this man. Not consort. I will not suffer your coercion. Am I understood?"

"You would say you don't want me?" Liam asked, his voice purring like a great cat's.

Orla laughed. "Don't be daft. A fairy would have to be ashes not to want you. But that isn't the point at all, now, is it, my lad? And sure, it can't be that you need to test for my chastity. If so, you should have presented yourself a good eon past, before I offered my maidenhead to the goddess on my Rite of Passage." She let an eyebrow drift north. "Or is it *your* chastity we're testing this day, lordling?"

She thought she actually heard a snicker behind her. The prince was not amused.

"We test your merit as the wife of the king's kin," he said.

Faith, he did know how to rile her, then, didn't he? "I am the queen's daughter," she said with every bit of imperious pride that had been bred into her. "You have no right to ask more."

All about them, the legion of faerie stayed silent and still. She swore they were holding their collective breath in dread of the heated words being exchanged. Orla paid them no mind. She was waging battle. And by the great queen Eriu, she thought wearily, wasn't it only the first? What had her mother brought her to?

Before Orla could think of another objection, her new husband reached down to grab the hem of his tunic. In one swift movement he pulled it over his head and handed it to the priest. Then, without taking his eyes from her, he divested himself of his leggings to stand before her as naked as she.

Ah, goddess, what an unfair advantage! He had to know he was magnificent. Orla heard the feminine sighs of appreciation from both sides of the border. She felt the unmistakable flush of hunger seep into her bones and flesh. He was granite and moonlight and the deep sounding of the sea. He carried new scars on his mighty chest and stood on the legs of a warrior. And his proud cock stood tall and hard.

"And I desire you, Orla, daughter of Mab," he said. "What is wanted is the ritual."

Orla had to wet her lips with her tongue so she could speak. "Then build me a hall, fairy prince. A grove of trees to rest in, so I know you honor me. I am not sport."

"No," he answered, his deep, deep eyes setting loose sparks in her. "You are not sport."

It seemed he was having trouble concentrating, as well. "Priest?" he asked without taking his eyes from her.

"We must have proof," the little man protested.

"Great-horned moon," a slim fairy chortled alongside him. "The sparks these two set off will make the fireworks of Beltaine look like wills-o'-the-wisp. I can live with just the imagining of it in my head. Can't you, old man?"

Orla chanced pulling her gaze from her new husband to assess this unexpected champion. "So you suffer no confusion, little man," she said to him, "my sparks will be the scarlet ones."

The fairy was slim and sweet-faced and almost comically dramatic. "Well, since our Liam's here will be a grand gold, we should have quite a show, then, shouldn't we?"

"Enough," Liam growled without looking away from her.

"And who are you who keeps track of a man's sex-lights?" Orla asked the newcomer.

The exquisitely pale fairy waved a languid hand that carried rings on four of its fingers. Excessive indeed. "My dear princess," he said with a sweet smile and a courtly bow, as if he were in a great hall rather than standing before two naked fairies in the dusk. "I am the Stone Keeper. It is I who will redress you to reflect the gifts you bring us."

I bring no gifts, Orla almost admitted. "Well, then, I'd best consider you a friend, hadn't I?"

He tilted his head and laid a hand on one slim hip. "Oh, I think there's no question about that, lady. Don't I just adore a bit of fire in a woman?"

"Stone Keeper," Liam warned.

"Well, didn't I need to have the time to have your hall woven, then?" he demanded. "It just needed a minute, and now it awaits you while you think more on setting the night afire. Now then, priest, what say you?"

Orla watched as the *Dubhlainn Sidhe* priest consulted with her priestess. She imagined they reached an agreement. She didn't care. Sure, the minute she'd turned back to her husband she'd found herself taken up with the heat of those eyes, with the wanting of those hips grinding against hers. Her mother might have taken the powers of the *leannan sidhe* from her, but, sure, she hadn't stolen the wanting. Orla hadn't wanted even the throne of faerie this badly.

"It is acceptable," the grave old man intoned. "We will wait."

Faith. Just in time. Liam said not a word, just grabbed Orla by the hand and pulled her after him into the deep shadows of the woods. Later, she was sure, she would think about how dark and cool it was here. Later she might wonder how she could be comfortable in a place with no light, no warmth and precious little laughter. Later she might even wish she could have pulled him into her light, instead.

Now she could think of nothing but wrapping her body about his. About mating with him, tongue and hands and cock. She lost her breath with the scent of him, a mixture of smoke and night and the sharp pines of the forest. She clenched her free hand to keep from reaching out to him first. She was hot and cold and hungry with the waiting for him, and she hadn't even taken the time to climb into his head for the beginning of the dance.

And she knew he felt the same. Goddess, it pulsed off him. It gleamed in the sweat on his skin. It vibrated in the very air about him. Orla wasn't sure they were even going to make it inside the small house he led her to. An upended basket of trees, it was, a simple shelter that

wore leaves for its roof. A holy place woven of the
sacred woods, the nine of life: oak, alder, willow, hazel,
hawthorn, birch, rowan, yew and elm, each waiting to
bless this union between the fairy clans, each demanding the acknowledgment of ritual.

Orla should have been afraid. She didn't know how to
mate without her gifts of seduction. She had no knowledge
of her own worth. Worse, she tasted yearning, and it was
a new and terrible thing for her. A *leannan sidhe* did not
yearn. She was the one others yearned *for.* This ache sat
uncomfortably on her, a wanting of something more than
flesh and heat and completion. This need to see his eyes,
to hear his cries, to hold him even when they were done.

She hated that—and she didn't care. She followed
him a step past the door and waited as he turned for her.
For a heartbeat, two, they stared at each other, eyes
almost black with arousal, nostrils flared to catch the
scent of it, bodies poised on the edge of insanity.

"You will accept my seed," Liam the Avenger demanded, not moving.

Orla battled back her uncertainty. "I will *take* your
seed," she countered, and prayed he didn't realize that
she trembled from more than wanting. She waited, the
breath caught high in her chest, terrified that this would
all go wrong.

He said not another word. Just caught her face in his
hands and opened his mouth over hers. He meant to
consume her; she could taste it. His lips were unbearably
soft, but they commanded; they seized rather than
courted. He pulled a response from her that all but
buckled her knees. She wanted this—she wanted *him*—
and was terrified with this wanting, but she couldn't let
him take control.

Reaching up, she grabbed fistfuls of his hair and pulled him hard to her. She met him mouth to mouth, tongue to tongue, hungry teeth to hungry teeth. They battled, they parried, they nipped and tasted and supped from each other until Orla could feel the velvet of his cock against her belly, until he captured her groans with his kiss, until she was melting with the taste and touch and scent of him. Fairy tastes, cinnamon and honey. Fairy scents, the clean pine of the forest, the air of the mountain, the salt of the sea.

He pulled her fully against him, and he measured the length of her with his hands. He was not gentle; she hadn't expected it. She didn't want it. She wanted him to challenge her to her limit. She wanted to match him move for move. She wanted his mouth and his satin-sleek hair and the powerful lines of his throat. She wanted to run her tongue along those new scars they had caused together and bite his belly where the skin was soft. She wanted him inside her, and she wanted it now.

There were no love words, no sighs of contentment, no laughter. There was a deep, intense silence broken only by the slide of hands, the moist music of kisses, the high hum of impatience.

Ah, goddess, his hands, his broad warrior's hands, his callused, clever hands, sweeping over her like a brand. Ah, his mouth, his hot, deep, sweet mouth, that marked every inch of her. His back and belly and thighs, sculpted from living flesh for the sole purpose of pleasuring her. He claimed her, but she claimed him, as well, marking every inch of his skin with her touch, claiming the sweep of muscle and tendon and the unyielding edge of bone with hand and tongue and skin.

She was so lost in sensation she almost failed to feel

him turn her, face to the wall. She felt him wrap his hand around the back of her neck and bend her over, so that he would mount her from behind. A position of submission. A statement more powerful than this mating. She was so lost she almost didn't care.

Begin as you mean to go on.

Goddess. She *didn't* care. She wanted him *in* her.

Within a breath of losing herself to him, she ducked under his hand and spun away from him. Panting as if she'd run all the way here from her own great hall, she balanced on her feet, prepared for attack. Her body screeched in impatience. *Now,* it demanded. *Satisfy me.*

"Did you learn your mating from the beasts, then, princeling?" she demanded, swiping her tangled hair out of her eyes.

Goddess, she didn't want to let him hear the fear in her voice, the overwhelming urge to just turn around and succumb so she could feel him impale her right there against the rough wood wall.

He was trying to keep his breathing still. She knew better. He gleamed with sweat, and his cock was rock-hard. He was no more in control than she was.

"You will accept me as I wish," he grated, reaching out.

She whirled away again.

"I think not. Didn't I tell you and all your friends already? I am daughter of the queen. Not a hot fairy's passing recreation. Meet me face-to-face or meet me not at all, lordling."

Her hands were clenched to keep from reaching for him. Her nipples were as taut as his cock. She could feel her own juices dampening her thighs. *Answer, damn you,* she wanted to shriek. *Finish this.*

He shook with the struggle to keep control. He glared

at her as if she were the enemy. "You are such a prude you cannot accept invention?"

She actually laughed. "I was *leannan sidhe,* lordling. I could shatter you with my invention. But now, my armies need to return home. Do we set off those lights or go home without honor?"

His movement was quick and hard. He reached to grab her. She stepped back just out of his reach.

"A fairy does not harm," she said, glaring herself.

"Well, that would depend on how well you accommodate me, wouldn't it?" he asked.

The size of him should have made her faint. It made her all the hungrier.

"Elven-made you are," she admitted, melting all the more for the sight of that size, "but I'm a strong woman, or else I'd not swear to defend you in battle. Now choose, princeling."

Another heartbeat. A breath. A stretching of the near-silence to tearing.

"I agree," he finally said. "Now come here."

She allowed him this small victory. She went to him. The minute they touched, lightning sparked fierce in them. They wrapped themselves in each other's arms and plunged into each other's heat. They found the earth somehow and stretched out on the sweet, soft grass so he could take his time savoring her breasts, so she could close her eyes against the exquisite pain of his suckling, so she could curl around him like a vine.

He slipped his cunning fingers along her belly and then down as she arched toward him, toward the hard ache deep in her, toward the empty ache of her, into the hottest core of her. He stroked, he slipped in and out, he tormented her to the point of madness until she could stand no more, so she pushed him back and went down on him, took that lovely hard length of him in her mouth, teasing it with her teeth, with her tongue and fingers and the flat of her palm, until he rumbled like a nearing storm.

The world went away, lost beyond her frantic need for completion, her hot craving for his touch, for the satin feel of him, for the slide of his skin against hers and his mouth on her mouth, for his fingers deep inside her and the arrogance of his cock in her hand. There was only the two of them and the sanctuary of this living hall in the deep woods, and the battle to meet as equals in this odd dance of dominance.

Again he pushed her legs open. This time she let him, welcomed him, pulling away from his kiss to meet him eye-to-eye as he paused, breathless, on the edge of that terrible precipice, trembling and hard-eyed. She smiled, but it wasn't a smile of submission. It was the smile of conquest, and he knew it, and he smiled back and drove into her.

Oh no, oh no, she thought vaguely, as he filled her, as he stretched her impossibly wide. He fits too well. He feels as if he belongs here, as if he's always belonged here, and how do I deal with that? How do I meet him as an equal when I know it will come to needing him? When it seems that after this I won't be whole anymore?

She wished she could close her eyes, wished she could just surrender and be done with it. She couldn't, though, could she? For he would never let her fight her way back. So she kept her eyes open. She met his black, black eyes with honesty, with the hunger she had for him, with the pride of her ancestry, with her challenge to his dominance, and she met him, thrust for thrust, reveling in the way he filled her, in the abrasion of the grass against her back as he rocked her, harder and harder, faster, until the hard, hot pain of arousal gathered, until it tightened, pulling at her feet and her arms and her eyes, until she saw his climax coming and knew that she would crest with him, a detonation of light and scent and lightning that would sweep everything before it.

And, oh, it did, obliterating the sun and setting off fireworks and splintering the day with white-hot light, until she keened with it, the joy too great to hold in, even as he reared back, his mouth gaping, and gave one great cry as he spilled himself deep, deep inside her where she would never lose him, not even if he lost her, not even then.

And then the two of them collapsed, still entangled with each other, arms and legs, hearts still thundering in tandem, bodies slick with sweat and sharp with the scent of climax, and lit by the dying embers of their sex-lights, a shower of red and gold sparks that floated away into the trees.

Orla lay there, surrounded by him, and she knew real fear.

She'd meant to show him that no one dominated Orla, daughter of a queen. She'd done nothing more than lose herself, and she had no idea what came next. She just knew that she could no longer be satisfied alone, and that was too great a power to give a man—especially an enemy.

"Is it enough for them, do you think?" she asked, her eyes closed and her ears filled with the sound of his slowing heart.

He made no move to comfort her or settle her. Orla thought his arms were still around her because he simply didn't have the strength to move them. "It'll have to be, won't it?" he said. "Sure, I'll not do it again."

Orla raised her head so she could see his expression. "Because you obviously found it so distasteful."

His hair tangled and his chest still heaving, he didn't so much as smile. "From now on our mating will be our business."

She nodded. "Ah, grand. I thought for a minute you'd gone all monkish on me."

"No matter if you were cross-eyed and spavined, I'd take you as is my duty to my king."

"And a way with the words on ya, too."

"It's all you'll get."

She closed her eyes again, wishing herself anywhere else. "Ah, and who could ask for more?"

For a second she thought he might actually have reached for her cheek. She swore there was a breath of movement against her. But when she opened her eyes, he was just watching her, his expression bemused.

"Well, if you bring nothing else to this farce," he said at last, "at least you bring passion."

Ah, well, then, and wasn't that just the sum of her life? And him still so magically wrought that she could drown in him like a fast-running river.

"So it's a romantic man they've given me, then, is it?" she asked.

"They gave you nothing," he said. Untangling himself from her, he climbed to his feet as if they hadn't just set the afternoon sky afire. "They imposed a life sentence on us. Get dressed, princess. We return to report this folly to the king."

Without so much as a look to where she still lay sprawled, heavy-lidded and flushed on the ground, he walked out of the hall and into the sunlight. Orla lay back and wished her mother had simply run her through with the dullest fairy blade in existence and been done with it. The pain would have been easier.

Chapter 3

The house of Liam the Protector reflected the man. Set between the hard rise of a mountain and the meandering dance of a stream, it was square and practical and spare. It wasn't that it was badly made or miserly, just the space of a man who put no store in comfort. Orla took one look at it and wondered what she was supposed to do with it.

"You're to be presented to the king tonight at the banquet," Liam said, setting down his sword and dagger on the bare wood table in his front room. There weren't even any rugs on the floor. "One of the women will bring the rest of your clothing. Since you will not be given your own raiment or stones until Eibhear names them, you will remain in the color you wear."

"Eibhear?" she asked, standing flat-footed in the doorway and feeling a strong lack of welcome within these walls.

Liam stopped where he was ladling himself out some water. "The Stone Keeper."

Orla couldn't help but laugh, thinking of the fussy little creature who had saved her from consummating her marriage in public. "Him? Named 'strong as a bear'? Sure, the goddess has a sense of humor."

Liam turned on her. "The god. The *Dubhlainn Sidhe* follow Lugh. You will also."

Orla bit her tongue. "He's that jealous of his power he can't acknowledge the creation of the goddess?"

"He has no need of her, as we don't."

Orla shook her head. "Well, sure, isn't that spoken like a man? And without the female, who would do the birthin', I'd like to know? It's a sure thing no man would."

Liam's frown was as mighty as his shoulders. "Don't be spouting such blasphemy beyond these walls, woman. It would be sore resented."

Orla raised an eyebrow. "More resented than it is inside them?"

Liam straightened and closed his eyes, as if praying for patience. "It's going to be a long life if we can't agree."

"It'll be a sure sight longer if you can't compromise. Faith, have you so soon forgotten the part about how I'm of your clan and you're of mine? Did it mean nothing to you?"

He let loose an inelegant snort. "By the great stones of *Cúchulainn,* you don't believe that drivel, do you?"

Orla fought for patience. Was this what the minutes of her life would amount to, then? Bickering over every word she uttered?

"Give me enough room to breathe, Liam the Protector, and I'll do the same for you."

He lifted an imperious eyebrow. "You'll do nothing

for me, woman, but cook and clean and be available for the convenience of my cock. Are we clear on that?"

Immediately images exploded in her head: the hot, carnal touch of him back in the little hall. The delicious pain of fullness when he drove into her. Goddess, he could coerce a woman into surrender, so he could.

But she saw the same images reach him, too. His eyes darkened. His pupils flared, even as he stood before her, tight-lipped and silent.

So even though her own skin skittered with the memories, she slowly straightened, her shoulders back, her head high. Sure, he didn't need to know she was sweating with the sudden heat—and more so with the fear of her next move. Would he take away even the lovemaking if she challenged him?

Ah, well, there was nothing for it but to find out.

"I'll be and do what the goddess wants of me," she said in her most regal tones. "When I have the time for your little friend Eibhear, we'll know just what that is, then, won't we?"

"What you were wasn't enough?"

Ah, it was all-out war, then.

"What I was, was criminally naive. Sure, didn't I let an enemy through my gates and count on his honor to protect me?"

He flinched as if she'd struck him. "I'm thinking we might not want to be discussing honor when the last time you saw me it was to ask me to drive a mortal to madness for you, princess."

Orla lost her breath entirely. Ah, he knew where to hurt, this beautiful man did. "And we were both wrong," she said. "He didn't have the protection for it, and it hurt him."

"I know it well, lady. I also know that if you'd been

in my place, you wouldn't have wasted your chance at the Coilin Stone, either. You think my people don't deserve it, after the site of the Dearann Stone has been hidden this long while?"

"I think you were inexcusably lax to lose the thing in the first place."

He leaned over her, as if his size would add weight to his argument. "I'd say that the jury still has to be out, sure, on just what word should be used in the case of the Dearann Stone. How are we to know, then, that the *Tuatha* didn't steal it themselves and aren't keeping it hidden away where its rightful owners can't find it?"

It was Orla's turn to do the eyebrow trick. "We know because if the *Tuatha* had had both stones, sure, we would have wiped you out of existence long since. Once we get it back when you've failed, though, we might just be kind enough to let you see it."

He laughed again and backed up. "You really think you'll find it when generations of *Dubhlainn* couldn't?"

She laughed right back. "I think you couldn't find the door if the knob's in front of you."

He leaned even closer. "Sure, I can find your cunny with my cock."

"Only if it's here to find. Keep speaking to a princess of the realm that way, little man, and you won't even have a sock to shove that thing into."

His laugh was full-throated. "'Little man'?" he demanded, incredulous. "You screeched like a mare in heat when you took me inside you, woman."

"Just as you did when you did the driving. When I say 'little,' I speak of your spirit, little man, not your various appendages. I'll blame that elven sire of yours for those. It certainly couldn't have been your fairy mother."

"You'll never speak ill of my mother."

"As you won't mine. And that includes accusing her of the petty theft of your stone. Are we agreed?"

"Great gods of thunder," a lilting voice interrupted from the doorway. "Agree on *something* before the entire village shows up outside for the entertainment. I could hear you all the way to the borderlands."

Orla turned to find Eibhear himself leaning his slim, puce-clad hip against the doorway, and wasn't he grinning like a fool?

"You feel you have the right to trespass on private conversations now, Eibhear?" Liam demanded.

Eibhear's laugh was tinkly and light. "Well, now, I'd say no, if the conversations were actually private. But your uncle the king asked me to break up the noise down here so he could get some work done."

For a second Liam just stood still, as if struggling for control. Then he grabbed his long gray cape and stalked to the door. "Grand," he snapped. "You keep her company if you want to. I'm full to my teeth with her."

Eibhear gracefully stepped aside. "From the looks of the fireworks over the ceremonial hall," he muttered, "I'd say it was the other way around, altogether, wasn't it?"

Liam screeched to a halt, mere inches from the smaller fairy, and bent over him. "And that'll be the last of our business you'll be involved in, Eibhear son of Bran."

Eibhear just grinned. "Not if you can't find a way to lower your voice when you share love words with your wife, it won't."

Liam evidently had nothing to say to that. He straightened and swirled his cape around his shoulder, barely missing Eibhear's nose. "I'll be with the *Coimirceoiri*," he literally growled. "And won't guarding the borders be a better way to spend the day than dancing with the likes of you two?"

"Borders?" Orla retorted, her temper lighting her fear. "What do you bother with the border for? Am I not enough of a payment for peace between us?"

Liam stopped stone cold. "And you think you're the only enemy that prowls the edges of our lands, do you?"

She blinked. "Aren't we?"

His smile was almost feral, and it frightened her all over again. "Ah, little fairy princess. Don't you have a lot to learn, now, about being a *Dubhlainn Sidhe?*"

"Well, she won't be learning it if you're out prancing among the high mountains," Eibhear said.

"You teach her, Stone Keeper. I have real work to do."

"Ah, sure, you already did the real work, lad. And wasn't the king fair generous to offer it to you?"

Liam's nostrils actually flared. But he said not another word, just pushed past the little man and stormed out of the house.

Left behind, all Orla could think was that the very air had left the room with him. That terrible thing returned, the yearning she wanted nothing to do with. It ached in her chest like an infection and robbed her of her breath. It made her watch him as if the mere sight of him were food and drink as he strode down the dusty lane, his stride long and strong, his shadow eating the ground before him.

She would *not* lose herself to him. She couldn't afford to. But goddess, it was all she could do to keep her feet where they were. She trembled with the wanting of him. Her body remembered him in all the private places only a fierce, hard man could touch.

Rather than make a fool of herself, she deliberately

turned away from the door. She looked around for a comfortable chair, but sure, there wasn't a one of them. She was reduced to the hard-backed little dining chair by the front window.

"A force of nature is our Liam," Eibhear said gently as he took up the other chair.

Orla's laugh sounded sore, even to her. "Well, speaking as the sapling in his way," she said, rubbing at the bridge of her nose, "I can't say I appreciate the grandeur of him."

"Ah, sure you can and all," Eibhear disagreed with a delicate wave of his beringed hand. "Doesn't he just take some getting used to?"

"Battle takes some getting used to, little man. Cataclysm. Disaster. He's beyond me entirely."

For a second she was greeted with silence. She looked up to see a curiously familiar light in Eibhear's eyes. Faith, didn't he have the look of Kieran himself about him?

"Ah," she said wearily. "You're going to be after tellin' me that it's up to me what I make of this particular disaster, aren't you?"

"Well, then, there's one stone you've already earned for your rings," he said gaily. "Sure, don't you demand the moonstone for the sight, then, girl?"

She closed her eyes. "There's no sight involved," she said. "Wasn't our own seer at this advice long before you?"

He was studying her; she knew the feel of it, even from behind her eyelids.

"What stones would you be wanting to replace your own, then, fairy princess?" he asked.

Finally Orla opened her eyes. "You ask me an unanswerable question, Stone Keeper."

"Can I ask what happened to the stones you had?"

She looked out into the afternoon, where the rhythms of a fairy village carried on beyond her reach. Gray-clad women gathered by the well. On the green, children sat in a little cluster around a gentle-faced old woman who was obviously telling them stories. A group of men passed on horseback, their black attire well matched to their black steeds, which were fiercer than any fairy horse she'd ever seen. Smoke curled from the little houses, and flowers topped the fences. This place looked so achingly like her own, but just that much different at the same time.

"The colors are so dim here," she found herself saying. "Does no one wear anything brighter than gray?"

"Maybe that's the task you're sent to perform, daughter of Mab. Maybe it's color you're bringing to this fairy realm."

Orla just shook her head, sure he was wrong.

"My stones," she said, looking now at her empty fingers. Every person outside this house had stones of their own, down to the tiniest children, whose first stones had been bestowed on their naming day. She had nothing. *Nothing.*

"Sure, didn't I lose them by making the fatal mistake of letting your protector prince into my realm in the hopes he'd help me secure my mother's throne?" she said.

Eibhear stayed still. "There's nothing a queen resents more than someone after her place, now, is there?" he asked quietly.

"Ah, no," she said. "I can't have you speak so against her." Orla smiled. "Sure, she's a proud one. Wily and sly and terrible in her times. But it wasn't the trying for the throne that condemned me. It was the dishonor I brought my people by torturing a guest at my mother's court. Worse, it was the death I brought to my clan and the forfeiting of our great Coilin Stone that cost me my place. Charges I deserved altogether, I'd think. Wouldn't you?"

"Aye," he said honestly. "I'd have to say I would."

She nodded, her gaze on the sky outside, her attention on her loss. "I was the *leannan sidhe*. It was my goddess gift and my purpose. And, oh, Stone Keeper, wasn't I the best, a legend among mortal men, proud of my own place and secure in it. Now, though, my sins have cost me all I know."

"You wore citrine and smoky quartz, then?" he asked.

She could do no more than nod, the missing gems throbbing on her empty fingers.

He sat silent a bit longer. "No," he said. "They're your stones no longer, fairy princess."

And didn't she know that better than anyone? It was a fair chore to keep her voice calm and even. "And how do I find new ones, Eibhear?"

"Ah, well, I'm afraid that's a question I'm not allowed to answer, princess. Isn't it my job to be watching only?"

Orla couldn't help but nod her head. "I know it, Eibhear. My sister Sorcha is Stone Keeper of the *Tuatha*. Haven't I grown with her responsibilities alongside me all my life?"

"Then you know I can do nothing to help," he said, reaching out to lay a hand across hers.

It was the first sign of acceptance she'd received in this terrible place. Didn't it almost bring her to tears, when the last thing she could allow in her life here were tears? Still, she couldn't bring herself to take her hand back.

"I've gone on alone before, Eibhear. I know the way of it."

"Well, then, for now you must keep the brown, Orla, and the empty fingers, although through my office I can gift you with plain silver to keep the place of the stones, if you'd like."

"I thank you. I've not been without my rings in my memory."

He nodded, growing brisk as he retrieved his hand and stood. "Orla," he said, and smiled. "As misnamed as I am, aren't you the same, girl? 'Strength of a bear' indeed."

Orla followed to her feet, offering a wry smile of her own. "Aye, and my name means golden lady. Faith, the only thing golden about me was my stones, wasn't it?"

Eibhear tilted his head, his eyes mischievous. "Ah, now, I'm not so sure. Black-headed and green-eyed you might be, but I'm thinking there's gold in there somewhere, Orla, Mab's daughter."

Again she fought the sudden tightness in her throat. "We'll have to be after seeing about that, now, won't we, little man?"

Offering his arm as if escorting her to the throne, Eibhear smiled. "That we will, Orla. That we will."

And the two of them walked out the door to meet the village.

He had to get away from her. It was all Liam could think as he stalked through the glen toward the high mountains. He would patrol the wastelands where he could feel the wind against his face and watch the hawks spiral, where he could escape the overwhelming urge to throttle her. To bed her until she screamed again. He would break something with his hands just to hear the splintering of it, instead. He would escape for as long as he could from the disaster his uncle created for him.

A wife.

Gods, even a consort would have been more than he could handle right now, and he was stuck with a lifetime mate. And what a mate she was. Argumentative and proud and hard as penance. But, ah, couldn't he still smell her? Couldn't he hear the soft, breathy moans she'd gifted him with as he claimed her lithe, bright body?

She'd humbled him with her hunger. She'd met him toe-to-toe, eye-to-eye, and demanded as much from him as she herself gave. He'd never known such soul-searing heat, not in his long life. It wasn't that he hadn't ever enjoyed sex. It was a celebration, after all, a gift and a reward from the god that every fairy cherished.

But no fairy had ever met him with such fury in her eyes. None had left him battered and sated the way Orla, daughter of Mab, had. Not one had tempted him to allow her anything if she would only lie down with him again, or pushed him until he stood mere inches from murdering her.

His wife.

If only they could leave it at the sex and jettison the rest. He didn't want her in his house, in his head, in his heart. There was no room. Not now. Not ever.

"Well, and why aren't you home enjoying the love-lights of your new wife?" he heard behind him.

He didn't even break stride. The last thing he needed right now was the cajoling of friends. "Why aren't you patrolling the eastern borders, then, Faolán?"

"I've just come in," his friend said, stepping up along-side him. "It's quiet, but by the shriveled balls of old Aengus, I'm feeling itchy out there lately."

A redheaded fairy who stood several inches shorter than Liam, Faolán had a voice that could soothe a mad bull, and a grin that was guaranteed to court a lady. He was also Liam's Captain of the *Coimirceoiri*, and his best eyes at the front.

"Aye, me too," Liam admitted. "That's why the patrols have been stepped up."

Faolán flashed him a brash grin. "Faith, I thought it was because you thought we were all bored with the Coilin Stone safe in the Treasury and all. Which reminds me, now. Have you seen Cian about lately?"

"Keeper of the Treasury Keys?" Liam thought back to the moment he'd handed the Coilin Stone to the king. Cian had been standing behind him, impatient to lock the stone away where it could be safe.

Faolán nodded. "The keys are in their place. But sure, the key keeper isn't."

Liam snorted. "Faith, he's forever sulking about something. He's probably run back to his mother. Set somebody to looking, anyway."

"I already did. For now, don't I have far more important matters to address?"

Liam looked over to see him lift a hurling stick off his shoulder. "Is it practice you're off to, then?"

"If you're not too exhausted from all your fireworks," Faolán said, "we'll be at the great field."

Hurling. Exactly what he needed right now, a bit of mindless violence and enough sport to work out his devils. By the time they were finished, he would have just enough time to collect his wife for the banquet.

"My stick is at the house," he said.

"And you're too afraid to go back and get it?"

For the first time since he'd gotten the dire news of his punishment, Liam managed a smile. "Wouldn't you be?"

Faolán slapped him on the back and turned them for

the hurling field. "Ah, well, I'm sure there's someone with an extra stick for you. Since you haven't worked off your bad humors yet and all."

"With that woman?" Liam asked as if he actually were amused. "Faith, she'd argue about the position of the sun. There's no rest in that one."

Astonishment. That was what was in her. Awe. The kind of raw sensuality that brought strong men to their knees.

"She can sure take the eye of a man, though," Faolán said, he who had been at the forefront of Liam's honor guard that morning. "You know what she reminds me of?"

"Full-pitched battle?"

Faolán laughed. "Ah, no, man. She reminds me of a bird, all bright plumage and fluttering wings. She makes you want to hold her in your hand and stroke her, you know?"

He was right, of course. Liam had seen it right away, even in the darkness when he'd first met her at the edge of a storm, and he wondered now what had happened to the women of his own clan that this one fairy should stand out so with her raven hair and hot green eyes.

An exotic bird, and Liam knew the exact one Faolán meant. They'd come across it on one of their forays into the other realms on a mission to maintain peace. It was in the world of the yellow sky, and the bird had landed on a blue branch right in front of them, singing its heart out. Its wings had been so iridescent you couldn't quite tell the colors between emerald and sapphire and amethyst, and its song seduced with a rare, harsh beauty. A feathered jewel a man wanted to possess with everything he had.

On that plane, capturing such a creature was a crime and carried a punishment of madness. He wasn't so sure it wasn't the punishment on this plane, too.

"Well, now, the problem with this bird," he said, walking purposefully down the lane, "is that she'll be after changing everything about me. I'll get home from hurling, and won't there be rugs on the floors and curtains at the windows? Lacy, flouncy things a man would destroy with one wrong swipe of his hands." Wouldn't she move right in and push him to the periphery in his own home? And if she met him again as she had in that little hall, sweat-sheened and panting, he might just let her get away with it.

"And have you never had such comfort before?" Faolán asked.

"Sure, my consorts knew better."

His consorts. Another topic Liam couldn't address right now, another weight piled on his sore heart, and didn't Faolán know that, too?

The redhead clapped Liam on the back and handed over his own hurling stick.

"Ah, well, at least she'll probably be able to cook better than you."

"She's a royal princess," Liam snorted, weighing the beautifully balanced ash stick in his hands. "You think she can so much as recognize an egg in its shell?"

"I think she can tell the difference between venison and pudding."

Liam shot his friend a dark look. So his brief foray as a housekeeper had been a disaster. It still wasn't enough of a reason to wish a wife on him.

"It's a wager, then. If she can manage a full meal within the week, I'll offer up my own hurling stick," he said.

Faolán actually stumbled to a halt. "The one handed down from *Cúchulainn* himself?"

Cúchulainn, greatest of hurling champions. And there were few things a fairy honored more than a great hurler.

Liam looked into the afternoon sun. "Ah, sure, if she takes over my life, I won't have time for the game, anyway, will I?"

Faolán's smile was wolfish. "You'll be after knitting doilies."

"Baking cookies."

"Leaving the milk out for the cat."

Decorating the night with red and gold sparks. He would make sure of it. If she took over his life, he would be sure to take over hers, as well, and he wasn't sure he would ever let her out of bed.

Unless they made use of the stream. Or the dining table. Or the rocky ledges of Sliabh Corcra.

He didn't realize he was smiling until Faolán smacked him again. "Ah sure, it seems your penance isn't as bad as all that, now is it?"

"Oh, it's bad," Liam disagreed. "It's the worst."

But couldn't he at least enjoy the one benefit of it while surviving the cost?

He almost turned back from the hurling field. It was only Faolán's arm guiding him in the right direction that kept him going.

Later. Maybe later. After he figured out how to tame her.

Faolán laughed as if he'd heard the thought.

Dusk was falling. Fireflies danced among the tiny sprites who dwelt within the leaves of the trees. The dryads who inhabited the great oaks whispered to each other, and the children murmured sleepily from the little houses. The moon had risen and peeked her silver face from behind one of the sharp mountains that made up this place.

Orla didn't like those mountains. They were too harsh, too unrelenting. Too sharp and bare, with no softness to them anywhere, their shadows consuming the land. Much like her new husband.

He'd left the little house early in the afternoon and not returned since. And now she stood alone in the doorway of that house she didn't really belong to, watching the people making their way toward the great hall where the banquet would commence soon, and there was no one to escort her.

Where was he, then, this husband of hers? Why hadn't he come to escort her to meet his king? And if he didn't arrive, what was she to do? She'd walked around a bit that afternoon with Eibhear, but he'd gone long since to see to the preparation for a new babe's naming day, leaving her in her brown robes and plain silver rings to wait for her husband.

Who hadn't come.

Just how long was she supposed to wait? Was there anyone she could call on to escort her, instead? Who would welcome her to this most cherished ritual in the fairy world?

Not the women she'd met already, sure. To a person, they'd watched her with wary eyes and still tongues, obviously waiting for her to betray her unworthiness to be among them. Pale wraiths who inhabited the long shadows of this place, they'd mistrusted her for walking in the sun. Walking in the sun, she hadn't understood their preference for the dark.

The *bean tighe* had welcomed her, true. A tall, dignified woman with cautious eyes and upswept silver hair, she'd been nothing like the healer in Orla's own plane. Her very own Bea had been the most untidy, unlovely little being the goddess had ever put on a plane, some kind of cross between a gremlin and a brownie, with pointed ears and sparse brown hair. But she'd had the dearest, most whimsical eyes a child had ever seen.

It had been Bea who'd dispensed comfort when Mab's daughters had needed it. Bea who'd dispensed the secrets only a woman would know or need. This healer of the *Dubhlainn Sidhe*—who was worthy, sure and competent, Orla made no mistake—this *bean tighe* wouldn't be the one to take the fear of a woman's changes from a child. Orla couldn't imagine sending anyone to her who needed comfort.

But the woman had offered the only welcome Orla had received besides that of the capricious Eibhear. Other than those two, the *Dubhlainn Sidhe* had made it a point to stay away from Orla's house.

Liam's house. It was what each of them had called it, as if Orla had no rights to it. She stood in its doorway now, more alone than she'd ever felt in her life, and wondering how long she should wait for the husband who obviously wouldn't come. Wondering exactly how she should present herself to a strange king's court without the escort he'd specifically chosen for her.

It had been a little while since she'd seen the last fairy flitter toward the great hall at the edge of the trees, and Orla was still torn. Which would be more humiliating— showing up alone, or not at all? Pretending her husband had kept her late, or disdaining his absence? And what if he were in the hall before her, conveniently "forgetting" to come get her?

Well, there was only one way to find out.

She'd always thought she had courage to spare. After all, she'd conquered innumerable men. She'd led the great fairy archers into battle, with only her elven armor and her strength to protect her. But the effort to take the first step out of her house was almost too much for her.

She did it. One foot, then another, clad in soft brown shoes, beneath a dun-brown dress, the color muting her into invisibility. Making her a brown wren. Worse, making her *feel* like a brown wren, and sure, what was she to do with that?

Only keep walking.

She'd made it halfway to the edge of the little village before she heard it, a splashing and a curse coming from the stream. So focused was she on her progress that she almost didn't stop. But then she recognized that voice and turned.

She froze.

He was naked. Stepping up onto the bank of the tumbling stream, he was wet, shaking his head so his hair tumbled in damp curls at the edge of his jaw. He was gleaming in the fading light, and the scar on his chest stood out like a brand. Suddenly Orla couldn't breathe. She couldn't move. She couldn't believe it when she saw his cock stir and rise.

Finally she looked up to see him watching her just as closely.

"You're going somewhere, then, wife?" he asked, his voice as dark as the shadows that collected along the edges of the stream.

"I'm accepting the invitation the king offered me, husband. I decided that since every other fairy in the realm had already left, rather than insult my host, I should go, as well."

"Even if it meant insulting your husband by showing up alone?"

"And how was I to know he was still coming to escort me?"

For a moment it looked as if Liam might respond with an attack. Orla could even see him rise to the balls of his feet. Instead, he turned abruptly and yanked on his clothing.

"I was just washing off the men's business I'd been about this day," he said. "Working to protect my new wife from threats she doesn't see."

"Threats I'm sure she'd like to learn about—if her husband would stay near long enough to inform her."

Clad again in his deep, dramatic black, her husband stalked over to her and grabbed her by the elbow. "When the time is right. For now, the king awaits."

Orla had no choice but to walk with him. "Indeed? Had I but known…"

"Don't push me, wife. I've accepted this marriage. I will participate. When we get home tonight, I'll even pledge my devotion by setting off a shower of sex-lights that will keep the village awake. Until then, try to behave."

I'm not ready, she couldn't help but think. *Stop here. Reassure me that everything will be all right. That somewhere I'll find acceptance, even if not comfort, in this cold, dreary world. Promise me I won't live in regret the rest of my days. Lie if you have to, but promise, just for tonight.*

But Liam, not hearing her thoughts, remained silent, and Orla had to find her own courage as she walked to meet his king.

Chapter 4

They were indeed the last to arrive. Liam fought not to curse out loud. He hadn't meant to be so late, but the practice had gone so well, the teams streaming up and down the field like a mad, noisy ballet that excluded all thought and regret, that he'd been loathe to leave. In fact, except for Faolán, he'd been the last off the field.

It had been Faolán who reminded him that bathing might not come amiss, both for his wife's benefit and for the king's. Liam had been dunking himself in the stream when he'd seen the last of the village stragglers passing on their way to the hall.

And then he'd seen his wife. Head up, stride purposeful, as dignified as a priestess on her way to ritual as she'd deliberately put one foot in front of the other on her way to the hall. Alone. Not one of his acquaintances, it seemed, had offered to accompany her. Even her husband.

For a harsh moment Liam had hurt for her. He'd been beset by the guilt of his own selfishness. He knew good and well how the village would have greeted her. He knew that without his support, she would remain a suspected outsider. And he'd come within moments of condemning her to presenting herself to the king alone.

"You will make your bow to the king as we enter," he said, his hand stiff around her even stiffer elbow. "He will undoubtedly question you a bit. Try to be polite."

She stopped so fast she all but yanked him off his feet. "Are we about to begin this again, lordling?" she asked, her voice deadly quiet.

Liam found himself staring.

"For the second time in as many minutes," she said, "you have insulted not only me but my mother the queen by insinuating I know not how to behave in court. Insult me at your pleasure. I can do nothing to stop you. But insult my mother again, and I promise I will mete out judgment on you that will merit mention in the history of the *Dubhlainn Sidhe* for centuries to come."

Again he fought that instinctive flush of pride in her. Caught alone in a strange and alien land with a husband who had been at best curt with her, she could still stand up to him. And not for herself, though she most certainly deserved it. For her lady mother.

He surrendered and offered her a genuine bow of respect. "You shame me with the truth, lady. I apologize sincerely. I can only blame my words on my own feeling of dislocation since the king bade me to marry."

For a long moment she just stood there, her eyes dark, her brow creased in a frown that only made him want to ease it with his hands. Or his mouth. Finally, though, she nodded and turned back toward the hall.

"Thank you, husband," she said. "It was a gracious apology. I think it would behoove us to at least maintain a semblance of civility before your court and king. They need none of our personal business before them."

"No more than they already have?" he asked, actually grinning a bit.

She flashed him an answering grin. "Ah, well, I have a feeling that for a Stone Keeper, Eibhear isn't as good at keeping the secrets that don't affect his position as my sister Sorcha."

"Eibhear is an old woman with his gossip," he assured her. "But for all that, he's harmless."

"And a good friend."

"Better than your husband, certain."

"He doesn't sacrifice as much as my husband," she said.

He was sure he needed to answer that, but they had reached the doors of the hall. Two of the house guard snapped to attention and pulled the doors open. Liam heard Orla draw an uncertain breath, and he gave her elbow a gentle squeeze.

"If there is a quality you don't lack, wife," he said quietly as he stepped over the threshold with her, "it's courage. It won't fail you now."

He caught the look of astonishment she shot him before facing forward again, and almost smiled. Was she so unused to kindness, then?

Or only from him?

"Well, then, Liam the Protector," his king greeted them from the high dais. "You have brought me a new addition to our family, have you?"

The aisle was long to the front of the hall, the tables full with fairies and elves and all manner of beings who passed back and forth across the borders. Liam gave

Orla credit for not stumbling to a halt in astonishment at the sight of some of them. Gremlins sat alongside satyrs, who supped with green-skinned scalewyngs, and more than one pukka nibbled at whatever their current form demanded. All paused in meal and conversation to watch the protector guide his bride down the hall to greet the king.

"I beg your permission to make known to you my wife, lord." Liam spoke in the most ringing tones he could.

His voice echoed up among the high branches of the woven trees that made up the hall. Tucked in among the leaves that formed the canopy, tiny flower fairies hovered with the sprites to get a better view. Stately marching fairies stilled in their seats and puckish brownies peeked around the benches. Orla's reception here in his land would depend on what happened in the next few minutes.

Seated at his high table among his high court, Cathal the King wore no more than a simple bronze circlet for his crown, even though the Coilin Stone rested in his vaults.

Rested. Not the right word for the Coilin Stone, sure. Throbbed, hummed, pulsated with a crimson energy that made a fairy want to claim nations and conquer all. It radiated strength and purpose and invincibility, and Liam understood why the gods had kept it in a woman's crown. Sure, it burned the hands with its energy merely when held, and didn't he know it too well. Even so, he longed to see it in the crown of the *Dubhlainn Sidhe,* who had too long been without a power stone of any kind.

The king, for now, didn't seem to agree.

"Approach, nephew," Cathal intoned in the prescribed manner.

Liam guided his wife to the front of the hall and

bowed low to his king. Before he could cue her, Orla detached her arm from his hand and dropped into the most graceful full court curtsy Liam had ever witnessed. Head down, skirt spread, hands tipped in a salute of impeccable grace.

"Your grace, may I present Orla, daughter of Mab, high Queen of the *Tuatha de Dannan*," Liam said, announcing her name to the farthest corners of the hall so all would hear his pride.

He heard the rush of whispers behind him. He saw delight spark in his uncle's quiet eyes. In the alcove, the harpist halted midtune. In an unprecedented move, the king rose from his seat behind the great table and came around to personally lift Orla to her feet.

"Rise, daughter of the *Tuatha*," he greeted her. "You honor us with your salute."

"I've heard much of you, King of the *Dubhlainn Sidhe*," Orla said, her voice gentle and respectful.

If Liam hadn't known her well already, he would have looked more closely to make sure it was still she. She was smiling on his uncle with an instinctive dignity that betrayed, more than anything, her rightful place in court.

His uncle smiled down at her and gave her his hand. "Come sit with an old man and tell him stories of your people, girl."

She dipped her head and put her hand atop his. "It would be my honor, my lord."

As they passed, the king turned to flash Liam a dry smile. "And you, Liam the Protector. Since you decided to present yourself to us before the great doors were locked for the meal, you may join us, as well. Especially since you've brought us such a pretty gift."

Behind him, the inhabitants of the hall went back to their meal. The court harpist plucked at his strings, and the air fairies went back to tumbling through the rafters. Liam stepped up to the high table and seated himself alongside his wife.

It was undoubtedly a mistake. Just her proximity was interfering with his temperature. He could smell the seductive, earthy scent of her, and he wanted to drop his face in her neck. Good thing the table was before him, he thought, gritting his teeth against his body's now predictable reaction. No one needed to know how he was beginning to crave his own wife.

He just wished *he* didn't know.

"I thank you for sacrificing your own stones and colors to come to us," his uncle was saying to her. "I hope you will find a true home among your husband's people, and that they will welcome you as fully as I do."

"I look forward to discovering my steps among them."

"And I will begin by making you known, if I may, to my own son, Owain, and his lady, Aifric."

Greetings were exchanged, although Aifric kept her eyes down and her voice so quiet it was scarce heard.

"It is on a bright day you join us, Orla of the *Tuatha*," the king said, reaching past his son to touch Aifric's hand. "For hasn't our dear daughter Aifric gained her place at the high table this very day by bestowing an heir on her husband?"

Liam saw his own wife's eyebrow rise at the statement and hoped she could keep her silence.

He shouldn't have worried. Not at the king's high table, anyway.

"Greetings," she greeted her new kinswoman. "Felicitations on your joyous day. Is your child named yet?"

"He is, of course, Cathal the Younger, after his grand-sire," the princess answered, eyes down.

Orla nodded. "A great name, then. Sure, I can't wait to meet him. Is all your time his, then?"

"I am the weaver," Aifric said, eyes still down. "A small skill, but one I cherish."

Orla stiffened again, but she merely nodded with a bland smile. "I see."

"Has Eibhear said when you will receive your new colors?" the king asked her.

Orla took hold of a goblet of mead in her slim, elegant hands and lifted it to her mouth. Liam couldn't take his eyes from her.

"Ah, no," she admitted. "I'm afraid I'll have to be finding out what other gifts the goddess—and god—have given me. Eibhear and I decided it would be less than appropriate for the wife of the king's nephew to continue her life as *leannan sidhe.*"

Cathal laughed. "If I know my nephew, sure, you won't have the time for it. But what else are you known for? Music? Poetry? Teaching?"

She squirmed just a bit in her seat. "I'm afraid you'd be badly used if you asked for music from me, lord. It's been said in my own hall that rats scatter at the sound. As for poetry, I've never had time. And no inclination for teaching."

"What else is there for a woman?" someone asked farther down the table.

Now there was no question at all. Liam definitely felt his wife stiffen. "Why, anything, I'd think," she said. "I imagine once I've tried everything I'll be able to choose."

Again the conversation stopped.

"Everything?" a woman asked in a hush.

Orla turned to Liam, as if checking her sense of reality. "Well, yes. Isn't that the way it's done here?"

"It is not," the king said quietly. "But then, my nephew will help you understand. We of the *Dubhlainn Sidhe* protect our women from the harsher tasks of life."

Ah, by the light of Lugh, Liam knew things were about to get sticky.

"Like what, exactly?" his wife was asking.

"And isn't that a lesson her husband should be giving her?" Liam asked, knowing perfectly well he was drawing her ire. Better him than the king, after all.

She swung her hot eyes on him, and he lifted a telling eyebrow. *Don't ignore me,* he wanted to say. *I'm trying to protect you.*

Amazingly enough, she seemed to understand.

"And it will be a lesson I'd very much like to hear," was all she said, although sure, didn't he hear an awful lot more?

"And you will, wife," he acknowledged.

"What about healing?" another of the court ladies asked. "We could always use help for our *bean tighe.*"

Orla's reaction was fleeting, but definite. "Ah, no," she said with a definite shake of her head. "I doubt it."

"Enough," the king said. "Such a discussion can wait for quieter moments. For now, we have court business to attend." And with that, he took his glass and rose to his feet. "First, I call on you of the *Dubhlainn Sidhe* to see here at the high table Aifric, wife of Owain, who has earned her place here with her deliverance of a son for the clan of the *Dubhlainn Sidhe.* I give her praise!"

Liam joined in the cheering, just as he'd always done. This time, though, he felt his wife's distress alongside him and wondered why he didn't feel the same pride as before. Another warrior for the clan. A man-child. The highest achievement a woman could claim. And yet his new wife clapped only politely as the hall thundered with foot-stomping and yells.

"Second," the King said, still smiling, "I give welcome to Orla, daughter of Mab, wife of my most beloved nephew, Liam, Leader of the Coimirceoiri. I ask all to rise and join me."

The king gave Orla an avuncular smile. "May she follow her new kinswoman's example and bear him many braw sons to follow in his way, and gentle daughters to comfort him as he grows old."

Liam saw that his wife was not quite enamored of the toast, but she kept her silence. He could just imagine what she would say to him later. Even so, he got to his own feet, silver goblet in hand. Mimicking his uncle, so all could see it, he turned to his wife and lifted his goblet toward her.

With an untidy shuffling of chairs, feet and wings, the rest of the hall followed suit, although not as quickly or as enthusiastically. They wouldn't, he knew. Not till enough time had passed that they could greet Orla not as a stranger from a warring clan, but as a neighbor. As close-knit as the *Dubhlainn Sidhe* were, though, even that might not ever happen. In the meantime, she would have to rely on him.

Mallacht. Why was just the thought of it enough to take his patience?

She was turning to look up at him. To seek some kind of emotional reinforcement, he thought. Comfort. Just the idea panicked him. Instead of meeting her gaze, he deliberately turned to the hall.

He knew he was being craven, but he was suddenly

feeling trapped again. Backed into a corner by the demands of politics and family, and chained by their expectations to a woman of neither peace nor gentleness.

If only she had been either, he could have incorporated her seamlessly into his life. In truth, he could have bedded her and forgotten her, her impact on his life so slight as to leave little impression. He would have left her to the women and gone on with his man's life.

Not so of Orla of the house of Mab. Like one of those rockets the mortals so loved to shoot off to celebrate their new year, she destroyed the silence and refused to keep to her place in the shadows. Even in her mud-brown robes and bare silver rings, she exuded a sensuality and life the likes of which he hadn't seen in his land in his memory. A bright, exotic, alien bird who carried the price of madness with her.

And he resented it. Even as he knew it wasn't her fault. Even as he knew she was braver than he'd expected, stronger than he'd hoped. But to survive here, she would need him. And he didn't want her to need him. He didn't want *anyone* to need him.

Not anymore.

"Do you drink the toast, husband?" she asked too quietly for anyone else to hear.

Liam shot her an annoyed look before lifting the cup to his lips. It would have been inexcusable to insult her in public by not drinking. It was more inexcusable, however, for her to remind him, and it set off his temper again, which was short enough on its own these days.

But he held himself still. He smiled and drained his cup, just as his uncle the king had done, and set it down on the linen tablecloth. And when it was filled again, he made his own toast.

"To my new wife," he said, lifting his cup, "who has promised to honor me until the day we leave for the West."

It was a direct challenge, but he couldn't help it. If she didn't understand her role here and now, would she ever?

Evidently not. For she rose to her feet right alongside him and lifted her own cup. She didn't seem to so much as notice the gasp of disbelief from the hall, or acknowledge the sudden frown from the king.

"To my new husband," she said, lifting her cup in his direction, "who has promised the same."

From the front table, Faolán let loose a bark of laughter. From farther back, one of the women *tsked,* an impatient, pejorative sound. Liam could almost hear her thoughts. *Pushy little thing. Who does she think she is?*

She thinks she's the daughter of a queen, he almost said out loud. The problem was, that didn't help her a bit here in the land of Lugh. In fact, he would have to say it was already proving to be a serious disadvantage.

He said nothing, though, simply drained his cup again and reclaimed his seat. Alongside him, his wife did the same.

"Are you sure you don't want to offer the court some music?" he asked as the food was presented.

"As sure as I'm thinking you don't want to lose your digestion."

He looked over, expecting to see humor in her eyes. Oddly enough, he caught a hint of bleakness.

Why? he wondered.

It didn't matter. He had no intention of delving into her character when that knowledge wasn't a need of any kind for good bedding, as they'd already proved. As he fully planned to prove again, and soon. There should, after all, be some benefits to this arrangement.

Just the thought had him hard as a rock. No one knew, though, but him.

And his wife. He knew she turned to him. He knew she saw the images in her mind of the earthquake they'd caused already and would again when they came together. He refused to acknowledge it. Instead, as if what was coming wasn't the only thing on his mind, he turned to the fairy on his other side and struck up a conversation. Orla was left to her wine and food, and the silence of his indifference.

She would murder him. She would take a horsewhip to him and tear nice long strips from his skin to weave a purse from. She would tie him naked to the tallest tree in his village and leave him there for the women to find so they could see him humiliated.

She reached for her wine, but her hand shook too much. She refused to let anyone in this cold, unfriendly hall know how sharply he'd cut her. How, even though he'd stepped into her mind to taunt her with the lovemaking she could expect later that night, he'd turned away as if it was beneath his notice.

As if *she* was beneath his notice.

It was hard enough facing all those unfriendly faces in the crowd. Even the king's words hadn't eased any of the expressions she saw. Her husband's toast, that goad to put her firmly in her place, had made things worse. How could she do aught but challenge him right back?

And it had set her even further apart from the people she would have to rely on for the rest of her long life. Sure, she didn't think there would be a woman in this benighted world who would seek her out now.

As if that mattered. After all, what would she have to

say to them, anyway? What kind of world was it that kept women from sharing the work of their own lives? Protecting them indeed. As if beings who gave birth and attended to the rituals of death were too fragile to face fear. As if they had nothing to offer but their wombs. And as if the only gift worth carrying there was a boy child.

Bah! Her mother had raised her better altogether.

Even so, she had to admit that her stomach crawled when she saw some of the guests in the hall tonight. She hadn't been certain when she'd walked in alongside her husband, but sure, weren't those gremlins sitting to the side? And, faith, was that a satyr? She swore she could see the hairy legs on him, and it was sure as Samhain he was leering at the blushing girl across the table from him.

What kind of place was this, where the inhabitants broke bread with such creatures? And what was she to do about it?

She wanted to rub at her forehead where her tension lived. She couldn't so much as fart in front of this crowd. She'd never been one for court etiquette. It had always seemed such a monumental waste of good time. But it had never felt so stultifying as it did now, when she didn't even have her sisters to talk to. The king was speaking to Eibhear, and Liam was talking to anyone in the room but her. If this was what their lives were to be, she wished he hadn't wasted his time being kind out on the steps of the hall. He'd apologized, and she'd believed he'd been sincere. She should have known better.

Sure, she hoped he didn't think he would actually live out any of those fantasies he'd planted in her head anytime soon. She would meet his next foray into lovemaking with an elven knife if he didn't remember soon how valuable a little sweetness was to his wife.

"If I may say so," a voice said in front of her, "he had no business taking so long bringing you here for us to fawn over."

Surprised, Orla looked down to see a handsome, red-headed fairy in attire similar to Liam's standing in front of the high table.

"He said he was doing man's work," was all she could think to say.

"If that means he spent the afternoon swinging across a hurling field like a young god, then he was, for sure."

Orla's smoldering temper flared. "Ah," she said, her voice dust dry, her expression rigidly neutral. "Hurling. Of course. I was wondering what would have demanded a dunking in the stream. Oddly enough, I thought it might have been *real* work."

"Ah, now, don't be fooled," the fairy said with a wide, easy grin. "That dunking was your fault altogether. If he hadn't taken the precaution, sure his own king would have recognized the lust on him."

"You can take yourself off anytime now, Faolán," Liam said suddenly.

"Ah, so it's your attention we have now, is it?" Orla asked gently. "Grand. You can be telling me, then, how a game of hurling protects us from all the enemies your people have amassed."

She took a bit of grim satisfaction in his quick flush of discomfort. "I don't think you'd understand," he accused.

"I didn't think you cared. But since we're about it, I'd like to ask your friend where it is the women play."

Even the redhead looked taken back. "Hurling?"

"Camorgie," she said, for wasn't it the same thing, but with the lighter stick for the women? "Sure, you can't mean to tell me that the women here don't play at all."

"He certainly can," Liam said. "Who do you think we are, to risk our women like that?"

"Ah, good," Orla said, clenching her fists to keep herself from rubbing her forehead. "And here I thought we might have run out of things to brangle over."

"There'll be no brangling," her husband warned.

"Careful, husband," she warned right back. "I'd think you wouldn't want to throw down so public a gauntlet on your first day of married life."

Their first day. Orla felt as if it had been days since that magic time in the little hall at the edge of the woods. Just the thought made her feel so very tired. The rest of her long fairy life stretched out before her, and it fair crushed her.

"Ah, good," Faolán crowed. "Finally, a woman who doesn't shrink before his infamous glower."

"Sure and you must have something to do," Liam threatened.

"Well, I have, but haven't I been standing here waiting this long while for you to introduce me to your good wife? I can't very well leave till you do, now, can I?"

"Orla. Faolán. Faolán. Orla."

Faolán gave Orla a big wink. "I can't think why himself the king doesn't use this one for diplomacy."

Orla found herself smiling at the handsome redhead. "Thank you," was all she could manage.

It seemed to stop him in his tracks. Worse, it stopped Liam, who was suddenly looking too closely at her. She wasn't about to betray how deeply he'd hurt her this eve. She wouldn't give him or any of them the satisfaction. But she would gift Faolán with her gratitude.

"I'm thinking it's going to be the highlight of the

court to see you seek your stones, lady," Faolán said, his grin not quite so brash.

"It's not an entertainment!" Liam snapped.

Faolán gave Orla another wink. "Well, if himself expects to be too busy to attend you while you do the searching, you can always call on me."

"Not if I send you to the twelfth realm, instead," Liam said.

Faolán laughed. "Ah, sure you won't be doing that. I'd never get back in time for the hurling championship."

"I wouldn't mind the help at all," Orla said just to see her husband turn colors. "After all, it's an entirely new life I'm facing here."

"And new challenges, sure," Faolán said, with a smirk at Liam.

Orla tilted her head in consideration. "Aye, I'd call them that, all right."

"And I haven't even mentioned the challenges of living with such a sweet one as your husband."

"An oversight altogether."

"Or his daughter. Now there's a challenge that'll earn you a stone or two."

Liam waved him off. "She's no account," he said. "For isn't she with her mother's people?"

Orla was struck speechless. Slowly she turned to see that her husband didn't seem to notice how stunning Faolán's statement was.

A *daughter?* Goddess, what was she to do about that?

At last she said, "She's no account? Would you like to tell me why?"

Faolán tilted his head. "She will never be heir," he said, as if it were perfectly obvious. "Not that you can tell her that, of course."

"Indeed," Orla said. "I'd love to hear about her, so."

Liam waved a languid hand at her. "It's not your business, woman."

She repeated in a voice that was deadly soft, "Still, I'd love to hear about her."

"Sure, and hasn't he told you?" Faolán asked, and for the first time it seemed his humor had fled.

"Told her what?" the king asked, suddenly interested in the conversation.

But Orla never had the chance to answer. Without warning, a ceramic bowl went whizzing by her head to crash into the wall behind her. Faolán ducked. The king stood. Orla faced the crowd and wondered who she'd angered now by simply sitting there.

The focus wasn't on her, though. Toward the back of the room, a fight had broken out, and a cluster of overlarge, overdeveloped fairy men were throwing punches and dishes and chairs, all yelling something about the hurling practice.

Orla gaped. Faith and the goddess, such a thing had never happened in her fairy life. No fairy had the disrespect to disrupt the queen's banquet. In this world, though, she was forced to duck rather than suffer a platter of butter in the face.

"What…?"

Suddenly she was being lifted from her chair and dragged off the high dais.

"Get to the side doors," he husband ordered, already heading for the melee.

Faolán was there before him. The sharp screeches of women tore through the hall, and air fairies chittered like agitated squirrels up in the rafters. Orla shook her head, completely stunned. What other insanity would she find in this benighted place her mother had sentenced her to?

Without another word, she rolled up her sleeves and stalked right down the center aisle. Not for the daughter of Mab to slink out the side doors as the shrinking women did. Not for the head of the archers, who had led the armies into battle, to retreat before a bit of a dust-up. Eyes blazing and back straight, she strode down the hall toward the main door. And if she had to knock some heads together on the way to get past, that was just what she did. Better than thinking about the latest revelation she'd just suffered.

A *daughter.* Less important, it seemed, than food and drink. Sure, even less important than an afternoon spent swinging a stick at a little leather ball.

Whack! Another set of heads suffered her fury.

Well, she would show *him* how unimportant his womenfolk were.

Whack! Whack!

And then she was through the crowd and out in the crisp evening air.

Alone.

Ah, well, she might as well get used to solitude. She had a feeling it wasn't going to change anytime soon. Especially if she took into account the looks she was getting from all those women who were scuttling out the side doors like roaches hiding from a bright light.

And because she didn't know how to act except as herself, she waved at every one of them and walked on home in the dark.

Chapter 5

"You shame me, woman."

Orla didn't even bother to look away from the view out the window. "You infuriate me, lordling."

She turned at last.

He stood just inside the doorway, disheveled and a bit bloody, his temper uncertain. Orla didn't care. She'd just spent her time inspecting his house again, and her impression had changed not a whit. There had never been a child in this man's home, and of a certainty no girl of any kind. There were two bedrooms, and both were as spartan as a military camp. No dollies or blocks or toys to soften the edges of a solitary life. No scrawled pictures or sloppy notes of affection left by a child who might have once lived here. Who might, by the goddess, be invited to visit her own father.

He was alone.

Which elicited the question, who was this daughter Faolán spoke of? And where was she? What else did Orla not know about this husband of hers that might surprise her when she could least handle it?

For a moment she didn't care. She could feel the heat of him no more than a foot from her. Her skin crawled with his proximity, and her mind sparked to life with the memories of him in her hands, of him inside her.

She wanted him. She *yearned.*

Goddess, she hated that word. She hated the feeling more. Aching and hollow-chested and impatient for the touch of his skin. For the taste of his mouth and the brush of his words against her ears: anxious words, impatient words, hungry words.

It took every ounce of strength she had, but she stood her ground at the window, her fingers splayed across the faintly uneven glass.

Faith, they didn't even know how to blow glass in this place so the world outside wasn't distorted and unreal. She should tell him that, right after she chastised him for allowing a melee to destroy the sanctity of the banquet.

"And I want *you,* as well," he said, his voice strained.

But he moved no more than she did.

"Not till we have the first discussion of our marriage," she said, finally giving in to the urge to rub at her forehead. "Oddly enough, I prefer to know the man whose cock I invite into me."

There was a pause, filled to bursting with electricity. "An odd thing for the *leannan sidhe* to say."

She closed her eyes at that. Ah, and didn't he know just where to plunge the knife? "Indeed it is," she said. "But then, I'm the *leannan sidhe* no longer, am I? I imagine this is part of learning my new gifts."

"I am no gift."

She actually laughed, even though it was a sore sound. "Ah, husband, how can a woman argue with such perfect logic?"

She heard him shuffle a bit. "You frightened me," was all he said, but it forced her to turn from the haven of the night.

"I frightened you?"

She saw the strain in his eyes and knew he spoke the truth. "Well, wasn't that you wading right into a mass of the biggest, most unpleasant hurlers in the fairy kingdom?" he demanded,

She still didn't understand. "And?"

"And they could have hurt you!"

Orla realized that she was gaping. "You really…"

Had feared for her. Something tiny and insubstantial broke loose in her chest.

"It never occurred to me that I might frighten you, husband. Sure, haven't I broken up my share of fairy fights in my time? Even a mortal fight or two, for you can imagine how surly they can get with a bit of competition for the *leannan sidhe*. I was more distressed that those men disrespected your king so much."

Now Liam seemed confused. "Disrespected him?"

Orla tilted her head, as if it could help her comprehend him better. "Aye, husband. Disrespected. How dare they destroy the banquet? Faith, the bard had not even sung yet."

Oddly enough, that was what broke through the tension on her husband's face. "By Lugh's light, woman," he said with a laugh. "What has the bard to say that's better entertainment than a good fight in the hall?"

She knew she was staring again. "Then this happens all the time?"

He shrugged. "Actually, it took longer tonight. Probably in deference to the king's welcoming of his new niece."

She couldn't seem to manage more than a shake of her head. "Ah, well, no wonder the women here all look as if they could do with a good meal, if they never make it through one uninterrupted."

"Sure, they don't mind. It's only the crockery that's annoying, as don't they have to rebake it again the next day?"

"And this happens every night?"

"As close as makes no difference."

Orla shook her head, amused. "Well, then, it seems I'll be knocking more heads here than I thought."

Immediately his good mood was gone. "That, you won't. Not when I'm there to protect you."

"Husband," she said, her voice patient. "I appreciate the help and all, but I'm perfectly capable of caring for myself. After all, haven't I taught the women battle tactics for years?" She stopped, considering, and smiled for him, finally seeing a way out of her loneliness. "There's none here to teach the women, is there? I could help."

"Teach the women what?"

"Well, combat, of course. Sure, didn't I lead the archers in the late war? Haven't I strapped on the shields and wielded the great *sidhe* sword when needed? I'll never claim domestic skills, husband. But by the right hand of Oisín, I can teach war."

For some reason, that riled him even more. Faith, his face was all but brick-red. "You'll do no such thing! You think we'd allow our women to set so much as a foot on the field of battle? Are you mad, woman?"

"And if the men are off on the battlefield, who is it, then, that protects the homes?"

"If the battle goes well, there's no need."

She laughed at him. She couldn't help it. "And how often has that happened?"

She saw it then, a flash of something in those night-dark eyes. Pain. Grief. Distress. But before she could say anything, he shook his head.

"Not while I live," he said baldly.

Orla slammed a hand on her hip. "I made a vow to you," she said. "It was to protect you as you protect me. I take no vow lightly, husband, or else what would I be doing here arguing with you over nothing?"

He actually waved off her words. "Ah, well, no one really believed that bit of nonsense. What woman would protect her husband, after all?"

Orla glared. "A *Tuatha* woman."

"Well, you are no longer *Tuatha*, are you?"

"Why, yes, I am," she retorted, unable to keep her eyes from his mouth. Faith, was arguing with him always this stimulating? Suddenly she was *yearning* again, and she hadn't even gotten around to the daughter business. "I might now claim *Dubhlainn* citizenship, but I'll be *Tuatha* till the day the West bids me come, and it wouldn't do any good for you to be forgettin' it. For aren't you *Tuatha*, as well, as is the way of my people?"

His eyes had grown even darker, and he stepped closer to her, ratcheting up the heat between them. "And where about you do you see these people of yours?" he demanded, reaching out to wrap his hand into the hair at the base of her skull. "Do you see them here, woman? Do you hear their music in our halls or their voices in this house? This is *my* house, and in it, my word holds. My wishes, my command. And it's an obedient wife that counts in my clan. A submissive wife. A wife who lives to please her husband—in everything."

Orla knew her own eyes had darkened. Goddess, she loved the challenge of him. "Indeed, husband. Is that the way of it?"

She set her own body flush against his, so that the heat of her skin reached him. So that she could feel the hard angles and valleys of his flesh. So she could know the insistent prod of his cock against her belly.

And she smiled. "Is it?"

His fingers still tight in her hair, he bent his head toward her. "It is."

She nodded, lifting her head. "Then what do we do," she asked, "about this?"

And then she reached between them to take hold of his cock.

Ah, delight, all that hard, sleek arrogance in her hand. Her husband's knees all but buckled.

"You…"

He could manage no more than that rasp, because she'd slipped right into his mind with her intent, and there she set her mouth hot and fast over his penis, her teeth nibbling at the soft, plum-shaped tip of it, her fingers wrapped around his sack until he dropped his head back in agony.

"Stop…"

Letting the images between them dissipate, she dropped to her knees and laughed. Tugged at his clothing until she pulled him free. Until she felt the trembling in her thighs that betrayed his effort to hold still before her. Until she could hear the harsh rasp of his breath as he fought for control.

"I don't think I will," she said, and settled her mouth over him.

Hot; he was so hot, sleek and long and hard, stone swathed in velvet, alive, twitching, seeking, as she licked and bit and sucked. Oh, she sucked, pulling at him as if drawing the very life force of him out through his rod. She gloried in the musk of him, in the salt of him, in the earth-solid weight of him.

She wrapped her long fingers around his balls and felt him shudder. She had him caught, right there in his window, victim to her ministrations, the scent of his sex rising around her, the urgency of his arousal inciting her.

"I'm not so sure it's about pleasing my man," she said, pulling back enough to run her tongue slowly up from the base of him to that delicious little ridge at the tip, "as it is about controlling him."

His hands tightened in her hair. His voice escaped in a low moan. His head fell back again, and she could feel his knees all but fail. The climax was coming on him, rising in waves, robbing his breath and his voice and his control. And she smiled and took him deeper, as deep as she could, so she could feel him at the back of her throat and know he was helpless in her hands, ready to do anything, *anything,* to please her in return for what she was about to accept.

She closed her eyes and reveled in the rasp of his fingers against her scalp, in the just-painful pull of her hair, in the sounds and smells and sensations of him as he lost control, as he ground out a deep, surprised cry, as he gave her everything she wanted, there on her knees before him with him in her sway.

And when the pulsing stopped, she slowly let him loose, letting him remember at the end what she'd brought him with her mouth and hands and teeth, and she let him crumble before her onto his own knees.

"Don't you *ever*..." His voice was husky, his eyes closed.

"Stop?" she asked, wrapping herself around him to kiss him.

She could feel his reluctant smile against her mouth. "Witch."

And oddly enough, that was what she took to heart. Not his arguments or his commands or his accusations, but the almost gentle word she'd surprised out of him that sounded as close to an endearment as she'd heard from him.

"We haven't finished this discussion," he assured her, pulling her into his arms where they knelt face-to-face.

"Indeed we haven't," she acknowledged, laying her cheek against his chest to enjoy the drumbeat of his heart. "We haven't even discussed this daughter business yet."

He bent down and claimed her mouth with a kiss that left her dizzy for air. "Later," he said. "Right now, I have a bit of tormenting to do myself."

And he did. Oh, by the strong hand of *Cúchulainn*, he did.

By the time she awoke, he was gone. Orla stretched, savoring the lazy-cat feel of a morning after hours of exhausting, mind-altering sex. Sure, she'd known it before, in her life as *leannan sidhe,* those moments when it had all seemed enough. When the sight of a man lying shattered and limp and smiling in the heather had been enough to make her smile. Now, though, there was more....

Maybe it was just that this time she hadn't needed to

rely on magic for what had happened, only her natural appetites. She smiled. Maybe she'd just needed Liam the Protector.

Faith and the goddess, she thought, closing her eyes over the memory of what he'd done to her the night before. *Sure I could get used to such a pastime. Such hands and words and the invasion of a cock that sure could challenge a girl's courage.*

She could still imagine him inside her, slamming into her, scouring her with sensation the likes of which she'd never known. He'd almost begged her pardon once. She'd shushed him and pulled him even deeper. And if she were any other being in the world of faerie, even herself only days ago, it could have been enough.

Unfortunately, now that she was no longer *leannan sidhe,* she suddenly realized that the sex, wonderful as it had been, was no longer enough. She needed him to offer more than his body. She needed his memories and his wishes and the sum of his days. She needed to know why it was he strapped on leather arm bracers and breastplate before slipping out into the predawn chill. She needed to know what Faolán had been talking about.

A daughter? How could such a hard, self-contained man ever cherish a daughter? Faith, in the heat of their own lovemaking, he hadn't given her a word of love, even as a sop to urge her on. His own cries had been wrenched from him, as if they were the last thing he would have allowed. How could he nurture a little girl? Sure it was obvious no one else in this benighted clan would ever think to value her.

How could he imagine that his wife didn't even need to know about the child? And how could he have left her this morning without giving her at least an idea of what she was supposed to do this day without him?

Ah, there it was again, that damnable sense of emptiness. That feeling that he'd taken a part of her with him when he'd crept out this morning. The wondering if he'd felt the same, or if he'd walked out with no more regret than the loss of sleep he'd suffered.

Just the thought was enough to take her breath. How could she bear to mark her days this way? Was this what her new life meant? Was this what she would face every morning for the rest of her days?

She gave herself a few selfish minutes to rub at her face with her hands and stare at an uninformative ceiling. Then, not knowing what else she could do, she rose and dressed. No matter what else, it wouldn't do to have this crowd think her weak and wanting, especially if she was. She would just have to see about getting on with things.

It was to be that brown gown again. She was afraid sometimes it was all she would ever don, a color that reflected nothing, that gave her no definition or distinction, even in this half-colored world at the edge of the mountains.

No, she thought, straightening her shoulders, then wincing. Her shoulders were sore with all the straightening she'd done this past day. Would it be enough to make them think she was brave? she wondered. Would it convince them that she could face their disdain with indifference? Would it incite them to welcome?

Well, there was only one way to find out. It was time to step out into her day.

Accompanied by his small squad of four, Liam stalked the sharp ridges of the Reeks as he had almost every day of his adult life. It was his gift, his purpose. He was a protector. He led the other protectors in their mission. He would never fail his people in this duty.

He'd thought, once, that he was impervious to temptation or mistakes. But the crimson throb of the Coilin Stone had called to him with the seduction of a sly woman. It had promised him power and independence and success. It had brought him Orla, daughter of Mab, instead.

"Sure, don't you think you want to save the scowls for the enemy?" Faolán asked.

"If I'm scowling, it's at the liberties you thought to take with my wife last night," Liam said as if it were true.

Fortunately Faolán laughed. "Ah, no, it can't be jealous you are, can it? I can show you how to woo her, all right, if you're unsure of yourself. And don't we all think her worth the effort altogether?"

"You'll think nothing or suffer my fist. She's naught but a pain in the arse, and you know it."

This time Faolán stopped right in the middle of the faint track along the bare mountain pass. "By the brave balls of Fionn mac Cumhaill, if you aren't a feckin' idiot for thinking that," he said, shaking his head in awe. "Did you see her banging those heads together last night? I couldn't take my eyes off her, and that's the honest truth."

"She shouldn't have had to do any such thing," Liam growled.

"Ah, but wasn't it a thing of beauty when she did?"

It had been. Even Liam had to admit it, no matter that she'd sparked a fury the likes of which he couldn't ever remember with her blithe progress through the thick of the fight, her back impossibly straight, her hair billowing out behind her like a battle pennant. The worst part had been the slavish looks of devotion her victims had turned on her before they'd slumped unconscious to the floor.

"They were ensorceled," he snapped. "Wasn't it the *leannan sidhe* they saw amongst them?"

Faolán frowned at him. "I saw no *leannan sidhe* in that hall, Liam. I saw a princess."

Liam glared at him, furious that it was Faolán who spoke the truth.

"You'll not say a word against that girl," Flann said, he who'd fallen first the night before.

"Not say a word?" one of the other guards retorted. "Were you blind, as well as deaf, man? She committed heresy. She should be stoned—meanin' no offense at all, Captain."

"And why would any be taken?" Liam asked drily.

"Heresy?" Flann yelled. "It was poetry, sure, to watch her. I was honored to feel her gentle hand on my head."

Liam all but growled as he whipped around on him. "And would you want your own wife to be buttin' heads together like a palace guard?" he demanded.

Flann looked stunned. "Of course not," he said. "But sure, isn't she of a different sort altogether, with those heathenish *Tuatha* ways?" Turning, he shook a fist at his comrade. "I'm tellin' you, you won't say a word against her or you'll feel my wrath."

"You and what troop of griffins?" the guard demanded.

"Enough," Liam commanded, raising his hand before the two of them set to brawling at the edge of a precipice. Faith, but it seemed there was no patience in the land anymore. The slightest excuse was enough to set the men off. And it had to be his wife, of all things.

"How could you speak ill of her?" Flann asked his outspoken comrade. "Wasn't she a fair sight, along with all her people, when they went into battle with the fairy gold glinting off their breasts?"

"Ah, well, that's true, then," another of the guards agreed in a dreamy voice. "And did you see herself your wife at the head of the archers with her proud strong neck and lithe arm and all?"

Liam glowered. "She told you she was there, did she?"

Both men blinked at him. "Sure, didn't you see her, man?" Flann demanded. "Isn't that why you chose her for yourself?"

Chose her for himself? Liam almost choked. Faolán, the traitorous sod, laughed until he was bent over double. "Ah, faith, but this just gets better and better, doesn't it? I don't suppose you lads were after tellin' the women of the village how magnificent our little Orla was at the head of battle, were you?"

The men exchanged bemused looks. "Why shouldn't we, so?"

Faolán turned less amused eyes on Liam. "If it's gentling her way into the clan you're wanting, I'd go home now and help," he said. "For it's a certainty that not one of those women will forgive her the men's interest."

Liam dropped his head, furious. All he wanted to do was walk his route with the men of his unit alongside. All he wanted was to fulfill his task for his clan. Not babysit that she-devil he'd married.

Instantly his mind filled with what they'd done the night before. He could see the impish delight in her eyes as she'd looked up from the unspeakable pleasures she'd visited on him right there in front of the window. His cock stirred. Worse, his heart did.

"And don't you owe it to her," Faolán quietly asked as if he'd heard him, "after your behavior to her in front of the assembly? She didn't deserve it, Liam, and so you know it."

Liam met his friend eye-to-eye and knew he was right. He'd shamed both her and himself, and then left her to suffer the consequences. He'd known better than to leave her to the mercy of his people. Slinging his great sword over his shoulder, he spun on his heel and turned back.

"Can you tell me aught about this daughter it's said he has?" Orla asked the little group of women.

She'd found them clustered in the square using the sun to help them see their work, weaving and knitting and mending the dinnerware back into shape. Their chatter had shut off like a water tap the minute she'd approached.

"That is for your husband to say," Aifric, the daughter-in-law of the king, said without looking up from her loom.

Orla fought the urge to rub her forehead again. She'd been at this for most of the morning, giving greetings and getting raised eyebrows, asking questions and getting puzzles, asking help and getting cold shoulders. She'd even seen a fight break out over whether she had the right to step into a smithy to look at a small sword. She'd had enough entirely.

"All right, then," she said, trying hard to sound friendly in the face of their hostility. "Would you mind if I sat with you a minute? I have to find my skills, so, and I can't think better to learn from than you. Faith, your weaving would make the goddess weep with wonder."

Her words gained her nothing. The women went back to their work as if she didn't exist.

She couldn't stand it anymore. "Do you all *like* my husband?" she demanded, fighting the urge to shred her plain brown robes in frustration.

Every head lifted. "Liam?" Aifric asked, eyes wide. "Who could not like Liam? We honor him. And sure, don't we care for his house when he is away on the borders?"

Orla nodded. "And if you like him so much, why would you wish him ill?"

Outraged, the pleasantly plump young princess with a goddess's hands at the loom, climbed to her feet. "How dare you say that to us? Who do you think you are?"

Orla managed to keep her voice even. "Ah, well, that's the problem, then, isn't it? I'm his wife. Whether any of us wants it—especially me—a queen and a king have so ordered it and two priests consecrated it. And so Liam is stuck with me. And the way I see it, those who love him here can either help him along to some peace and harmony, or make certain he lives the rest of his long life in misery for having a wife with no skills, no life and no idea of how to go on in his world to make his way easier."

"Why don't you just go back where you belong?" demanded a woman with wet clay on her fingers.

Orla straightened yet again, and made sure her eyes were as calm and placid as she could as she sadly shook her head. "Ah, I didn't know…"

"Know what?"

"That this was a land where an oath holds no honor. It's sad I am at that."

Now all the women were on their feet. "How *dare* you say such a thing of the *Dubhlainn Sidhe, Tuatha,* when you stole our stone?" a woman demanded, pointing knitting needles at her.

"I say such a thing," she said quietly, facing the older woman without apology, "because you have just asked me to break an oath held sacred in two worlds. Since no *Tuatha* in the history of the world would ever have thought to do such a thing, I find I'm fairly flummoxed by the idea of it." She shook her head again, as if too perplexed to understand. "Faith, I'm not sure it's something I'll be after getting used to anytime soon."

"I challenge you to say that to the menfolk," an older, sterner woman snapped. "Sure, they'd break you in two like a stick."

"And further disgrace their family names?" This time she didn't have to pretend sadness. "Mayhap this isn't a place I want to know, after all."

And then, taking one of the greatest chances of her life, because she just didn't know what else to do, she turned to walk away.

"You ensorceled my husband!" the knitter accused, and Orla heard real distress in the words.

She turned back and saw that the woman meant it. Worse, that it really hurt her.

"Ah, now, how could I?" she asked. "Didn't you see my fingers when I came, the shame of having no stones? Didn't you hear that because I allowed Liam the Protector to steal away our beloved Coilin Stone, I was stripped of my skills as *leannan sidhe?* I no longer have the power to ensorcel anything."

"Then why is it that my husband hasn't stopped talking about you since you knocked his head in the hall last night?"

Orla considered what the woman said. If it was true, it was unknown in her experience. In her world, what she'd done simply wasn't that unusual.

"Could it be he just wasn't used to seeing a woman exerting her rights?" she asked.

She got more than one bemused look.

"Your rights to do what?" Aifric asked.

Orla snorted unkindly. "My rights to finish my dinner in peace, if you must know. Just how long have that lot been making mice feet of your banquets now?"

The knitter shrugged. "Ah, sure, they've always been easy to rouse. It's the warrior in them, like."

"It *has* been getting worse," another woman admitted. Her compatriots glared at her.

The woman shrugged. "Sure, couldn't we do with our dear Dearann Stone to soothe things a bit? It's getting fair fractious these days, is all I'm sayin'."

She was smiling, as if her words held no import. Orla saw the strain in her eyes, though. Faith, were things worse than the odd dinner brawl?

"Well, and whose fault is that, that we have no Dearann Stone?" the knitter demanded, glaring at Orla again.

"I'll say this once, and then be done with it," Orla said, already vastly weary of this line of thought. "No *Tuatha de Dannan* stole your stone. If we had, sure, wouldn't we be wearing the bloody thing for all to see?"

Her vehemence seemed to surprise them a bit. The square was silent with resentment.

"Do the women often get caught in the middle of the dinner brawls?" she asked, instead, hoping they would follow her change of topic.

Oddly enough, they did. "It's just a matter of getting free before the worst," Aifric said. "Sure, they'd never hurt us."

"Not intentionally," another offered. "Sometimes, though, if you're in the wrong place and all..."

Orla looked around at them and wondered whether they were ready for her in this place, after all. For sure, she wasn't going to stop knocking heads together any-time soon.

"Well, then, don't you think it's something you might want to change, now? If nothing else, sure it's a criminal waste of food."

"And just how do you expect us to do that?"

Orla ignored the sudden acceleration of her heart. Could it be this easy? Would she find a purpose here?

"I know you heard it last night," she said, "but my name is Orla of the Clan of the *Tuatha.* I'd be happy to tell you what I think. I'd just like to know who I'm after telling it to."

Aifric, obviously the ringleader, turned to silently consult the others. The women kept silent, but they must have passed some kind of information, because she turned back.

"You know that I am Aifric," she said. "Wife to Owain, heir to the king, and weaver to the *Dubhlainn Sidhe.*"

Orla smiled, trying hard not to betray the real relief she felt at this small gesture of welcome. "Greetings again, Aifric."

"And I am Tullia," the pretty, thin woman with the clay offered. "Consort to Flann of the *Coimirceoiri* and potter."

Orla grinned. "Ah, so it's you always tasked with replacing all the dinnerware, is it?"

The potter blushed hot. "Ah, no. Not all."

"I give you greetings, Tullia." Evidently none of the others were ready to make the same gesture, so Orla nodded, knowing she had to move on. "May I ask a question of you all, since I'm new to the land of the *Dubhlainn Sidhe?*"

It seemed Aifric had to consult her friends once more. *Ah,* Orla thought. *Definitely a qualified acceptance.*

In the end, they pointed her to the edge of a wall

where one of the knitters sat. Orla accepted the invitation and settled herself on the warm stones.

"There truly aren't any *camorgie* teams here?"

"Not for years upon years," Tullia said, wiping her hands with a towel. "It has been deemed unwise."

Orla nodded. She was beginning to see, indeed. "And which women on the council thought this?"

"Women on the council?" Aifric asked. "What women?"

Orla kept her outrage to herself. If her mother the queen had indeed known where the Dearann Stone was all along, she had a lot to answer for to these women, who had no feminine power to offset their men's aggression. Sorcha had been sent to find the stone, but there was no guarantee she would succeed.

"You truly don't know how the Dearann Stone went lost?" she asked.

Tullia shrugged. "Well, my Flann says that he heard it went missing during the last Realm War."

"Realm War?" Orla asked. "We've fought no Realm War."

"Ah, no, *you* wouldn't. Isn't it the task of the *Dubhlainn Sidhe*, then?"

"Some say the stone was spirited away for safekeeping, but that the keeper himself was lost before he could return her," another woman offered.

"Our bards say it's in the land of the mortals," Orla said.

The woman nodded. "It seemed odd to us."

This time Orla gifted them with a grin. "Much more believable to think a *Tuatha* spy had crept in and made off with it, I'd think."

Aifric, at least, had the decency to give a chagrined smile. "More enjoyable, at least."

Orla found herself grinning back at Aifric's honesty. "Sad to say," she said, "we weren't smart enough to think of it."

What this *Tuatha did* think was that even without the help of their Dearann Stone, the women of the *Dubh-lainn Sidhe* could use a bit of power. And helping them might just earn her a stone.

"Would you let me help you till we can get the stone back?" she asked.

"How?" Aifric asked.

Orla looked around to find the women at least listening. "Well, sure, I could teach you how to do what I did last night."

"You could not," her husband said suddenly, and sent the gaggle of women into chaos.

Orla was almost amused. To a woman, they couldn't decide whether to be frightened, outraged or titillated. Yes, she imagined, her husband had the same effect on women everywhere. Especially when he was clad in his leather arm bracers and breastplate, standing not a stone's throw from where they sat.

"Greetings, husband," she said, not bothering to get up. Ah, faith, he had legs on him. If only he hadn't brought them here just now, when she finally had something to do. "Have all the enemies of your people been vanquished this quickly, or is the hurling practice merely over?"

She knew better, so. She could see the fury gathering in his dark eyes. Still, she had the feeling no one in this world ever pushed him except his friend Faolán. Certainly none of the women would think to challenge him, now, would they?

Certainly not these. They were all straightening dresses and patting hair, as if waiting to be asked to dance.

"What are you about, wife?" he demanded.

She gave him a languid look. "Why, trying to earn my stones, husband. What did you think I was doing?"

"Fomenting rebellion." He held out his hand. "It's time you came with me. We have a discussion that's overdue."

She raised an eyebrow but didn't move. "Indeed. And here I was about to get to know the women of your village."

"You need to get to know *me* first."

That actually made her laugh. "And that, Aifric," she said to the plump little weaver, "is a man for you. Haven't I been after begging him to do just that since we met at the border? But it seems hurling and fighting are more important—until I offer to teach the women of the village some of my own skills."

"Are you coming?" he demanded.

"Are you finally going to tell me about this daughter of yours?" she demanded right back.

"I told you—"

"That it's not my business?" She shook her head. "Then you offer me nothing, husband. I'll stay here with my friends."

Her *friends* looked pitifully uncomfortable. *Faith,* she thought. *I hope he relents, so I don't put them in an untenable position. And oh, I hope I can hold out till he does.* Her breath was getting short again.

"Fine," he finally snapped. "I will tell you of my daughter. I'll tell you of my favorite horse and the apple tree I raided as a child. Just come along. *Now.*"

Even though her legs were trembling after the chance

she'd just taken, Orla gracefully rose to her feet and settled her brown dress around her. Then she gave the women a regal nod.

"It would please me to visit later, if I may," she said. "I thank you for your gracious welcome."

More than one of them blushed with the knowledge that they'd given her nothing of the sort. But Orla was building bridges this day, and she gave them each a huge smile before taking her husband's hand and following him into his house.

Chapter 6

Liam had already unbuckled his breastplate before it dawned on him that it might be better not to do so. He couldn't predict this wife of his, and he'd learned to his chagrin the night before that she wouldn't hesitate to fight back if riled.

Again the thought made his cock stir, which made him frown all the more fiercely. Sure, he couldn't be after lusting for a sharp-tongued woman. Lugh knew he'd never done so before. He'd never allowed that kind of behavior in his consorts.

Even so, he'd come back to make some kind of amends, if he could, for his behavior. He bent to pull the leather off over his head, all the while trying to gauge the mood of his wife. She was sitting in one of the two straight-back chairs he'd crafted when he'd reached his majority, and somehow she made it look like a throne.

He would have to do something about that, too. He had to impress on her what her place was in this house, and it wasn't to take over what was his and make it hers. He needed to remember that. But first he needed to control his unruly manhood and its tendency to interfere with his purpose, as it had the night before.

Ah, the night before. He couldn't help dallying with the memory of it: the weight of her perfect, full breasts in his hands, the feel of her sleek waist and legs, the sight of her hot, impatient eyes and hands. Her hands, which had traveled over every inch of him as if memorizing him. Faith, he didn't know the paths of the Reeks so well, and he'd walked them for decades.

"And sure, won't we be after revisiting such a delightful pastime later," Orla said, because, of course, she could see perfectly well what he could. "But for now, we need to talk."

Liam was relieved that he wasn't one to blush or she would have caught him at it. Battling well-deserved frustration, he set his armor down and settled into the other chair across from hers at the front window.

"Well, then," he said, rubbing a bit at his now bare wrist. "Have at it, woman. You've already managed to interrupt the brunt of my mission by bringing me home before I could successfully scan the borders. What more can you do to disrupt my life?"

"Bringing you home?" she echoed. "I called no husband to me."

"The other wives did. Sure, couldn't I hear their distress all the way to the wasteland? How is it that in a matter of less than two moonrises you've managed to sow discord in this perfect village?"

He could tell by the renewed fire in her eyes that she

had something to say to that. He never gave her the chance. "Sure, isn't every woman here outraged at your behavior at the banquet last night, striding through the hall like a warrior and making their husbands look ridiculous?"

"Oh, I think their husbands managed that quite well enough all on their own, don't you?" she asked, her voice suspiciously silky. "As for the women, faith, I think they were intrigued, not outraged. At least I hope they were, for sure, they need to be."

"What would you know about it?" he demanded. "You have no concept of what life is like on the borders, what we need from the men and expect from the women of the *Dubhlainn Sidhe*. And yet you presume to judge?"

For a moment she just looked at him, obviously chewing her words over. Then she got to her feet and crossed to the door.

"Grand," she said. "Show me." And without another word, she pulled the front door open and walked out.

For a moment all Liam could do was gape. *Mallacht,* he cursed silently. What next?

What next was her leaning her head back into the doorway so her hair swung behind her like a sable curtain. "Well, then, husband? Are we to go about your business, so I understand?"

He felt as if somebody had just pushed his head under water. "I thought you were after wondering about my daughter."

She lifted a wry eyebrow. "And who's to say we can't talk about her as we walk? You're the one said I needed to know the borders. Well, here I am, all right, and ready to learn."

Liam battled a surprisingly strong urge to throttle her. Right after he took her to the floor and impaled her with himself so that her eyes widened as they had the night before, hunger and surprise and just a little fear darkening them as she'd realized the force of his hunger.

He closed his eyes against the image and counseled himself to be patient. And faith, if she didn't wait there without moving, the picture of forbearance.

"Soon you'll go too far, woman," he growled, and climbed to his feet.

For just a moment, too quick to be sure, when he opened his eyes, he thought he saw it on her again. Fear. Uncertainty. Vulnerability. It stopped him, just for that long. He had to be mad. This wife of his was about as vulnerable as a wolverine, and he'd best not forget it.

"The borders," he said, stalking past her with every ounce of military presence he could muster, "lie out in the wastelands of the Reeks. You see them rising behind the village like sentinels."

"Or prison walls," she muttered, following along.

Liam swung on her. "Those prison walls keep more than just the *Dubhlainn Sidhe* safe. They also keep the *Tuatha* from knowing the perils of the other worlds, and the mortals even more."

"What other worlds?" she asked, looking around.

"Sure, you've been through the gates at Carrowmore," he said. "The twelve gates into the other worlds?"

"Well, yes, of course. But those gates lie in the land of the *Tuatha,* not the *Dubhlainn Sidhe.*"

"Those are only the front doors, Orla."

That stopped her, sure. She stared at him as if he'd run mad. "But some of those worlds—"

"Are too terrifying to contemplate. Don't you think we know? After all, isn't it the *Dubhlainn Sidhe,* the Fairy of the Dark Sword, who have been given the task of keeping our world safe from them? Haven't I mourned more than one warrior of my clan who perished in that defense or, worse, lost his soul?"

"But the world knows nothing of this," she protested. "Sure, it's nowhere even in the mortal tales."

"Because mortals have not the defenses to protect against even the least terrible of the other worlds. Why do you think the *Dubhlainn Sidhe* learned the art of dream-invasion? Why do you think we sow nightmares that would shake a sane soul? It is our most effective way of keeping mortals in their own plane, never to wander too far and stumble over a door that must never be opened. The dreams—the terrible dreams you sought me out to provide for you—are the best protection the mortal world has."

She looked truly shaken. Oddly, he wasn't sure that made him feel better. Ah, well, how long would she survive without knowing the worst of his land?

Before he could think better of it, he took her hand and drew her along. They didn't walk down the meandering lanes of their little village, though, toward where the women were gathered at the old well exchanging the information of the day while they pursued their stone gifts. Instead, he turned her onto a narrow track that led through the birch and willow trees that lined the tumbling stream.

Here the world was soft and gentle. Here it seemed ludicrous to think that only a moment of inattention could bring nightmares down on this little glen that would shatter the strongest of hearts.

"That's the real reason you stole the Coilin Stone," Orla said suddenly.

Liam didn't bother to look away from where a doe dipped her delicate head to the stream to drink.

"This place is called Gleann Fia," he said. "Glen of the Fawn. Appropriate, isn't it? Walking in these shadows, it's hard to think that any bad thing could happen."

"Wolves can come and take down that doe as she drinks," Orla said. "A bear could come eat the wolf. And a mortal with one of their fierce weapons could destroy them all. Don't think I don't comprehend risk, Liam."

He kept walking, their footfalls hushed in the grass. "Yes," he said. "It's one of the reasons I took the Coilin Stone. I thought that the added power might help bolster the borders."

"Has it?"

He looked over at her. Damn the woman for being so perceptive. "Not appreciably. But it's only been here for a bit now, and during much of that time we've been meeting with the *Tuatha de Dannan* on the field of battle."

"Why?" she asked. "You already have the stone."

"Because we thought you really did have the Dearann Stone, as well."

She shook her head. "You lot need better bards. Ours could tell you plain well that one of the *Dubhlainn Sidhe* carried the stone over to the land of mortals in the days before my life began and lost it there. Your women think it was to protect it during a war. Well, and isn't my sister Sorcha off now, trying to recover it even as we speak?"

He shook his head. "You *must* have stolen it. Sure, we've tried for long seasons to find it without luck."

She flashed him a grin. "Ah, well, but you're men, aren't you? Haven't we all seen that men have trouble finding the mead on the banqueting table unless a woman points it out?"

They'd begun to climb now, the way a bit rockier as they neared the high gray shoulders of the mountains that defined the land of the *Dubhlainn Sidhe,* an empty, endless horizon of ragged old men who stood guard over the gentle green land. Liam moved to help Orla over the roughening terrain. He needn't have bothered. As lithe as the doe they'd seen, she hopped effortlessly over the rocks and hollows of the path.

"Have you actually had incursions?" she asked.

Liam almost smiled. Leave it to the girl to stay on the point. "Regularly," he said. "We barely fought off an attack from the Seventh Realm only a short while before you contacted me."

"The Seventh Realm." Her eyes were wide and stark.

The ghostlords lived in the Seventh Realm. Blood seekers. It seemed she needn't have faced them to know their threat, he thought.

She looked over at him. "Why did you agree to my request to torment the mortal?"

He shrugged. "I was in the mood for a bit of chaos," he said. "I'd lost a friend in the high ridges."

"I'm that sorry, Liam. I didn't know."

She'd surprised him again. "And how could you?" he asked. "Was part of the power of the *leannan sidhe* that of seer?"

"Faith, no. The queen already has a perfectly good seer at her disposal, and he'll be around long into the reign of whomever my mother appoints to follow her."

He considered Orla. "Was the chance to be queen so important to you?"

"That I would invite disgrace and exile for it?" she asked, and took his hand again to climb some boulder steps. "It wasn't the power," she said simply. "It was the fear that my mother was deserting her people and leaving them in incapable hands."

"Your own sister?"

They'd reached a ledge, and she stopped a moment to look out to where the sea waited at the horizon beyond the harsh tumble of mountains. "Ah," she said. "I do love the high places."

Liam climbed up to stand beside her. This was *his* place, where he came to cleanse away the filth he sometimes brought from other realms. It was a place where the god Lugh could see him and bestow blessings for the hard work he did. And now she'd put her imprint on it. It would never be the same.

He was surprised he wasn't angrier about it.

"My sister Nuala, who was heir to the throne," Orla said, her head back, her eyes closed, "is the best of our clan. She is gracious and brilliant, and so compassionate the animals come and lay their heads in her lap."

"But she isn't a queen."

"Not the queen the *Tuatha* need. Especially not if we share the burden of protecting the world from the other realms."

"You don't. That is the work of the *Dubhlainn Sidhe*."

"I'm not so sure we can divide the load that easily anymore, Liam. I'm not sure we should."

"It isn't your choice."

She sighed, her eyes still closed. "No," she said, sounding unspeakably bleak. "It isn't, then, is it?"

And again, in that moment, he grieved for her.

"What will happen now?" he asked.

"To the *Tuatha*?" She shrugged. "You've just said it. It isn't my business to know anymore. I pray my mother the queen doesn't leave for the West soon, though. Whoever becomes queen needs the training of it, altogether."

"She is ready to go?"

"She has been for a bit. She was just waiting to train Nuala." Her smile was wry. "Or whomever else she chooses now. Sure, I see no one in my clan worthy of it."

"Did you see yourself worthy?"

"I saw that I had the hunger for it, the love of it, the ruthlessness for it. I saw that what I cared about most was the clan, at least in this." She shook her head and walked on. "I was wrong about that, too, though, wasn't I? None of it was enough. *I* wasn't enough. A sad indictment on a princess royal, altogether."

He could think of nothing to say that would salve that wound. So he kept climbing to where the mountains gnawed at the empty sky. The air was thinner, the breeze sharper, the horizon stark and silent. This was the place where peace lived. This was where the lords of the Seventh Realm had tried to tear him apart like a braised rabbit.

He scanned the horizon for his squad of protectors, but saw nothing but a spiraling bird and a long-haired mountain sheep. Today, the mountains appeared friendly.

"Why don't we sit down somewhere?" he suggested.

Orla made it a point to look around at the inhospitable landscape before lowering herself onto a flat boulder as if it were a presentation throne. "I'm not sure if it's a compliment and all, Liam the Protector, but these crags become you. I can see, all right, how the *Dubhlainn Sidhe* belong here as much as the *Tuatha* belong to the softer hills of the North. For aren't we the caretakers of the earth?"

Liam chose a nearby boulder and joined her. "And we the defenders."

She nodded, eyes squinted a bit as she took in the range of mountain peaks before her. "And the intruders appear here first?"

Liam gestured across the echoing spaces. "Anywhere along the line of the Reeks. The edge of our world is porous and ever changing, it seems, and they are adept at finding the gaps."

"But you go across, as well. I saw the satyrs at dinner."

He nodded. "The king has been brilliant at forging treaties with those who also need help against the likes of the berzerkers and the scythies."

Orla sucked in a breath, as well she might.

"I stepped into the world of the scythies only once," she said. "It was a dare, and a stupid one at that. I've never been so frightened."

Liam couldn't help offering a smile. "You, frightened, wife? After your exhibit in the hall of the king, sure I find it hard to believe."

She snorted inelegantly. "Ah, well, there's nothing so daring about clunking some sense into thick fairy heads. But to withstand the invasion of scythie tongues so they have no chance to clutch on to your brain…" She shook her head again.

"You've done so?" he asked, knowing how horrifying it had been when it happened to him, the sticky, barbed tongues wrapping and slithering and invading his mouth. But sure, far better than the sticky barbed threads that wove agony and madness into your brain, so that your thoughts were removed and the horrors of scythie dreams inserted. None survived that. Not intact.

Not intact at all. And didn't he know it better than most?

"But sure, isn't there the Fifth Realm of the magic-colored skies, and the Third, where the animals speak?"

He nodded. "To be protected as assiduously as ours. Can you imagine what would happen to those worlds if mortals invaded?"

She shook her head. "Faith, they'd make the whole thing into one of their theme parks. It is why we guard the Carrowmore Gates with our lives and honor."

"And we the Reeks, as well."

She shook her head again, and brought her knees up to wrap her arms around them, a little girl sitting in a magic place. Liam almost smiled. Her question, when it came, was nothing childish, though.

"Is it because of the Dearann Stone that we haven't worked together as a protective force all these long years?" she asked, her gaze still focused over the wasteland.

Liam looked his fill of her as the sun glinted raven-blue in her hair and her skin glowed an otherworldly porcelain. "Ah, well, I think it's been many things."

She flashed him a dry smile. "And my mother, the queen, had nothing to do with it, I'm sure, since once the Dearann Stone was gone, she had the lion's share of power in the realm of faerie."

He smiled back. "She might have been a wee bit arrogant. But our Cathal can be pigheaded, as well, and has kept refusing help he felt a warrior king shouldn't be after asking for."

"If I were queen, he wouldn't ever have had the chance," she said under her breath.

"If you were queen, I don't believe he would," Liam agreed.

For the first time since they'd met on that fairy plane alongside their honor guards, the two shared a look of perfect accord.

"How can the two of us help, then?" she asked.

He lifted an eyebrow. "The two of us?"

"Well, do *you* think we should waste a perfectly good chance to teach our two clans cooperation?"

Liam couldn't help it. He laughed. "Faith, woman. Do you never sit still?"

She gave him an unrepentant grin. "I used to, sure. But I find that without the never-ending effort of seducing mortals, I have vast reserves of energy and nothing to do with them. I think I could fit a wee bit of détente into my schedule."

"And you think, after all this long while, you and I can heal the rift with honeyed words and…what?"

Her grin was pure deviltry. "A force of women archers."

He scowled.

"At least allow them the right to defend themselves," she insisted.

"I have no say in it. Only the king can so decree, and isn't it himself who forbade any woman from sitting at the high table who hadn't birthed a male child for the clan?"

"Sure, that can be changed, too. Didn't I claim a seat there myself?"

"Not because you're a princess, Orla. It was in honor of my marriage."

She glared, then she huffed, then she simply dropped her face to her knees. "Ah, Mother, what is it you've done to me?"

And oddly enough, Liam wanted to touch her, to soothe the weight from those frail-looking shoulders. "Is it so very bad, then?" he asked.

She didn't bother to lift her head. "Did you happen to hear the gentle words of welcome the women in that square shared with me, then?"

"Ah, no. No, I didn't. I came in just as you threatened to raise your own army."

"Still not a bad idea. But not with that crowd, I'm

thinking. Sure, they'd rather I break my vow and slink away in defeat than share any of their skills so I might gain my stones."

Ah, he hadn't realized it was that bad. And as proud as his Orla was, it must have cut her deep.

Almost as deep as his behavior at the banquet the night before.

"I'm—"

That fast her head was up and her eyes blazing. "Don't," she said, lifting an imperious finger, "apologize. Not till you can mean it for more than the length of a conversation."

Ah, now, didn't that make him feel better? He wanted to kick himself. "For that, too. You're not the only one uprooted and turned about by this, Orla."

"I seem to be the only one treating it with grace, though, don't I?"

By Lugh's left hand, how could she set off his temper so fast, when all he wanted was to comfort her?

"Define," he grated out, "grace." Thinking, instead, of how she'd stood toe-to-toe with him, screaming like a fishwife.

Sure, she lifted her head at that one. "Well, now, I'd have to say that grace is not calling your king a backward, bigoted blowhard for all that nonsense he spouted about how I'd finally be worthy of something after shooting a boy—and only a boy, for faith, what are women for anyway?—from my loins. *That,* fairy, is grace. For wasn't I eyeing the very sharp lance of the closest elven guard to show the king exactly where his heart would have been if he'd had one? And I never—" she jabbed him in the chest for emphasis "—*never* grabbed it."

Gods, he wanted to laugh. He wanted to pummel her. How could it be both? How could he survive this?

"Well, glad I am you've found the high ledges of the Reeks," he finally managed. "Sure, outrage like that would never be safe any closer to the village."

"And *you*," she reminded him with another poke, "were going to tell me of this daughter you have."

"After I tell you this. I'll not have my wife shamed before the women. I'll be speaking to Bevin, Siomha and Binne by sunset tomorrow, and you'll find your skills with them."

"And who are they?"

"Those women you were tormenting today, wife. The leading women of the clan. It is they, along with Owain's wife, Aifric, who make the women's decisions."

She went wide-eyed on him. "Those really aren't their names, now, are they?"

"And why shouldn't they be?"

She snorted and shook her head. "Goddess, with names like that, it's no wonder no one stands up to the stupidity of the men around here. Quiet, sweet and pleasant? *These* are the names of the women of power? Faith, the first thing I'd do if I had any say is rename them Bride, Brina and Macha. Strength, protector and battle. *That* is what I'd call your women, and maybe then they'd learn to stand alongside their men when the world is threatened. Maybe then they'd demand the men afford them a bit of respect for the terrible task of raising their children, boys *and* girls." She wound down, then, her shoulders slumping as she came flush up against the reality of Liam's world. "That's what I'd do."

And Liam was stunned to realize that he believed her. Worse, he was sad that she would never get to realize that dream, for she was a bright-plumed bird caught in a dull brown cage. And there wasn't a thing he could do about it.

"You might want to rename my girl child, as well," he said.

Her head snapped up. "Haven't you heard me at all, then? You speak of your child as if she's livestock. Is that all she is to you?"

"Nay." At least in this he could be honest. His daughter was the constant reminder of his sins. She was his penance and redemption. And he couldn't bear to look at her most days. "What would you have me call her?"

"By her name, I'd think."

He found a small grin. "She doesn't like her name."

Orla tilted her head. "Well, if it's anything like the other names in this village, I may already respect the girl."

"It's Binne, as well."

She actually rolled her eyes. "Well, the girl has sense, sure. She shouldn't have to bear such a burden."

"Her mother chose her name."

"Her new mother will give her a second name, then."

"And what will that be?"

"Isn't that for us to find out when we meet?"

He was getting uncomfortable again. "It was never my plan you should," he said. "She is content with her mother's clan."

"So content she wants another name? She'll come to us. She should at least meet her second mother, no matter if she stays with the first."

Liam opened his mouth to protest. Maybe even to explain. But for the second time in two suns, he was saved from having to anger his wife.

"Berzerkers!"

It was Faolán, and suddenly Liam could see him racing over the hills, the other three men of their unit close behind.

"How many?" Liam demanded, jumping to his feet.

"Enough for the troop! We have a bit of time and all. You want to raise them?"

"You're secure in defense?"

"Aye."

"I'll stay," Orla offered as if they were discussing dinner preparations.

"You'll not," Liam said. "My men can't fight with a woman in their midst." He caught her hand as she was about to take exception. "Even a woman versed in the arts of war. Help me warn the village and gather the men."

She couldn't argue, of course. Taking one last look to where Faolán and the men were choosing their defensive positions, she whipped around and leapt off her ledge. All Liam could do was run down the mountain after her.

Chapter 7

Orla wanted to scream. No, maybe she *would* scream, just to see if it would get a reaction out of any of these women. Liam had led a troop of mounted warriors off into the mountains what seemed like eons ago, and not a word had been heard since. And the women seemed oblivious.

No, she couldn't actually say that, either. Here they sat in the main square of the village, where a lovely fountain sparkled in the diffuse light of late day and flowers ran riot before the cottages, and where all of the *bean tighe*'s equipment lay gathered and sorted to the side: salves, potions, bandages, instruments.

Orla had recognized them from seeing them just recently when her own *bean tighe* had dealt with the terrible injuries her people had suffered in battle with this very clan. She still couldn't look at the awful things without remembering the stifled cries, the groans and, worse, the terrible silence of failure.

Sure, the women of this village must have suffered the losses of that same battle. Orla herself had seen the *Dubhlainn Sidhe* dead lying crumpled on the beautiful plains of Sligo. But not one of these women had said a word about their losses. None seemed to worry about the men now fighting. Not one paced or so much as stopped to look south to where the men had disappeared.

Didn't they wonder? Didn't they, in the name of the goddess, know fear?

No, they sat in sight of those terrible instruments working at their own crafts as if nothing were at stake. They conversed about the chores of daily life and bestowed passing hugs on bright-eyed children as they ran by. And they passed Orla from one woman to the next in an attempt to identify her skills.

It had taken no more than a look from her husband to set them to the task, and they'd done it with a will. Hadn't she already molded a set of misshapen bowls that would hold no more than air and embarrassment? Hadn't she knitted a scarf that had somehow come out with angles to it? Hadn't she tried to make a loaf of fairy bread, only to set the baker's house on fire?

If she took to measuring Liam's absence in the number of tasks failed, it would be six. If she measured it in the levels of frustration and patronization, it would be crippling. Her fingers were pricked and burned, her hair knotted, and her dull brown dress singed and stained.

"How long does it usually take to fight off such an incursion?" she asked, settling herself next to Binne, the tanner's consort, who was to show her how to prepare skins.

A tiny wren of a woman with chapped hands and a shy giggle, Binne opened her kit of tools. "Ah, well," she said, "I've never known Liam to miss more than a meal or two."

Which said nothing to Orla.

"The king does not come to wait?" she asked, as Binne sharpened one of her blades.

Binne looked up, puzzled. "Sure, whatever for?"

Orla opened her mouth and found she had nothing to say. Was it this commonplace, then, this invasion from the realms of nightmares? Was she to expect to pass her days waiting for word of Liam's safety?

She would never be able to stand it.

At one point she'd even briefly thought to go visit with the horses, just to take her fear where it couldn't be witnessed by the women. Sure, she was going to have to get used to the beasts sooner or later, anyway. It seemed there wasn't a person in the place who didn't revere them.

Maybe if she crept away alone to get used to the horse they'd gifted her with, she wouldn't be as likely to humiliate herself later in public by falling off. Especially since they'd thought to honor her with an animal named Breeda. Brilliant. They name the *horse* strong. Exactly the companion a fairy who was terrified of the awful things needed—a princess who would have had her tongue cut out before admitting it.

But Binne said that the women never left the square while the Guardians fought.

"Not since what happened to Aghna the last time, anyway," Binne said, her attention too much on her work to see the startled reactions of the other women.

"Aghna?" Orla asked, eyeing Binne's instruments with trepidation. How exactly would she ruin *this* project? "Who's that?"

"Oh, Liam's consort. Sure, we lost her, and her little girl so brokenhearted and all."

Orla knew she was gaping. "*Lost* her? Great goddess, how?"

Binne looked up quickly, her expression chagrined. "Oh…oh, well…it was…I'm sure Liam will tell you, now. I just know a bit and all."

Which was a lie, of course. Orla was going to say something, but suddenly Binne's mate, the tanner, was looming over the little woman.

"You've a mouth on you, don't you, woman?" he barked, startling a few birds.

Binne flinched. "Forgive me, Peadar. I just—"

His motions jerky and impatient, he crowded her even more. "You just *nothing*. Control your tongue."

Instinctively Orla stepped up. "Ah, now, wasn't she just helping me see if I could work the skins and all?"

The husband straightened, and Orla saw a flash of raw rage in his eyes. "I thank you for your help," he said, his voice not much calmer, his meaty hands fisted at his side, "but it is my word Binne needs about her behavior. Isn't that so, Binne?"

The little woman's head was bowed, almost in a defensive position. "Aye," she whispered. "So it is. It's that sorry I am, Peadar."

"And why aren't you working on the feast?"

"The *Coimirceoiri* are in the hills."

That seemed to be enough. He straightened and patted a bit at his leather apron and huffed. "You'll be at the home on time, then."

"Oh, aye." She never lifted her head to see him leave.

As silence returned to the square, the women all bent back over their work. Orla just stared after him. What had she just seen here? No fairy man should so disrespect his lady, especially in front of her friends and neighbors. She looked around, but not one of them looked surprised. Not one seemed to be fighting the same urge as she, to give the bully a piece of her mind.

Sure, she'd seen mortal men harass their wives just so, pushing their bulk around and stealing a woman's space and pride. But a fairy!

"Would you…uh, like to try the scraper?" Binne asked her.

Taking one last look toward where the tanner had joined a knot of other tradesmen farther down the lane, Orla found she could do naught but nod. Sure, she would take it up later with Liam. For now, though, she had more time to waste and another puzzle to solve. Taking a calming breath, she bent to her new task.

It was hard to ruin a goat skin, but Orla managed it. She stank of acid and animal fat and had cut another hole in her dress, and had nothing to show for it but an untidy lump of hair and a shriveled…something. And still she saw nothing from the direction of the mountains.

"It'll soon be time for the meal," she said, gazing off toward the Reeks.

Several of the women looked up. "Aye."

Then bent back to their work. Orla thought she might scream.

"Would you like to—" Aifric swallowed and considered her loom like a fragile child "—weave?"

Orla looked at the fairy-fine lilac wool on the frame and swallowed, as well. "Ah, no, Aifric. Not today, I'm thinking. The piece you have in there is too exquisite altogether for me to lay hands on it. Why doesn't someone show me a piece of furniture that needs destroying or a house that needs being brought down? I think I'd excel at that, now."

And for the first time, she actually got the women to smile for her. Sure, a few even laughed.

"Ah, now, it can't be that bad," Aifric offered unsteadily. "Sure there's something we can find for you."

"Not unless it involves tormenting mortal men evidently," Orla admitted without enthusiasm. "And sure, haven't I given that up as a bad habit?"

"And you won't help the *bean tighe?*" that severe gray lady asked from the side of the square.

"Ah, well, since I'm being honest and all," Orla said, "you should know that having my hands in blood doesn't just make me faint."

"No?"

She closed her eyes, remembering the very uncomfortable moments when she'd seen to her archers after battle. "I vomit."

The women actually arched away a bit, as if afraid she might demonstrate. The *bean tighe* bent a small smile on Orla. "And don't I prefer the honesty over the surprise?" she asked.

And of course, wouldn't that be the moment the Stone Keeper made his dancing, flitting appearance? "Ah, grand, Orla. You're learning the women's skills."

The women all laughed again, so hard that Aifric dropped her shuttle, then had the grace to look chagrined.

Until Orla laughed the loudest. "Ah, brilliant. Come, Stone Keeper, and see the miracles I've wrought with base clay and flour. Bestow on me so many stones I may not lift my hands."

Eibhear entered the square with a beaming smile that

lasted only as long as it took him to reach the wall where Orla's attempts had been displayed.

"Great goiter of Goneril," he breathed, wide-eyed.

Orla bent to consider her lumpish ceramic attempt. "Why, Eibhear, I think you have it entirely. Doesn't it bear the butter stamp of the thing, for sure?"

She got another burst of laughter from the women.

Eibhear turned distressed eyes on her. "And you look—"

She spread her arms out and twirled, knowing precisely how she looked and smelled. "As if I've survived an attack by marauding monkeys?"

"Ah, no," he disagreed. "Sure, monkeys are much tidier altogether."

Pushing her drooping hair out of her eyes, she grinned at him. "And they smell better."

He shrugged and grinned back. "Ah, well, I didn't want to say anything, in case you'd fallen in the cesspit and were embarrassed."

"Not any more embarrassed than I've been by my attempts at the womanly arts."

"You've really…tried."

She nodded. "I really have."

"And you don't want to, maybe, try again?"

Three woman cried "No!" so loudly that Orla burst out laughing again.

"Only if you want every other woman in this village to beat you like a rented dwarf."

"Did you have any ideas of your own, then?" he asked, looking truly perplexed.

"Besides forming the women into an army of archers? Or raising a rousing game of *comargie?*"

"Aye," he said very drily. "Besides that."

"Archery?" Aifric asked.

Orla smiled on the women. "Sure, isn't it part of what I spoke of before, teaching you how to do what I did at the banquet. Now, *that* I would delight in doing."

"Well, *that* would get me pilloried not only by your husband, but the king himself," Eibhear protested. "Is there another task you might want?"

She sat on the fountain wall, suddenly tired. "Nothing comes to mind, I fear. But sure, I'll be after letting you know when it does."

Alongside her, Aifric got to her feet. "She *did* try, Eibhear," she said. "I will attest to how hard she worked."

Binne rose, as well, and the *bean tighe* herself. One by one, the women joined her. "Aye," Binne said. "Take nothing away from her for the attempting."

Orla was just tired and dispirited enough to find herself beset by the sting of tears in the back of her throat. "I thank you all," she said, confused by a sense of camaraderie she'd never known before. "Especially for your great patience."

"Ah, sure, it's no problem," Soimhe, who'd tried to teach her knitting, said with a grin. "Where else would we see such unique creations, then?"

It was then, finally, that they heard the horses approaching from the south. To a woman they turned, slipped aprons over their fairy dresses and gathered over by the *bean tighe* in a curious choreography. Orla stood where she was, her heart racing and her hands damp with sweat. She could see no farther than the first curve of the lane out of the village, for the great oak sanctuary grew close and tall there. She could hear the quiet talk of the women and had nothing to say to them. Goddess, how did they stand this, the not knowing, the

terrible fear that the one you waited for would not turn
that corner?

How did *she* survive it, who hadn't yet had the time
to grow used to this terrible thing, this anxiety she didn't
want at all? How did she wait time and again for him to
return to her?

She refused to think what that meant. Faith, she
hadn't even known how to think of a man as anything
but a toy until recently. She was an infant to her emotions, and she felt she would burst with them.

And then she saw him. A bit battered, a bit bloody,
grinning like a boy after a good hurling match, as he
deftly guided his great warhorse down the lane at the
head of his troop. The thunder of them echoed through
the little village. The women strained to see each man
who progressed toward them. The *bean tighe* waited
patiently by her instruments, her hands hidden inside the
sleeves of her blue robes and her features quiet.

Liam pulled his horse up not a foot from the gathering and grinned down at the women. "We'll be in need
of a bit of bandaging, *bean tighe*. The ghostlords thought
to make a feast of us this day. They went home with
empty bellies."

The *bean tighe* nodded. "Well, then, it's to the banquet you'll all be going as soon as you're cleaned up and
presentable. There will be singing in the halls tonight,
all right."

"Singing indeed, *bean tighe*. And where is my lady
wife? Does she wait also?"

"She's been busy destroying your village while you
played soldiers," Orla called out to him, rigid with the
effort to keep her knees under her.

Goddess, he took her breath all over again. Sleek and

strong and supple atop his prancing horse, his hair tumbled back and his eyes glowing with the exhilaration of a battle well fought. She wanted to pull him off that horse and take him in the dirt. She wanted to weep with relief. She wanted to pummel him until he promised never to frighten her again. She was weak with the surprise of it, and furious that she wasn't stronger.

He laughed as his troop clattered to a halt around him and began to dismount. "Did you miss me, wife?"

"Like a rash, husband."

With the agility of a cat, he vaulted off his horse and gave him a swat on the arse. The horse gave him a big shove in the back and then turned to trot off to the stable, where the horsemaster would praise and reward him. One by one the other horses followed. Liam paid no attention. He was stalking his wife.

"By the light of Lugh, woman, isn't it an adorned and sweet-smelling wife a husband should be able to come back to?"

"By the sweet hand of Danu," she retorted, feeding off the sudden heat in his eyes, "if that's what you're wanting, you should give me fair warning of when you're due home. Sure, I've had my hands full tormenting your clanswomen. I can't be expected to bathe, as well."

He reached her, sweaty and grimy and streaked with blood from a long cut on the side of his head that should have set her stomach to roiling. Curiously, it didn't.

Grinning, he bent that head to her. "In that case, we'll just have to bathe together."

She smelled him, now: salt and earth and wind. She fed off the exhilaration in his eyes. She *yearned*.

"Are you sure there's a river in all the land of faerie deep enough to dunk that great head of yours?" she asked.

He laughed, his teeth gleaming in the failing light. "It's not my head I'm thinking of dunking, woman. And sure, not in a river."

She actually felt like blushing. She, Orla, who had said and done things that would have made this man blanch.

"Ah, no," she said, physically turning him back toward the other women. "You get yourself over to the *bean tighe* first. Once she's had her way with you, then maybe I'll have mine."

He actually waggled his eyebrows at her. "You're not coming along, then?"

"No," she said, giving him a bit of a push. "I'll wait right here where I'm not in the way."

"So it's not a *bean tighe* you'll be, then?"

"Sure, why would I wish to replace the good one you've got?"

He stopped and considered the state of her dress. "Then what skills do you bring me, wife? What womanly arts to soften the edges of my home?"

Ah, didn't the man know how to deflate her mood, even when he wasn't trying? "No skills, husband. No arts."

And that was the sum of it, wasn't it? The only thing she thought she could do, she wasn't allowed to. Other than that, she had nothing to bring to this man or his clan. Ah, well, she'd at least had some moments of hope this day. She'd had the camaraderie of the women, which she'd never enjoyed before, not even with her sisters. If she had nothing to give in return, what did that matter?

All the other women had gathered to welcome their men, clucking and patting and tending with gentle, practiced hands. With a flashing smile, Liam joined them. Aifric chastised him for taking risks, and the woman who had such clever hands on a potting wheel closed the wound on his head.

And Orla, unable to take a step closer, stood alone at the edge of the evening and watched. And when she knew her husband was well cared for, she turned and walked away.

"You didn't wait for me."

Orla looked up from where she was washing her hair in the stream behind their house to see her husband standing on the bank.

"Ah, well, you were in good hands. I had nothing to do but make myself sweet-smelling for you, now, did I?"

Did he hear the unpardonable uncertainty in her voice? Could he tell how suddenly isolated she felt, even after a wonderful afternoon in which her disasters seemed to have at least succeeded in weaving some kind of bond with the other women of the village?

But the waiting for him had changed her. His return had cemented it. She needed him. She fed off the sight of him like honey and berries. She feared for him, and ached to stand by his side when he put himself in danger.

And he wouldn't let her. More, he didn't wish her to. He didn't need her, for what was there to need?

"Well, wife," he said, shucking his clothing, "I've done as you said and presented myself to the *bean tighe* for her torture. Sure, don't you think I deserve a reward for it?"

The shadows had collected in the glen, the mountain eating the late light so that Orla could see him only in patterns. The slice of a thigh, the curve of a shoulder, the spark of animation in his eye. How could those alone set her pulse thundering again? All right, then, those and the suggestion in his words. The potent grace of his movements. The purr of his voice.

"And a reward you shall have, husband," she said, knowing that her voice was breathy with hunger. Suddenly the air chilled her and the water swept too strongly against her. Every inch of her skin was sensitive. Her body, once wholly her own, burned for the meeting with his.

Naked now, a work of art painted in shadow and sinew, he bent at the waist and dove into the deep pool by the willow. Orla turned to meet him when he rose, and thought how different her life had become in a matter of days. Then she felt his hand curl around her calf, and she thought of nothing at all.

He swept his hand up her leg as he rose from the stream. He wrapped his hands around her waist and pulled her to him, as if even air was too thick a barrier between them. He bent his head to her and just looked.

"Was it a hard fight?" Orla asked, lifting a hand to trace the injury at the edge of his face.

He smiled at her and let his own hands wander. "Ah, wife," he mourned. "Am I going to have to be instructing you all the time? No fairy wife would ever ask such a question when her husband comes to court her."

Orla smiled back, still anxious about her own lack. "Well, I'm no ordinary fairy wife, then, am I, husband?"

He settled a hand around her breast and simply warmed her. She shivered anyway, but sure, not with cold. Her nipples pebbled hard, and her belly ached.

"Aye, then," he said, kissing her eyes closed. "A hard fight we had, but a good one all the same."

She arched her neck to give him better access. "I'm not good at the waiting, Liam."

He thumbed her nipple and kissed her behind the ear. "I know, Orla. I thought of you up there on the ridges. We could have used an archer or two."

She took her own turn, spreading her hands over the warm planes of his back, memorizing muscle and tendon and spine. "And I would have been happy to provide them, so."

He sipped the water off her throat. "But you can't," he said.

She curled her fingers into his hair and thought she might weep. "I know. Sure, and haven't you men fallen into some bad habits since you lost your female stone?"

She could feel his smile against the sensitive hollow between her collarbones, and it set off fireworks down to her toes. "Ah, now, you can't think this is a bad habit."

Then he tasted her with his tongue.

"I can think of…worse," she managed, even as her knees threatened to fail her. Ah, he felt so fine beneath her hands, all sleek lines and solid angles. How perfectly he fit her, hip to hip, thigh to thigh. How deliciously her body anticipated his.

"Will you celebrate with me, then, Orla?" he asked.

Opening her eyes, she saw that he was serious. It was a request, sure, something she had never thought to hear from this proud, self-contained man. Just the thought of it threatened whatever defenses she had left. She couldn't even think to be flippant.

"Aye, Liam," she said, meeting his gaze with certainty. "I will, and gladly."

His smile was slow and heated and, goddess help her, relieved. He said not another word, just bent to her, his mouth a hair's breadth from hers.

"Open to me," he whispered, and she did.

"Let me touch you," he pleaded, and she did.

"Come to me now," she begged, and he did, lifting her in his warrior's arms and begging her to put her legs around his waist, then dipping his fingers into her, spreading her, settling the tip of him against her. Taking his face into her hands, she met him openmouthed and sucked on his tongue. She wrapped herself around him, rubbing her breasts against his chest. She inhaled him, and she tasted him, and she took him deep into her, sliding down on him until he was fully joined to her, stretching her, filling her, surrounding her with his heat and life and delicious, silken strength.

Let me love you, she almost said, but didn't. For sure, why should he want that? She closed her eyes, instead, so he couldn't see the words in them, and she laid her head against his and rocked in his arms and pulled him into her and discarded every sense but the sense of him, the rightness of him. She collected his groans to her heart, and she gathered her own arousal, able to weave this at least from sight and smell and the agonizing anticipation of his touch.

She felt his climax coming on him, gasping and straining so that he filled her, oh, aye, sating her with the great strength of him, so tight, so deep, that she felt her own body clench, felt the stars and colors and scents of the earth spinning into her, through her, setting her to shuddering and sobbing there, her face in the crook of his neck, her ecstasy cradled safe in his arms.

The stream burbled around them. The water washed them, and the cooling evening air gentled them. And still they stood as they were, Orla wrapped tightly in his arms and in turn wrapping him tightly in hers. And never did she want to move from this place again.

"Orla," he said into her hair, his breath tickling her.

She held her breath, not sure what she wanted him to say. Not love words, sure. But maybe comfort words, or words of welcome?

"Yes?"

"I leave in the morning for an extended number of sunsets. I need you to behave while I'm gone."

That quickly, the night became cold and Orla remembered her place.

Chapter 8

It was to be a long patrol, he'd said to her, taking him and a large contingent to the far reaches of the mountains. It was his duty and right as head of the *Coimirceoiri* to lead them so, and he was honored to do it. He'd swung into his saddle and trotted out of the village at the head of his elite troop and said not a word of missing her. Of looking forward to the day when he could return to her arms.

And now, more than a moon cycle later, Orla decided that he could stay on his benighted patrol until he turned to dust, for not only had he forgotten to leave her with kind words or suggestions of what to do when she continued to fail in finding her stone gifts, he'd also forgotten to leave her with instructions for what to do when his daughter suddenly appeared on her doorstep.

"Sure, and didn't the beast so much as say he'd sent for me?" the little girl demanded, her pack of clothing at her feet, her gaze reflecting supreme childish disdain as she took in Orla's aborted attempts at housekeeping. "He said it was your idea and all."

"Ah, no. He didn't," Orla said, stepping down from where she'd just hung the curtains she'd woven on Aifric's loom. She had to tilt her head to appreciate them, since, sure, hadn't they refused to stay a uniform length or use up all the yarn she'd introduced? Their color was grand, but she wasn't sure what to do about all the little knobs of material that lumped the things up so.

"Faith, you're more useless than I am," her new daughter said, hands on small hips.

Well, Orla was in a surly enough mood for both of them. She needed no help from a child. Taking a good rub at her tense forehead and forgetting what the elder Binne had told her, she sighed. "Do you speak to your own mother so?"

The little girl lifted an imperious eyebrow. "And why on the god's earth would I be after talking to *her?* She's been dead these many seasons."

"Ah, I'm that sorry for it."

She cursed herself for forgetting. She knew so little about this child, but the name she didn't want. But it wouldn't do for the child to know. And child she was, no taller than Kieran back in the land of the *Tuatha.* Maybe eight summers? Nine? And sure, a beauty she would be in a few more, as dark-eyed as her father, with a thick ebony braid that reached to her waist, palest porcelain skin and a bow-shaped little mouth that would probably do better for not pouting so much.

"How long has it been since you've seen your father?" she asked, bending to pick up the girl's bag and heading for the second bedroom.

"Since he threw me out, I imagine."

"Sure, he did nothing of the kind. What do men know of raising a little girl, now?"

"Little girl?" the child echoed haughtily. "I am no little girl. I am the daughter of the Avenger."

Orla turned back to her. "I thought he was a beast."

"Well, it doesn't keep him from being a great warrior, now, does it?"

Orla gave her a wry smile. "I'd say it should help greatly. What do you wish to be called?"

"You know not my name?"

"Of course I know your name. The question is, does it fit you?"

Liam's daughter gave an inelegant snort. "Not if I were hit on the head with a mallet and lost all memory. Sure, wouldn't I have to be a ninny to choose a name like Binne for myself?"

"You don't see yourself as the sweet type, then?"

"It's a silly name."

"Was it your mother's choice?"

The little girl scowled, looking oddly vulnerable for all that. "I'm thinking it might have been more like wishful thinking."

Orla smiled. "And if *you* wished? What would you choose?"

She'd made it all the way inside the second bedroom, where more of her artistic efforts were on display. Sure, it looked as if someone had left behind all the rejects from the artisans' guild.

"By the light of Lugh," the girl said, staring in awe at one particularly vile attempt at glassblowing. "How did you get my stone trials here before me?"

Orla took another look around, and then at the

stunned look on the little girl's face, and couldn't help but laugh. "Ah, now, I think we're going to get along fine, daughter of the Avenger. For isn't all this the unfortunate result of *my* stone trials?"

Liam's daughter stood in the doorway, staring in disbelief at the mismatched, miscolored room Orla had put together with her own hands. Then she burst out laughing.

"Well, now, doesn't that just pay him back in full coin, then?" she said, and stepped inside.

"Pay him back for what?"

"For discarding a gentle consort who lived only to please him."

Faith, was every creature in this realm so good at driving knives into her chest?

"You defend your mother well," Orla managed.

Binne shrugged. "Someone has to do it. She never managed on her own, sure."

Orla had no idea what else to say. She had a good idea that small chat was over, and what else was there for her to offer? She was sure the child would know better than to anticipate any food prepared by her stepmother's hand. Sure, wasn't that same stepmother teaching the baker a few tricks of self-defense in exchange for a bit of bread and honey? Come to think of it, she'd done the same for Siomha the knitter and Bevin the herbalist, all behind Eibhear's back. After all, what the Stone Keeper didn't know, the king didn't, either.

What did one offer a child? It had been her sister Sorcha's gift, to always know what to do with them. Not hers. Wasn't the only child she'd ever spent any time with the seer himself? And sure, Kieran was older in spirit than any other child she'd ever met. Except maybe her new daughter.

"Deirdre," the little girl said suddenly, her gaze fixed solidly on Orla's curtains. "I'd be Deirdre."

Orla all but held her breath as she gave a slow nod. "How long is it I've known you now, daughter of the Avenger?"

Finally the girl looked over, and Orla caught the lonely little girl in those challenging eyes. And she knew that no matter what else, she wasn't about to let this child be tossed aside again.

"It hasn't even been a sun-quartering, why?"

And wasn't she balanced for flight when she said it? Orla thought of a fawn caught at the edge of safety, an eye always to the forest. If fawns had teeth and claws, at least.

She smiled at the child. "Ah, sure, and wouldn't I say I can't think of a more perfect name for you if I worked for my life."

The girl stiffened. "You think 'one who rages' appropriate, do you?"

"Ah, no, I'm not at all fond of that meaning. I much prefer 'fearsome one.' For haven't I been looking this long while I've been in your realm for another fearsome creature to talk to?"

Still the child didn't relax. Orla didn't mind. She knew where she was going with this girl, even if the girl didn't. She *liked* her, and wasn't that a rare thing entirely?

"And is it as Deirdre you'd like me to introduce you to the women of the village?" she asked.

The girl snorted again, waving a dismissive hand toward the town square. "Sure, they already think they know Binne."

"But Binne was her mother's obedient daughter. A

girl who protected the one she loved with silence. I'm thinking Deirdre might be the perfect daughter for this new…" No, she couldn't claim mothership to the child, or she would lose every trace of progress she'd made. "What?" she asked, tilting her head to the girl. "How is it we should be known to each other?"

The girl still looked skittish, but at least she also looked intrigued. "They tell me he married you."

"By edict of your king and my queen."

That earned a few moments of silence. Orla waited them out without moving. The girl gave another look around the room, around the village, as if she could see it through the walls. "I imagine himself would have an opinion on what it should be. Where is he, then, when I come at his bidding?"

"Guarding the borders so you can rest peacefully in his house. And no, I know not when he'll be back."

"Well, there's nothing new, then."

"Would you have him sacrifice his mission for the pleasure of a selfish child?"

Orla almost didn't hear the girl's answer, so struck was she by her own words. Here she'd been grousing and fretting this long while since she'd last seen Liam, and sure, wasn't she acting like a spoiled child herself?

It was no help that she wished she could have been out on those borders with him. Or that she'd thought she could have done a better job than some she'd seen mount their horses that last morn. For now, her job was to wait.

"I'd say I'd want to be your friend," she said to his daughter. "But that won't sit well at the times when I need to tell you nay. For no matter how well I like you, it won't change my mind."

Oddly enough, that seemed to intrigue the girl all the more. "I could call you Stonebarren."

"You could. But then I'd have to call you the same, and I thought we'd settled on Deirdre."

The girl flushed and turned her head. "You'll not be my mother."

"Nor did I ask to be. But I'd like to be more than your father's wife."

The girl shook her head, as if Orla had just taken one step too many. "Let me think on it," she said.

Orla actually felt relieved. "Ah, grand," she said. "Let me know at any time. I'd say we're going to have plenty of it."

That quick, the fawn threatened to flee. "I'll not be staying," she said, her voice high and shrill. "I *have* a place in the world to be."

Orla nodded. "And so you do. I'm hoping after you get to know your father *and* his wife better, you'll have two places in the world to be. But this is no prison, Deirdre. I would never take that choice from another, since it was taken from me."

"You don't want to be here?"

"I wasn't given the chance to decide. I'll do well with it. But sure, choice is a precious thing to have."

"So you don't wish for his attention, either?"

Ah, how easily one lost the advantage with a child. "For all his fierce reputation," Orla said, as if musing over a decision long made, "I'd have to say I've seen nothing but honor in him."

"He's abrupt. He thinks of nothing but his mission."

Orla shrugged. "He's a man. If you can change that, sure, I think you might change his character."

Finally, *finally*, Orla got a slow, sly smile from the

girl. "And wouldn't he look ridiculous in a woman's dress, now?"

Orla laughed. "I'd say he'd run neck and neck with Culley the butcher for ugliest woman in thirteen realms."

They shared a moment—only a moment—of accord.

"Would you like to go outside and see the women?"

"I'd like to set up my room. Sure, it looks as if half of what's here will end up in the trash."

"Only if you want to sleep there with it."

The little girl just stood there, chin up, Liam's midnight eyes challenging Orla to force her into something. Orla felt unbalanced again, frustrated with her foray into the unknown. One minute fine, the next bog land, and goddess, wasn't she overcome by the urge to rub at her forehead again? Maybe it wouldn't be a bad idea to have a break from Liam's daughter for a bit.

Was this what Liam felt when she sparred with him? Was she just as wearing on a man's patience and tact? Would he toss her aside, as he had his consort, when she finally wore him out?

With no answer to any of it, she left the room and closed the door behind her. It was as well she had an appointment with Bevin the herbalist. Sure, she wasn't needed here right now.

Orla sneezed, and the ground comfrey disappeared into a cloud.

"Ah, well, here's another notch on my belt," she said, brushing the powder off her face. "Eibhear can keep the jade for earthweaver in his store room. Sure, I'll not be wearing it."

"We could try again," little Bevin offered.

As tiny as Deirdre, Bevin had a high, breathy voice

and moonlight-pale hair to go with her dark brown eyes. Her dress was a mottle of moss-green and goldenrod, and her hands bore the herbalist's jade.

Orla didn't like cooking, and she certainly didn't take to the healing that might demand any of these plants, but she wouldn't have minded at all coming away from this little house with at least one skill under her belt, especially since Bevin had been so patient with her. Faith, Orla was certain she'd condemned Bevin to days back up the hill replenishing her sneezed, spilled and crushed supplies.

"I'll come for the picking," she offered, trying her best to scoop up a bit in her hands to put back in the bowl.

Bevin's laugh was anxious. "My thanks, Orla, but prayers are needed, and ritual, to retain the perfect properties of the herb in its taking."

Translation: Orla would royally bollocks-up that task, too. "Well, then, why don't I take a bit of time to show you a new trick or two?"

Again Bevin looked anxious. "Oh, I shouldn't and all," she protested. "It's unseemly…."

"But?"

Orla had been waiting for the answer to that question for days now. After all, Bevin had sought her out as she'd wandered in the deep shade along the stream, and pleaded with twisting hands for help in learning just enough to protect herself from…

From whom? She'd never answered.

Bevin tiptoed to her window and peeked out along the lane. She checked the door. "Please," she said, turning. "Just one or two more."

Orla wasn't about to refuse. "Well, then, Bevin, for the next trick, I need to know if you have the courage to do it."

Bevin actually paled. "I…I don't…"

"It's not difficult. It doesn't even take much strength. You just have to be willing to inflict pain."

"Oh."

Again the other woman's hands were twisting in front of her as if anxious all on their own. Fleeting emotions sped across her features, and then she straightened her shoulders. Well, Orla might not recognize the emotions, but she recognized the actions. She stepped close, for close was where secrets were safest.

"It's so easy, you should know it already, sure," she said, then took one of those flighty hands and led Bevin to the window. "Faith, we all should. Now, do you see Culley the butcher there?"

Bevin peeked and ducked, then nodded. Well, it would have been tough to miss him. Orla suspected he'd traded his patience for food, for sure, wasn't he forever bellowing at somebody and munching on something?

"I know he seems fierce," Orla said. "Faith, he's got a bellow on him stronger than his own bulls."

"He's too big," Bevin whispered. "They all are."

"Not at all, and I'm about to tell you why. See where his legs come together there beneath that great wobbly belly of his?"

Bevin blushed, then nodded again.

"Grand." Orla took hold of her hand. "That's where the most sensitive part of a man's body lies, Bevin. His stones. I promise you, if you want to stop any man in his tracks, all you have to do is kick up with your knee as hard as you can right into his stones. He won't expect it, and after, he won't be in any shape to chase you for it."

Bevin kept watching the butcher, who seemed to be browbeating his helper.

"You're sure."

"Oh, aye. Hasn't the *leannan sidhe* had to have recourse to the trick a time or two, when a man insisted his rights were the only ones to be considered?"

Bevin chuckled a bit, the sound almost a gasp. "Kick," she said.

Orla grinned. "Up."

"Does anyone else know about this?"

"Well, if I have my way, now, by the time I'm finished, every woman in the land of faerie will."

Bevin gave a quick, jerky nod. "I hope you do, so."

In truth, Orla thought as she left Bevin's home, she was considering doing just that. She wasn't sure if she was only noticing because Liam was gone, but it seemed lately that the mood of the village had turned sour and fractious. Sure, no one was waiting for the banquet to fight anymore. She saw a lot of finger-jabbing and flying spittle, and weren't the women clustering a bit closer together as they worked? Hadn't they been getting the brunt of the bad tempers?

She could see no reaction in them, sure. Nothing except the rare incidence of somebody like Bevin asking for surreptitious help. But she was beginning to feel… nervous.

And the trees were turning. Nobody noticed yet, she thought, because they would never have expected to look for it. But Orla knew. She saw. As sure as day, the world was fading without the Dearann Stone to counteract the Coilin.

Her mother had warned her about the effect of Coilin energy in a masculine world. Was that what she was seeing? Maybe she should take some time and question some of the dryads in the trees. Sure, they had the measure of the earth better than any. They would know whether Orla had the time to wait for Sorcha to find the lost Dearann Stone.

She could just steal the Coilin and run, then, couldn't she? Get it back to her mother's crown, where it would at least stabilize the slide till Sorcha found the Dearann Stone. Sure, there was nothing keeping her from it.

Only her oath to honor and protect her husband. And a fairy did not honor her husband by stealing something so precious and then leaving him behind to take the blame. All she could do was pray that Sorcha knew what she was doing so far off in the land of mortals. And wish she knew exactly where it was that Sorcha had been dropped, so she might use the back door to the land of mortals and help her look.

"Any luck, then, girl?" the *bean tighe* asked from her customary place of waiting while the *Coimirceoiri* remained away, her chair settled against the front wall of her house, where the sun could warm her and she could smell her roses.

Orla gave the old woman a wry smile. "I'm afraid you'll not be getting your herbs from me."

"Ah, well, it's a painstaking job, anyway. Did I hear you have the Protector's daughter with you?"

"Well, if locked in her room is with me, then so I do."

The *bean tighe* smiled. "Sure, she'll escape her den when she gets hungry. All healthy animals do."

Orla smiled back, thinking of the fierce pride in those young eyes. "She must have been a surprise to her mother, altogether."

The *bean tighe* just shook her head. "Sure, everything was a surprise to Aghna, I'm afraid."

"She's been gone awhile, then?"

"Awhile. And wasn't Liam grateful to her people for

taking the child, as he's always gone? We offered, but he felt it better that way."

"I'm that sorry for them both."

The *bean tighe* squinted over at her, as if assessing her words. "I'm not sure he's ever forgiven himself for what happened."

Orla took a step closer. "Can you tell me?"

The woman shook her head. "Ah, no. That's for your husband to say."

And wasn't it what she'd expected? "The girl wants us all to call her Deirdre now," she said.

"And it'll be Brigid next week, so. Such is the way of children."

Orla nodded, already distracted by the emptiness of the paths. "Where are the men?" she asked, turning around to take in the whole empty village.

"Can't you hear them, then? Hurling practice at the field."

Orla stood very still and then heard it. She cocked her head, trying to arrange the men's voices into coherence.

"For an afternoon of hurling, they don't seem very happy."

The *bean tighe* shrugged. "Sure, I'll have some heads to stitch this day."

Orla considered the other woman's passive countenance. "You stitch heads every day lately."

For the first time the old woman met Orla eye-to-eye. "And I'm thinkin' I'll be stitchin' until things change, too, won't I?"

Orla sucked in a breath, meeting those calm green eyes. "It'll get worse."

The healer nodded. "No one will believe if you tell them, you know."

"But they have to see the leaves falling."

"Ah, no. They only see what they want to. Especially the men."

Orla's laugh was sad. "Isn't that just like them, then?"

The *bean tighe* shrugged. "And has your mother been after acting any better?"

Orla's instinct was to jump to Mab's defense. She knew, though, that the old woman was right. "Save me from the holding of power, *bean tighe*. I'm beginning to think it more destructive than poison."

And yet she'd sought it hard enough that people had died. Now the thought made her tired.

"If I'm not mistaken," the *bean tighe* said, looking off toward a growing noise, "we're about to be visited by more blood than your stomach can stand."

Orla followed her gaze to an untidy gaggle of dirty, sweaty men marching their way, voices still raised. "Hurling's over, is it? Well, then, I'll be off to try to draw the daughter from her nest." She was about to walk away when she turned back to see the old woman watching her. "It occurs to me I don't know your name."

And for the first time she got a real smile. "Why, I'm called the same as your own *bean tighe,* girl. Bea."

"Farewell, then, Bea. I hope the hurlers keep their brawling to the field."

She hurried home. But she stopped long enough to look out to the high road, which remained stubbornly empty.

By the time Liam reached the last turn in the road four days later, he was filthy, frustrated and exhausted. It had been a hard time out in the wilderness, and he was looking forward to a bit of peace and quiet.

"My bed," Faolán groaned alongside. "All I need is my bed."

"And a willing partner," somebody said.

"Two willing partners," somebody else added.

Even the bantering was halfhearted. They had just spent one too many nights sleeping on the hard ground and dodging the rain, which was even worse. By the hand of Lugh, he was no flower fairy to thrive on a waterfall in his face. He preferred the nice, dry environs of his house, especially since he now had a very willing wife waiting there for him.

It was the only thing that had gotten him through when the days grew long and muddy, the memory of Orla in that stream the last night he'd been home. He couldn't help recalling it now, how her body had shone in the faint moonlight, how her hair had tumbled over her lush, high breasts and fallen like silk through his fingers. How her sighs had sounded like music above the chatter of the water. How tight and hot she'd been, as if made just to sheath his cock.

That thought alone was making him hard again. He could hardly wait.

"I hope there's venison at the banquet tonight," Faolán said.

Maybe, Liam thought, he was close enough to slip into her mind. Let her know he was coming. Tease her with what to expect. He could almost taste her excitement on his tongue, the anticipation almost better than the act itself.

"I hope the wine barrels are bottomless," Uaine said, tipping back his waterskin for the last drops.

"I hope Tullia is waiting naked in the road," Flann said.

Liam hoped Orla was waiting naked in the stream.

Maybe he would suggest it to her while he was still out on the road. Sure, it would give her time to get ready, then, wouldn't it? He was close enough now. All he had to do was set his mind to it. Find her mind and settle the idea right into it. He was sure he would be able to sneak in under her guard before she knew he was there. Sure, she would be delighted to welcome him.

"You shouldn't speak of your consort like that!" Uaine snapped.

For a second Liam thought he was talking to him.

"She's *my* consort," Flann said. "I'll talk of her as I want."

"Not if a better consort for her comes along."

By the gleaming balls of Silverhand, Liam thought. Here we go again.

"Enough, you two," he commanded, losing the link he'd almost established with Orla. "You've already bloodied each other's noses enough for this trip."

"He has no respect—"

"He has no right—"

"You have no permission to annoy me!" Liam yelled, turning in his saddle. "Have you two always been this juvenile, or is this just the season for it?"

Odd how two of the fiercest fighters in the *Coimirceoiri* could pout like toddlers.

"We are the *Coimirceoiri!*" he called loudly enough for all to hear over the jangle of harnesses. "We'll enter our village in a formation to make me proud or I'll know why!"

For the moment it was enough to shut them up. It was too late, though, for him to reestablish his faint link with his wife. Just as his men collected themselves into a uniform trot, the village came into view.

"Where are the women?" Faolán asked, looking around.

"Where is the *bean tighe?*" Liam echoed.

"You filthy son of a dockside troll!" he heard from down one of the lanes. "You'll pay for this!"

A woman screamed. Another, who sounded suspiciously like his wife, cursed. Liam kicked his horse into a canter. The rest of the troop followed, hands on swords.

Aifric stood at the edge of the square, her nose bleeding and her loom splintered on the stones. Two men were wrestling in the dirt alongside, and the other women had backed into a corner, out of the way. Not Liam's wife. She was stalking up to the men with a bucket of water in her hands.

"Orla!"

She looked up, and he saw the stark shock on her face. "Welcome home, husband," she greeted him.

Then she threw the water over the men. There was much howling, but the two broke apart. One even managed to notice Aifric's loom.

"Ah, ma'am, I'm that sorry," he said, standing there dripping water all over the destroyed frame.

Aifric was crying. Orla was standing with her hands on her hips.

"And what are you going to do about it, Culley?" she demanded.

"Wife," Liam said, swinging from his horse. "This isn't your business."

She glared at him. "And whose would it be, then, husband? I see no one else trying to protect Aifric's stone gift from these great louts. Most of the rest of the great louts are down at the hurling field, fighting there."

His head was beginning to throb. "They'll pay restitution."

"Ah, well, grand," she said, her voice dripping with

disdain. "That'll get the banqueting cloths made in time for your return, and take away the injury to an innocent woman, now, won't it?"

Throbbing turned to outright pain.

"And haven't I been thinking this long while of the sweet greeting you'd give me, wife?" he asked, his voice not much more patient.

She didn't even look away from where she was bent over Aifric. "It's delighted I am you're home unscathed, husband. If the great hall still stands at dusk, we'll have you a fine banquet. But before we can do that, I have to get Aifric settled." Bending down, she helped the young woman up. "Come along, *a chuisla.* Look. Isn't Owain here now to help you to the *bean tighe,* for I'm thinking you'd better get there before the hurlers do, or she'll be too busy to see you. And by the time you're finished, sure, won't Culley have asked Seannan the Master to make you a new loom?"

Culley stood alongside, head bent, like a chastised three-year-old. "Yes, ma'am."

"You bloodied her nose!" Owain yelled at him, shoving right past Aifric to get to him.

Orla grabbed him by the sleeve and spun him back to his wife. "Sure, and you can bloody his right back after we see to your lady wife." Focused on pushing the prince toward his wife, she didn't even waste a glare for Liam as she said, "I'll be home by the time you settle your horse."

He actually thought she added something under her breath like, "Although I'm not sure you'll be very happy about what you'll find there, either."

Then she walked right up to Culley and gave him a push. "And you. You let your fight spill over and hurt a good woman again, and I'll take your balls with my own knife. Do you hear me?"

Without another word, she stalked off.

"What in the name of Lugh is going on around here?" Liam demanded.

"I'd say your wife has begun to make her mark," Faolán said behind him, sounding suspiciously amused.

Liam was just about to yell at him when he was distracted by another scream, this one from a man. Half his force leapt off their horses and pounded after him down Tanner's Lane to see tiny Bevin jumping up and down, her hands over her mouth and tears in her eyes.

"Oh, I told you to stop," she sobbed, backing away.

Liam reached her to see Peadar the tanner curled up on the cobbles screeching in pain, his hands tight against his crotch.

"You vile bitch!" he screeched, rocking back and forth.

"I *told* you," she insisted on a hiccup. "I told you I'd learned to protect myself."

Faolán began to laugh. The men alongside winced in sympathy for the man in the dirt clutching his privates. Liam closed his eyes, suddenly certain he knew what had been happening since he'd been gone.

"Wife!" he bellowed.

Chapter 9

"And what did you expect me to do?" Orla demanded, her hands yet again on her hips as she faced off with Liam back in their house. "Leave these women defenseless against attack?"

"That was not an attack, Orla," he said, trying hard to keep his voice down as he battled an old surge of panic. "It was an accident. You know the men would never have targeted Aifric."

"And Bevin? Was she not a target?"

He squeezed his eyes shut and counted to thirty. Ah, sure that dream of Orla naked in the stream was waning fast.

"Peadar will be chastised by the council. You had no right to teach Bevin something so hurtful."

"You mean something that saved not only her honor, but her fairy soul? Peadar has been after her since before you left, Liam. She wouldn't tell me. You know what a gentle soul she is. But I got it out of her today. He's been harassing her, as if harassing his *own* consort weren't enough."

"Did he physically attack her?"

"No. He entered her mind."

"Then he didn't hurt her."

She seemed incredulous. "And you don't think that forcing your way into another's mind without welcome and attempting the taking of her is an invasion?"

"Isn't that what *you* used to do?"

She flinched as if he'd struck her. "No. It isn't. I was always welcome, husband, and if I wasn't, sure, I left right away. Liam, the tanner wouldn't let her alone. She hasn't slept for the past three or four days, so afraid she's been that he'd appear and try to force her."

"But a fairy can't force himself on another, Orla. You know that."

For the first time since he'd stormed into the house after her, she looked vulnerable. "I'm not so certain anymore, Liam. I swear I'm not. I see disaster coming."

That unfamiliar panic spread tentacles through his chest. Lugh, she was asking him to let her act, to step into dangerous situations, as if it were her right. He couldn't allow it. He *couldn't.* Not when tensions were escalating across the frontier.

"You're exaggerating," he said. "You know it can't really happen. It's against every fairy oath and principle. So teaching Bevin to inflict such cruel punishment is just petty."

That quickly, her spine was back. "And why don't you hold your opinions until you've watched things a bit yourself?"

"Are you saying I've been neglectful for having to be out in the wastelands?" he demanded, furious.

"I'm saying you should keep an open mind. You haven't seen the escalation in violence since you've been gone. The aggression the likes of which I've never witnessed before, except in the nightmares sent by—"

"The *Dubhlainn Sidhe.*" He turned to look out the window, suddenly even more exhausted than ever. "And you expect that we're every one of us capable of unimaginable evil, I guess."

"I expect nothing of the sort. Am I not the same woman who lay with you willingly, not once, but a dozen times? Do you really believe I think so little of myself that I would take a monster into my body without objection? Stop assuming all is well, Liam. Take a new look at your people and tell me I was wrong. Tell me the women here should be happy with their lot."

He swung around on her, finger in her face. "The women are *not* allowed to use force. That's the end of it, Orla. I'll hear no more. Do you understand?"

"Well, sure, and aren't I that glad I let you talk me into visiting?" a new voice interrupted from the front doorway.

Liam turned and went stupid. He knew he blinked a couple times. He was sure he opened his mouth. But he was just too distracted and too bloody tired. Suddenly there was a furious little girl standing in his front door, and for a moment he couldn't think why.

"Binne?" he said, even more stupidly.

"Ah, well, it's good to see you, too, Liam."

That sarcastic voice simply didn't fit that tiny body. He turned to Orla, as if this surprise were all her fault.

"By the way," she said in deceptively dulcet tones, "did

I tell you that your daughter has accepted your invitation to visit? She's been here about two moon cycles now."

He could do nothing but close his eyes. "I forgot to tell you she was coming."

At least Orla had the decency to keep silent, he thought.

"Well, so much for the hearty welcome," his daughter said.

That got his eyes open. "Is this what your mother's people have taught you?" he demanded. "Disrespect to your elders?"

"If you didn't want me to come, why did you send for me?"

Ah, the unanswerable question.

She was so little, he thought. So proud, her shoulders back and her little pointed chin up. Lugh, she looked like him, and already she had the heart of a queen. She was squeezing his heart with the sight of her, because he knew what she thought of him. Worse, he knew he deserved it.

"Why don't we all go back out and come in again fresh?" Orla suggested, her voice so suddenly calm and reasonable that Liam had to overcome an urge to stare at her. "Then we can greet each other with the happiness we really meant to."

"You still haven't answered me, Orla," he said. "I want to know whether you understand that women are forbidden from resorting to violence."

"After you've sat at the banquet tonight."

"You know there'll be a brawl at the banquet. It will tell me nothing."

"I think it might tell you more than you think. Now, say hello to your daughter."

He felt caught, as if his feet had gotten stuck in a bog. He was aching for his wife's touch, and who would have thought it? He'd always sought out quiet consorts, meek women with soft words and a passive way in the bed bower. Not termagants with a knack for a bucket of water over the head. Yet he wanted her to soothe him home from his long mission. He wanted to climb from his horse to find her safe in his house where she belonged.

And then there was his daughter, whom he hadn't seen since his last long mission, and she was glaring at him with justified accusation. He wanted to gather her into his arms, feel that whipcord little body against his and smell the little-girl smell of her. He was beset by a fierce need to protect her from everything. By the gods, he'd missed her.

"Hello, little cat," he said.

"I prefer Deirdre," she said with great dignity, her little spine straight enough to snap, her tone centuries too mature for her size.

He couldn't help but grin. "Ah, and didn't I tell your mother you'd be after demanding a second name for yourself?"

He hadn't even gotten the words out before he realized his mistake. Orla actually flinched. His daughter glared at him, and suddenly her eyes were bright with tears.

"She's *not* my mother!" she yelled, and bolted back out the front door.

Liam closed his eyes, completely defeated. "Well, *that* went well."

"Ah, don't feel so bad," Orla said. "Most days I don't do much better myself."

He positively ached for someplace to simply lie down. "I've just been so bloody distracted by the incursions...."

"I know. There's been no harm done here. Sure, it's probably been better that she and I had the chance to find our way together before you appeared to muck it up."

Liam opened one eye to find her smiling.

"I am doing my best, Orla."

"I know, Liam. Why don't you go bathe off the road dirt? I'll bring out your clean clothes to you."

He got both eyes open. "You cleaned my clothes?"

She huffed. "Don't be daft. I destroyed your clothes trying to clean them. Aifric rewove them on that loom that's now being used for kindling for tonight's bonfire."

He didn't want to talk about Aifric again. He would much rather think about Orla. Especially Orla in the stream. With no more than a few words, she'd resurrected that image of them making love in the water, and it hit him hard. It might have been the smell of her standing near him, spice and clean air and sun. It might have been that he'd been without a woman for at least three moon cycles. He didn't care. He was suddenly hard as a rock.

"Come to the stream with me," he suggested, and that quickly, the images materialized in his mind.

There she was, walking down the back lawn toward the streambed, the last of the sun glinting off her hair and pouring over the lush curves of her body. She was smiling, and Liam could feel that smile all the way to his toes. He hurt with that smile. It was a smile of promise, of provocation. There in his mind she reached down and took the hem of her dress in her hands, and slowly, gods, oh, so slowly, she began to draw it up. Past the sleek perfection of her legs, the dimples of her knees, the milky cushion of her thighs. Past that tantalizing triangle of hair that was so baby fine a man almost couldn't feel it against his fingers, that sweet nest that protected the greatest mystery of the universe.

The alternate realms were nothing, the miraculous design of days and seasons meaningless, compared to the wonder of that hot, tight refuge. She kept the hem of her dress right there, just where her belly rose toward her breasts, and she began to sway. Just a little. Just enough to set him on fire.

"Lift it," he said to her in his mind. "Lift it away and let me see your breasts, Orla."

"Why?" she whispered, and he knew she'd joined him there in his head, so that the two of them stood in the stream with the breeze cooling them and the shadows protecting them.

"Because I've thought of nothing else since I galloped away on my horse all that long time ago."

It seemed to be the right answer. Her smile broadened, and she continued to lift, gently pulling the material up so that it swept slowly over her taut, hard nipples, so it framed her flushed, hungry face, so it floated back to earth away from her.

He heard her sigh. "It doesn't matter how mad I am at you," she said in his head, her eyes dark and her breasts flushed with arousal. "I can't say no."

Without taking his eyes from her lovely, luscious body, he stripped off his clothes, too. "Then don't," he said.

It wasn't enough. He needed to be inside her, not in her head. He vaporized the images in his mind to smoke to find her standing before him smiling, her eyes hot with arousal, and by the bright eyes of Lugh, wasn't she still wearing that awful mud-brown dress? Well, now, he would have to do something about that. Taking a moment to secure the door against surprises, he stripped off his clothes.

"Forget the stream," he said, and stepped right up to her.

She lifted her face to his kiss. He lost his patience. He lost his taste for seduction. He needed to be in her. He needed it *now*.

"I'm sorry," he groaned against her mouth, and then he reached down and ripped her dress all the way down the front.

"Faith," she gasped, leaning even closer. "There's another task for poor Aifric. And her without a loom and all."

"I don't care. I need you, Orla. Please."

It was the last thing either of them said. They never even got as far as the bed. Liam was frantic for her, for the welcome he knew he would find inside her. He knew he should have taken more time. He should have gentled her with his hands and courted her with his words, but he could do no more than grab her and pull her to him. And she met him, kiss for hungry, ravenous kiss. He ran hard, impatient hands over her, squeezing her breasts to feel the unbearable softness of them, curling his palm over her pelvis to cherish the angle and strength of it. She pulled and scratched and claimed as fast and hard as he did.

And when he turned her this time, bending her over the table, she went gladly. And when he stepped up to stand just behind her and slide a finger deep into her, only a finger, no other touch, she trembled. And when he took a second too long to plunge into her, she yelled at him.

So he didn't wait. He drove into her, and she arched

If offer card is missing, write to Harlequin Reader Service, 3010 Walden Ave., P.O. Box 1867, Buffalo, NY 14240-1867

NO POSTAGE
NECESSARY
IF MAILED
IN THE
UNITED STATES

BUSINESS REPLY MAIL
FIRST-CLASS MAIL   PERMIT NO. 717   BUFFALO, NY

POSTAGE WILL BE PAID BY ADDRESSEE

Silhouette Reader Service
3010 WALDEN AVENUE
PO BOX 1867
BUFFALO NY 14240-9952

Get FREE MERCHANDISE!

CROSSWORD GAME

Scratch the gold area on this Crossword Game to see what you're getting... **FREE!**

YES! *I WISH TO CLAIM MY FREE MERCHANDISE!*
I understand that my Free Merchandise consists of **TWO FREE BOOKS** and **TWO FREE MYSTERY GIFTS** (gifts are worth about $10) — and everything is mine to keep, with no purchase required, as explained on the back of this card.

338 SDL ES2E   238 SDL ESL3

FIRST NAME	LAST NAME

ADDRESS

APT. #	CITY

STATE/PROV.   ZIP/POSTAL CODE

Order online at:
www.try2free.com

to take him deeper. She called to him, urging him on. She reached around to grab his hands and wrap them around her breasts, and then she rocked back against him, and rotated and swayed, so that he was bathed in her, he was drowning in her, he was impaling her, spreading her legs wider so he could drive deeper, bending down to inhale the salty musk of her as she started to come. And then, as if he were indeed a stallion, he bit her on the neck, right there at the most tender spot at the arch of it, and she screamed, convulsing around him, milking him until he thought he would die. She laughed until he clasped her shoulders and forced her down, and then he pumped into her, all of him into her, and he cried out— once and only once—her name. And when he collapsed over her damp back, he laughed, too. And then he took her again on the table, and again on the floor.

It was some time later as he lay there panting and sweating in repletion that he realized that whatever he was lying on was unbelievably lumpy. And he'd made nothing lumpy in his house. His hands still wrapped around his wife's warm body, he finally took the time to consider the changes in his home.

Ah, well, hadn't she been after doing just what he feared, for weren't there rugs and curtains and breakable glass things on the tables?

On the other hand, she'd surprised him, as well. As he scanned all the disasters that decorated his home, he felt the laughter bubbling up in him. He couldn't help it. There wasn't a thing in this house that wasn't hideous.

"Can you tell me," he barely managed, knowing his voice sounded strangled, "what color my curtains might be?"

She actually turned to consider them, as if she could

tell. "I think maybe it's a brand-new color, husband. Do you like it?"

He burst out laughing, and then ran for the stream before she could dump something over *his* head.

The banquet fight broke out while they were still eating, which meant that not only fists flew, but food and crockery and, at one point, almost the harp. The women ran, the king retreated, and much to her husband's displeasure, Orla knocked a few more heads together on her way out the door. This time, though, what she heard on her way out was, "Interfering bloody woman."

Then she saw one of the men running out the door after a girl barely past her Rite of Passage. He was laughing, a skin of whiskey in one hand and reaching for the girl's hair with the other. The girl was crying.

Orla wished her husband had made it outside to see this. He persistently refused to believe her when she told him of the escalating problem. Of course, she hadn't gotten much of a chance to talk to him, because, as was his right, he sat at the head table with the King. As was her place, lacking a male child to her name, she sat with the women.

Well, one of the women she'd been sitting with was this sweet girl. So as the girl and her pursuer passed her standing there in the shadows, Orla put her foot out and tripped the bastard. The girl kept running. The man thumped to the ground and skidded a few feet on his stomach, howling epithets by the bushel. Orla bent close to his ear and whispered worse epithets.

"And if you think to go after her again with such little respect on you, I promise I won't wait for the king to make the judgments."

"You broke my knee, you madwoman!" he roared.

"Better than your bollocks, I'm thinking."

Which inspired him to silence. Every man in the village knew who'd taught the women their new trick.

Orla straightened and walked off. She ignored the vicious "Bitch!" behind her back. She was just glad that Liam's daughter was too young for the drunk men to notice.

Since it was useless to wait for Liam, she walked on home to Deirdre. She'd made another miscalculation that afternoon by letting her hunger for her husband outweigh the little girl's need to be found when she'd run away. Now Deirdre was hiding back in her room, and Orla was the enemy.

Ah, sure, it would all be so much easier if she had any control at all around her husband. She didn't, though. Faith, if he hadn't ripped her dress off that afternoon, she would have done it for him. And it was getting worse, entirely. It wasn't just the wanting of him, it was the needing of him. It was the fact that one smell of him had her skittish as a mare in heat.

Just the thought almost brought her to blush. Well, she'd told him that she would be happy to play that game when it was her choice. And Danu knew it had been. She could still feel the sense of helplessness as he'd bent her over, easily controlling her with his big callused hands, taking her so hard that she almost couldn't breathe.

She'd never allowed it as *leannan sidhe*. Hadn't she been the one in charge at all times, after all? But with a man she yearned for, it was a variation she could very easily come to crave. Oh, all right, then, more than crave. It might be her favorite thing to do. Except for making love in the stream. And on the settee. And the floor. And to be truthful, in that big, soft bed that barely contained him.

Faith, couldn't she easily get lost in the man and never find her way out again? It was a tempting thought. No worries, just Liam. Just his comfort and his smiles and his big hands on her to make her feel wild and safe at the same time.

But it wouldn't—couldn't—be enough, and she knew it. Her mother would have expected more, especially if she'd seen the state of things with the women here.

"Who's there, then?" a man called through the darkness.

"Orla," she said, squinting to see a familiar crop of red hair. "A good evening on you, Faolán. And why aren't you in helping to wreck the great hall this night?"

"Ah, well, haven't I been about the king's business and too busy to join the fun?"

Sure, he'd cleaned up from the long ride, but he didn't look rested. Or, come to think of it, easy.

"You bring unhappy news, I'm thinking," she said.

"If you consider another patrol unhappy, then aye. I do."

"But we've just had the satyrs in for treaty talks."

He shook his head. "Not the satyrs, I'm afraid. An advance party from the army of the Twelfth Realm has just been repelled by our border sentries. If that isn't enough, now, hasn't the king demanded we track down his keeper of the Treasury keys?"

"He's still missing?"

"Ah well, didn't we think he was with his mother's people. They claim no sight of him. Me, I'm thinkin' because they can't tolerate the little whiner any more than we. But sure, isn't he the king's nephew, and a monarch gets uneasy about people going missing if there's a scuffle of any kind. Especially since it happened to him and all."

"Great goddess. When was that?"

"Well, it was during the last great Realm War, then, wasn't it? Sure, I've only heard the tales, but it's told he was separated from his contingent of *Coimirceoiri* and lost in the Sixth Realm with no way back. They found him wandering the land of the scythies with no memory on him."

Orla shuddered. She simply couldn't imagine. "He was so lucky to come out whole, for he regained his memory, didn't he?"

He nodded. "Most of it, all right. As unpleasant as his nephew is, we can only hope he loses a bit of his memory, as well." He squinted at her. "I don't suppose you've seen him, now, have you? Skinny lad, dark, always with a scowl on his face?"

Orla huffed in frustration. "Isn't that every fairy in this realm lately?"

Faolán gave her a wry smile. "Aye, well, you might have something there. Is Liam still in with the king?"

"Ah, sure, all the crockery isn't broken yet. He'll be heaving away with the rest for a while yet, I'm sure."

"My thanks." He started along, and then stopped. "And while we're next gone, wouldn't I appreciate it if you weren't after teaching too many other pretty lasses that trick with the knee? Sure, my mother wouldn't mind a grandchild or two."

Orla grinned at him. "Don't deserve it, and you won't have need to fear it, Faolán."

Because he was Faolán, he chuckled. "Are you sure you haven't gained a stone yet?"

"As sure as empty hands can show me. Why?"

He shook his head. "I'd think you'd at least get one for strategy."

"I'll take that as a compliment."

He laughed again. "I'm still not sure whether I meant it so or not."

Despite that, Orla smiled as she walked away into the darkness. At least she smiled until she realized that, come morning, Liam would be off again, and she would be left with a worsening situation and no power to change it.

When Orla let herself into the house, it was to find Deirdre sitting in the front room reading. "What are you doing here?" the little girl demanded.

Orla made it a point to look around. "Well, now, I think I live here," she said.

In answer, the little girl slammed the book shut and stalked off to her room. The last sound Orla heard was a definite slam of the door.

Perhaps she needed to talk to her mother about raising girls, after all.

Liam did leave the next morning. The seeming fragility of the border worried the king, and there was none but his Protector who could advise him on it. Orla was still exhausted from their lovemaking all the night before as she watched him strapping on his breastplate before the sun rose.

"Will it take long, do you think?" she asked.

"I don't know. I'll try to send word, so." He bent down and cupped her face in his hands. "Try to keep from taking over the kingdom while I'm gone, then, would you?"

"I'll do no more than what I need to."

He lost his easy manner. "Don't disobey me on this, Orla."

She looked up into his weary eyes and knew better than to lie. "Go make your farewells to your daughter."

He nodded and kissed her. Then he kissed her again, and she knew it wasn't enough. It would never be enough.

It was curious, she thought later, as she watched him lead his band back out of the village, the horses huffing at the early-morning chill, the bridles jangling. She and her husband seemed to do nothing but argue and have sex. Even so, she couldn't wait to see him return. She couldn't even think about his getting injured again, or worse. She felt connected to him in a way she couldn't remember feeling connected to any other in her life.

Even odder, she realized that she was no longer terrified of being left alone in his world. The goddess knew she hadn't exactly found any new stone skills, but she did feel that she had a purpose. She had friends. She had the pride of knowing she was Liam's wife, and she had Liam's daughter, who kept forgetting to go back to her mother's people.

It wasn't her world. But she was making herself comfortable in it. As comfortable as she could be, anyway, with the world at risk and a husband blind to it.

There was no question now. She could see the yellowing leaves that lay across the lane. More incursions would come across their borders, and the gracious society of faerie would decay further. Soon even the king would be unable to deny the change. It was only a question of what he would do about it.

Please, Sorcha. Find that bloody stone.

Orla stood in the lane until the last man left and then returned to the house.

In the days that followed, she kept herself busy. She taught more tactics to the women and asked the horsemaster to keep her fear of horses secret. She went out riding with Deirdre, who was, of course, a natural horsewoman. It became a way for the two of them to bond, since Deirdre couldn't bear anybody not loving horses as much as she. She would be the next horsemaster, she insisted, much to the present horsemaster's amusement. Orla told him not to get too comfortable in his job and forged a tentative friendship with her new daughter.

The days passed, and Liam returned with news that the Treaty of the Twelfth Realm had indeed been broken. Parties met to reinforce it, and Liam left again. Orla tried farming and apothecary and sun-signing and scrying, and failed at them all. If the Stone Keeper had seen her training the women, he would have seen her real skills, but the sessions were secret, carried out when the men were at hurling, which was much of the time now.

By the time Liam came back for the third time, he had to admit to Orla that there was something wrong in his world. He saw that the border was becoming a fragile thing that needed constant surveillance. And he saw the increased aggression even among his own men, who couldn't seem to manage a patrol without at least one knock-down, drag-out fight.

While Liam was gone, Orla had several times attempted to present to the king and his court the women's petitions for protection against unlawful aggression. Each time she was sent away, not only without a hearing, but with a metaphorical pat on the head, and told that no fairy man would ever hurt a woman. So the next time Liam came home, she waited till he left for the hurling field, then borrowed his short sword and began to show the women how to use it.

The women trained each day when the men left on patrol or for the hurling field. They weren't discovered in their illegal behavior until the day Orla and Deirdre were out in the fields cultivating the wildflower crop for the perfume makers. There were about fifteen women there, along with a small swarm of flower fairies and a boggart, who was chasing the shrieking children around the field.

Orla felt oddly content. The sun seemed to shine more warmly on her back, and several of the women were singing old songs as they bent over the variegated blanket of flowers. Liam would be home soon, and Deirdre had actually just run up to her with a straggly bouquet of violets clutched in her hand.

"It's for you," she said in her odd, abrupt way, as if ashamed of her gesture.

Orla gave the girl her best smile and a quick hug. "It's a treasure I'll cherish, Deirdre." And then she wove them into both their braids.

"We should get some to decorate the house."

Orla took a considered look around. "You're right. Faith, it's one thing I don't think I can bollocks up, isn't it?"

"We'll see if Liam notices when he comes home."

"Stop calling him Liam. You don't call your mother by her name when you speak of her."

"I'm not mad at her." Suddenly the girl's face grew solemn. "I can't be, can I? It wouldn't be right."

It occurred to Orla that neither Deirdre nor Liam had ever discussed the girl's mother. "How did she die?" she asked.

Deirdre looked startled. "Sure, don't you know?"

Suddenly there were screams. Orla spun on her heel to hear the thunder of horses and the raucous yells of men. The boggart was screeching like a parrot, and the flower fairies lifted in an agitated cloud. The *Coimirce-oiri* had returned. Except they weren't in the lane, as they should have been. For some reason they'd decided to ride right through the field where the women were harvesting.

"Get the children!" somebody yelled.

Orla didn't see Liam or Faolán. She recognized Tullia's consort, and he was laughing and swinging his sword as if he were charging an enemy line, instead of a field of women. Chaos reigned before them. The children had frozen in place, and their mothers were grabbing them and running.

"Stop!" Orla screamed as she ran toward the horses, waving her arms. "Turn around or you'll hurt the children!"

But the men didn't seem to hear her at all. They were too busy trampling the last of the flowers and swinging their swords at the bushes. The women were making for a thick stand of trees. Orla wrapped an arm around Deirdre's waist and carried her over.

"I want to help!" Deirdre protested.

Orla patted her cheek. "Next time. Now stay here."

Then she ran back into the field.

"Form up!" she called to the women. "Stop them!"

Aifric and Tullia and two others joined her, and they headed for the horsemen. Keeping half an eye on the other women, Orla chased down the first horse she saw and jumped for the man's sword arm. She didn't grab for the sword; she pulled the man from the saddle.

The man, a surly second-liner, thumped to the ground. His horse immediately stumbled to a halt.

"You should be ashamed of yourself," she snapped at the great black beast, giving him a smack on the muzzle. Obviously contrite, he bowed his head and backed away.

Then she turned to the man, who was struggling to get up. Planting a foot squarely in his chest, she gave him a great shove. Then she grabbed his sword and turned it on him.

He shrieked.

He shrieked again when Orla reached down and cut off one side of his mustache with his own sword.

"Where is the Commander of your guard, you slug?" she demanded, resting the sword point against his throat.

"The...hall," he gasped.

"Well, then, we'll go speak with him."

She looked up to see at least three other women in the same position.

"Is everyone safe?" she called.

"Aye!" Aifric called back.

Orla turned back to her captive. "Which of you will tell the horsemaster and Liam the Avenger that you have participated this day in reckless, senseless destruction in defiance of fairy law?"

"What law have we broken?" the man at her feet demanded.

"You put your own children at risk, you *cac*. You're going to pay for that, too."

She never heard her husband approach. "I think first you're going to have to tell me exactly why women of the *Dubhlainn Sidhe* are holding swords on their men," he said next to her. "It is a violation of every statute in the realm."

The man at her feet gave her an evil smile. "I think it's you who'll be paying."

Ah, and wasn't he in the right of it?

Chapter 10

It turned out that the king was no more pleased with her than her husband was. They were gathered in front of him at the great hall: Orla, Liam, the other women and the man whose mustache she'd severed, with none but the sprites to witness from the high rafters.

"Now," the king said, his entire body rigid with affront, "you may explain to me what possessed you to instruct the women of this clan in swordfare."

"Someone has to protect them," Orla said, thinking it better that they not know how badly she was shaking. Not just with fear, but with outrage. Kings, it seemed, were not fond of outrage, either.

"The *men* of this clan protect the women." He stood, hands clenched. "You put those women in jeopardy, and that I can't tolerate. We have our statutes for a reason, Orla. They are to protect our women against rough ways and injury."

"And how do we protect ourselves from a band of drunken *Coimirceoiri* who think it sport to trample a year's supply of flowers?" she demanded, her own hands clenched at her sides, head held as high as her mother could possibly want. "Not to mention the clan's children, who were playing there while we harvested."

"They will be dealt with," the king said with great patience. ·

"With all due respect, your grace," she said, her voice trembling, "they needed to be dealt with *before* they threatened their children. Not after."

"Ah, sure, we're the best horsemen in thirteen realms," her victim blustered. "None would have come to harm if this harpy had just kept her hands to herself."

"You'll speak when *I* say!" Liam bellowed at him, giving him a clout on the head.

"She cut off my mustache!"

"You're lucky she didn't cut off your cock, you idiot! What were you *thinking?*"

The man at least had the sense to cower before Liam's wrath.

"We'll be after getting to him in a minute, Liam," the king said. "Right now we must settle the question of the women. They used swords."

Orla was losing whatever was left of her patience. Was he serious, so, that he thought that the most important problem?

"May I speak, your grace?" she asked.

Cathal pulled at his earlobe as he looked at her. Finally he gave a wave of the hand and sat back down. Orla had to assume that was consent.

"We've tried to speak to this council and were turned away," she said. "We petitioned the high court, with no better results." She saw Liam's surprise, but knew she would just have to deal with that later. "Myself and Aifric and Tullia, at least. We've expressed our fear of the escalation of violence in the villages, in the rough treatment women have been suffering. None have seen fit to listen."

"Ah, now, Orla, you are new to our way of life," the king said, smiling. "Sure, it's a different place altogether than the peaceful glens of the *Tuatha*. A harder life, I'm afraid, this close to the border. It needs strong men, and that those men become boisterous should be no surprise. Sure, they bring no threat to any of my people."

She didn't believe that, either. Still it wouldn't be politic to say so. "But if they get unruly and cause unintentional harm, there is no recourse for the women," she said, instead. "No way to protect them against injury or insult."

"Which will not come. You know as well as I that a fairy man cannot force a woman. It is against every law."

"The laws were written before the Coilin Stone lived with you," she said quietly.

That fast, the king was on his feet again and her chance was over.

"That is not the business of women!" the king snapped. "Even you."

She briefly closed her eyes. "If you don't feel the same, your grace, why don't you wear it? Sure, the power stones are made for crowns."

"It is not for you to know!"

"I fear it," she said, facing him with the last of her courage. "I know its energy, and I think it begins to poison us."

"Liam," the king said, no longer looking at her, "you

"Only the furniture that's broken."

She actually got a faint grin out of him. Ah, faith, but he looked strained this day. Tired and stretched, as if all his time at the edge of other worlds was literally pulling him apart.

"I'm sorry, Liam," she said, lifting a hand to his face. "Sure, I don't mean to sow dissention wherever I go. I don't mean to cause you more strife."

He bent his head to hers. "Ah, well, doesn't it add a bit of spice to my life? Faith, before you came along, the only surprises I ever got were out on the frontier."

She scowled, her fairy heart melting with the gentle light of his deep, dark eyes. "And I suppose there's a compliment in there somewhere?"

"Aye, wife. There is. Suffer us some patience if you can, Orla. Try to bear with edicts you think barbaric. At least until I can present a case the king can't ignore."

She looked hard at him. "You believe me."

He straightened and looked off over her shoulder. "I've been Commander of the *Coimirceoiri* since my majority. Sure, in that time, I've never known them to do something as monumentally stupid as they did this day. Faith, even the horses joined in, and sure, don't they have more sense than most of the men? As for the war…" He shrugged. "I'm afraid it's not such a stretch of the imagination. The women have to be protected."

"You'd actually speak for us?"

His smile was even gentler. "And why wouldn't I when I find I have a wife, not to mention a daughter, to protect?"

Orla studied him. "And would you let us protect you back?"

It was as if a light went out in him. "Never!" He shook her again, and Orla was getting fierce tired of that altogether. "Never, do you hear me? It's not right, it's not needed, and it's not *wanted!*"

For a moment she could only stare at him, stunned to her toes. He almost looked dazed with the emotion of his words.

"But why?" she had to ask.

He actually drew a deep breath and passed a hand over his eyes. "Forgive me," he said. "I wasn't after trying to frighten you. It's just you must know that it would upset the natural order of things. It would bring more destruction than any war ever could."

She saw so many emotions cross his usually stoic features that she couldn't separate them. But surely this was about more than laws or tradition. "What is it makes you so afraid, then, Liam?" she asked.

That quickly, the mood seemed to pass, and he smiled. "You," he said, cupping her face in his big hands. "You make me afraid, Orla, with your foolish bravery and your sharp-edged righteousness. Faith, girl, you could have been killed out there today, and then what would I have done for new curtains when ours fell apart?"

For the first time since she'd known him, Orla saw a hint of vulnerability in his dark eyes. Uncertainty. Pain. She knew there was more. She also saw that he'd already closed the door on her chance to find out, especially here in the middle of the street.

"It's not curtains this time," she said, her voice unpardonably breathless. "It's gardening."

He grinned, and she saw relief in it. "Grand. I'll have flowers in the kitchen and *webwoogs* in the dirt."

"Deirdre thinks we could make a go of geraniums, so… Oh, faith," she gasped. "Deirdre. She's going to be frantic."

Liam turned her down the lane. "Bea has her. We'll go get her."

They did, to find a pale-faced little girl pacing the small cottage.

"Oh, you're here!" she cried, throwing her arms around Orla. "Are you well?"

Orla almost didn't respond, so shocked was she. Just in time, she bent over her new daughter and wrapped her arms close about her. "Ah, sure, hasn't your father come to my rescue, just as he does all his people?" she asked, her voice deliberately light. Goddess, but Deirdre smelled of grass and sunshine and little girl. Orla found she could gorge herself on such a scent.

Deirdre pulled back far enough to consider them both. "Truly? You won't be punished?"

"And how could the king punish a warrior who defends children?" Liam asked beside her.

"You should have seen her," Deirdre told him, eyes fierce. "Faith, my heart was in my throat the whole while. She faced down a soldier on a stallion, Father. She pulled him *off*."

"I know," Liam said, smiling. "It might not have been a good idea, but she had the courage of a lion, didn't she?"

"I want to learn how to do that."

Orla couldn't help but laugh. "Goddess, child, there was no learning about it at all. There was just rage. He might have hurt you, and sure, I wasn't about to stand for it."

The little girl actually had tears in her eyes. "I've been so mean."

Orla thought her heart would simply explode. "Ah, no," she said, kneeling down before her, her hands on her shoulders. "You've had quite a lot to get used to, now, haven't you? Sure, when I tell you more about the *Tuatha de Dannan,* you'll know that there's nothing we prize in a woman more than the courage to speak for herself. I'd expect nothing less from the daughter of Liam the Avenger."

"But I was so afraid," Deirdre whispered.

Liam dropped to his haunches right in front of his daughter and gently took her from Orla's hold. "And who said there was anything wrong with that?" he asked, brushing her hair off her forehead. "You aren't after thinking Orla wasn't afraid out on the field, are you?"

Deirdre's eyes grew wide. "Was she?"

"Petrified," Orla assured her.

"Fear protects us, Deirdre," Liam said, pulling his little girl into his arms. "Sure, if I had a man enlist in the *Coimirceoiri* who said he never felt fear, I'd kick him out faster than Orla could slice off his mustache."

Orla could tell that the little girl didn't quite believe them. Even so, she dug her face into her father's shoulder and hugged him hard. "I missed you," she said.

He dropped his head right over hers. "I missed you, too, little cat. And now, wasn't I afraid, as well?"

That got her head back up. "Of what?"

He stroked her cheek. "Faith, of you, of course. What is a man of the *Coimirceoiri* supposed to know of a little girl, then?"

She glared at him. "He should know she'd want him to teach her to ride, of course. Show her what he does and tell her stories of his great deeds."

He closed his eyes. "Ah, *mo chroí,* I didn't need to wait for a wife to find a brave woman, now, did I?"

"You did not," his little girl said very gravely. "Besides, you already had a brave consort."

His features were even graver. "Aye, lass, I did." He dropped a kiss on the girl's head. "Grand, then. We'll all go for a ride up along the high paths. That should be fun."

And Orla knew that they'd made their first tentative bond as a family, for didn't Deirdre shoot her a conspiratorial grin? "Ah, brilliant," she said. "Wasn't Orla just saying how much she likes her new horse?"

Behind her husband's back, Orla stuck out her tongue. He didn't understand why his daughter broke out into giggles. But Orla, standing there with her new family, thought she'd never heard a sweeter sound.

Liam lay in his soft bed next to his wife and found himself sleepless. They'd set the room afire with their lovemaking this night. They'd been hungry as ever, but there had been a new excitement, a new gentleness he hadn't recognized, from the both of them. And he realized as he looked down at Orla's face, peaceful as it seemed only in sleep, that he wouldn't have it any other way.

He had come to their wedding wanting nothing of her. Not her name, not her body, certainly not her bold, challenging ways. And yet, suddenly, he couldn't imagine his life without them. Sure, his brightly plumed bird had such a fire in her that it could warm the world, and he was a blessed man to be able to warm himself at it. He was privileged to be able to see her find her new colors.

It had been at the banquet that night that she'd received her first stone. Liam looked at the beautiful new ring on her right forefinger and smiled, for hadn't Eibhear surprised them all as he'd stalked up to the high table before the meal had even commenced?

"What is your need, Stone Keeper?" the king had asked, his goblet halfway to his mouth.

Eibhear bowed to the king and then to the assembly. "Well, now, didn't I think I'd better be taking care of business before the furniture started to fly, your grace?" he asked, his hands fluttering about him. "You'll see, then, I'm in my robes of office, which means I have a stone to give. And when better to award a first stone than at banquet?"

Liam had been sitting next to the king and never anticipated what came next.

"I call Orla, daughter of the *Tuatha de Dannan,* wife of the Protector," Eibhear sang out, his hands spread, his green cape flowing behind him, his cornsilk hair gleaming.

Her eyes wide with shock, Orla looked around as if waiting for the rest of the joke.

"Come on, then, girl, get up here," Eibhear said with a mad grin. "Before the rest of them have a chance to interrupt."

And so Orla stood very carefully and walked up to where the Stone Keeper stood just before the king.

"I, Stone Keeper of the *Dubhlainn Sidhe,* so discharge my office this day," he intoned, hand out to her. "I have watched and listened, and I have seen the first stone that belongs on Orla's hand."

"Well, sure, it can't be for decorating!" one of the men called.

"Maybe barbering!" another answered.

Eibhear snapped his fingers, and a bolt of thunder rocked the hall. "You dishonor the ceremony by your words, which could cost you your own stones," he said, and suddenly his voice carried iron in it.

It was all Liam could do to keep from grinning himself, for wasn't the Stone Keeper as much of a surprise as his wife? Sure, it was enough to quiet the crowd. That and a few well-placed smacks from a woman or two.

"Come forward, Orla, and receive the iolite this night," Eibhear said. "For isn't it the stone for those who teach?"

"Teach?" the king asked with deceptive mildness. "Even though what she taught was forbidden?"

"Shooting stars and sulfur," Eibhear said with a chuckle. "There's nothing says the skill has to be approved, only beneficial. She gave the women of our clan guidance, and they learned."

"And you think she succeeded?"

The little man laughed again, and raised a gleaming iolite and silver ring over his head. "By the light of Lugh, did you see those women in the field today? Sure, they took down the best of our warriors without so much as rumpling their clothes. They were taught well, and I'm thinking the training might not be wasted in days to come."

"Not you, too," Liam heard the king mutter to himself.

Liam sighed, for hadn't he been at the king himself in furthering the women's cause? Sure, if the council provided better laws to protect them, they wouldn't feel forced to do it themselves. The king, though, hadn't been ready for it. The king, Liam was beginning to fear, was altogether too close to the Coilin Stone to remember reason.

But he hadn't wasted much thought on it, not then. For hadn't it been more important to watch as his wife held up her hand and accepted the sleek silver-and-iolite ring she would now wear for the rest of her days? He'd felt his throat tighten with the pride of it and smiled when he'd met her gaze, and wasn't it a shock to see the tears on her face, even as she beamed?

Ah, she'd been sweet tonight, hugging him and then holding the ring up, and then hugging him again. Hadn't he been fit to burst for her, and even prouder when they'd arrived home to share the moment with a crowing Deirdre? And later, when they'd gone to bed to share her triumph alone?

A simple thing, a stone. Something he'd always taken for granted. Sure, hadn't he been bestowed with his first stone on his naming day, when the Stone Keeper had held him up before Lugh and called him Liam, Resolute Protector? He'd been gifted then with the adventurine for steadfastness, for it was the backbone of mountains, the heart of all fairy life. That was later joined by the emerald for leadership and the onyx of strength.

He couldn't imagine not having them. He hadn't really considered what it had been like for Orla to lose hers until the moment she'd been given a new one. She'd been radiant. And the first person she'd turned that radiance on had been him. In that moment he thought he might have fallen in love with her.

Which was why he had to stop her. He knew what she was trying to do. She was working to gain permission to fight. To don a breastplate and bracers and lift the heavy sword. He could see it in her eyes, hear it in her impatience.

He should probably tell her why. He should tell her the story of Aghna's destruction. He was a coward, though. He didn't want to be reminded of his failure. Faith, hadn't he even ignored his daughter rather than be faced with it?

He had to tell Orla or face failure again, and this time he wouldn't survive it. He would tell her.

In the morning. For now, he thought he just might hold her as she slept and pretend that all would be well.

"We have to do something," Bevin said.

The women were sitting around the fire at the home

of the *bean tighe,* where they collected and prepared the equipment for her work. Aifric was there, and Tullia and Maeve, the little thing Orla had saved from the drunk at the hall. Others came and went, and then stood outside to offer a bit of protection.

Liam was gone again, and things were worse. Just the night before, the women had presented a petition to keep the men from practicing their hurling in the vegetable patches. Three of the women working the fields had tried to chase them off, but the men had laughed and whacked away at the pumpkins and gourds and late lettuce as if they were the ball, not the little leather *sliotar* that lay unnoticed on the ground. And instead of the help they'd asked for, the women had been threatened with a ban on gatherings for harassing the council.

And sure, that wasn't the only problem. Orla suspected that the ban on forcing might have been breached. Binne, wife of the tanner, was even more skittish than before, and Orla could have sworn she'd seen bruises on her arms. Binne had denied it. She was here, though. Orla hoped it meant something. She was relieved that so many of the women had gathered.

"We have no legal recourse," Orla said now as she rolled the bandages she hoped would never meet any part of Liam's body. "And sure, the more we complain the worse it gets."

"Is there no one who would stand up for us?"

"Oh, aye," Orla said. "Liam made an attempt before he left this last time. The king would not hear of it."

There was a general sigh of disappointment in the cozy room. Even though she had no skill to help the *bean tighe,* and even though this *bean tighe* was so different from her own, she found comfort here. She had grown fond of the smell of the herbs that hung drying in the kitchen, the overstuffed furniture that seemed to embrace a person, the bright yellow-and-orange rugs on the hearthstone floor.

"We need leverage," she said, her focus on the white linen in her hand.

"But what?" Aifric asked. "The men control everything."

Orla nodded. "True, they write the rules and enforce them. They pardon each other for their crimes and name new ones for us. As it stands right now, they lack nothing."

"We could stop their food."

"They'd just raid the mortals."

"We'll stop the cleaning."

Orla raised a wry eyebrow. "Sure, and you think they'd actually notice?"

She got a round of chuckles for that.

"Well, what else is there?" Bevin asked.

Orla thought on it for a long while, coming up with options and discarding them just as quickly. The problem with men who were sliding away from their gentler natures was that they stopped noticing the gentling gifts women brought. They preferred the harsher edge of existence.

There was one thing, though, that not one of them would wish to live without. Orla sat up straighter. The idea was ludicrous. Dangerous. She met the *bean tighe*'s gaze and thought she saw the answer reflected in those calm, gray eyes. It was so simple, really. It was the only thing men couldn't do without and that women could remove.

"Sex," she said baldly.

Tullia blinked. "What about it?"

Orla was busy thinking. "We'd have to stand together on this. There can't be a single holdout or we'd be lost."

Aifric rose to her feet, aghast. "Sure, you're not saying we stop the lovemaking? But it's our most cherished ritual."

Orla stood to face her. "And don't you think I'd rather not give it up, either?"

"*Fuist,* it's a fair bit drastic, isn't it?" one of the other women murmured.

Heads nodded. The women stilled.

"Which means it can only be our last resort," Orla said.

Because the last thing she wanted was to lose the comfort of Liam's arms. And if she was going to ask the women to swear off sex, sure, she would have to swear off it, as well.

And goddess, if it wasn't unfair, for it seemed she'd just found her comfort there. She suspected Liam felt the same, and she simply didn't want to hurt him that way.

"*Last* resort," Aifric said. "Who decides?"

"Orla," several women said at once.

"Ah, no," Orla said, hands up. "I'm no judge. We need to agree."

"We need to agree we'll do it," Bevin said, her voice stronger than Orla had ever heard it before. "You decide when it happens. We all trust you."

Orla looked around the room, even more stunned than she'd been when Eibhear had reached out to her in the banqueting hall. Oh, she cherished her new, beautiful ring. But not nearly as much as the calm acceptance of the faces turned to her this day. She almost smiled, because it occurred to her that this was what it was like to feel humbled. Sure, she'd always thought she would hate it. She couldn't believe she'd been so wrong.

"Are you sure?" she asked.

"We need a list of demands," Maeve said.

"Requests," Orla corrected.

"Requests, then."

They wrote up their list, and then voted on it and the sex ban throughout the afternoon. There was never really a question of it, of course. The women were past frantic. Even Aifric, ever-aware of her position at the high table, cast her vote without hesitation. By the time the banquet came, every single woman close enough to contact had agreed to the measure. And every one had left the timing of it in Orla's hands.

Orla prayed it would never come to it. She hoped Liam would return from the borders soon, so she could at least warn him about it before it happened, since he would be caught in it, no matter his innocence. It had to be *everyone*.

Unfortunately she didn't get her wish. It was no more than two days later when everything came to a head, and it happened in her own house. It happened to her new daughter. And it happened while Liam was still away.

Chapter 11

Orla might have waited if it had been anything else. But by the goddess, some man invaded Deirdre's mind.

Orla had been sitting by the steam with the girl late in the afternoon, watching the dragonflies dance among the sprites along the riverbank. She had her bare feet dangling in the water alongside Deirdre's and her ear cocked to the high road, listening for Liam's return. She prayed for it, since just that afternoon she'd finally had to bring Binne's situation to the court's attention. The bruises had been real. Her husband the tanner had actually been hitting her when she'd balked at lovemaking. *Hitting* her, which was against every law of faerie. And what had the council done when presented with the evidence? Tsked and said they would investigate. Orla had barely kept herself from leaping across the table and showing them how pleasant it was to be beaten.

Ah, Danu, but didn't she wish her mother were here right now? Didn't she wish Liam was? The goddess knew *he* would take charge of matters. He would find a way to protect them.

It was amazing. Before coming here, she would have looked to none but herself for solving a puzzle. But now she wanted Liam's help, his insight and calm judgment. And she wanted his arms around her while he was exercising them. She wanted his arms around her even if he wasn't. She missed him.

She forever found herself looking down that long road and felt lost every time she didn't see him there. She wanted to share her bed, but more, she was beginning to feel she wanted to share her heart. And what frightened her about that was that she wasn't frightened.

"Orla?" Deirdre suddenly asked. "What happens at a girl's Rite of Passage?"

Well, she hadn't expected that one, sure. Eyes to where a school of minnows nibbled at her toes, she did her best to sound offhand. "Well, it's when she is officially a woman in the land of faerie. She is assessed again for her colors and life stones, taught the things she'll need for adulthood and celebrated for her wonderful childhood."

The little girl tossed a pebble into the water. "Is that all?"

"Of course not. You know as well as any that it is the day you first welcome the joy of life-making. Sure, haven't your mother's people spoken of it? There's no hurry about it, though, for, sure, aren't you a few years off yet?"

"Are you certain?"

Something about the tone of her voice caught Orla's attention. "Deirdre?"

The little girl wouldn't look at her. Her head down, she was picking at the grass as if it were a school lesson. Orla's heart hit her stomach. She couldn't think of a child braver than Deirdre, and now she was hiding from something.

"What's wrong, *mo chroí?*"

Deirdre shrugged. "One of the men…" She drew a huge breath. "He was in my head. Can he do that?"

Orla stopped breathing.

Calm. Stay calm. "He shouldn't be able to. Do you want to tell me about it?"

Deirdre lifted confused eyes. "He said he wanted to show me what happened on my Rite of Passage day."

Orla could hardly get her voice to work. "And did he?"

"No. I think I slammed a door on him."

Rage hit Orla like a storm. She was shaking with it; she actually saw Deirdre through a red haze. That anyone would so blatantly violate the most sacred of the children's laws in the world of faerie, and that he would dare try to do it to Deirdre…

Orla had never murdered. She would this day.

"Do you know who the man was?" she asked with careful calm.

"Somebody on the hurling team. He has whitish hair, and his ear is funny-shaped. And he had a griffin on his tunic."

Orla wrapped her arms around the little girl and pulled her close. "You did exactly right," she said, resting her cheek against Deirdre's sun-warmed hair. "He had no right to come uninvited into your mind, especially to be expecting you to—" it was her turn to draw the breath "—have him show you what he knows is too old for you. I'm so proud of you. And I'm so very, very mad at him that I could carve him up like a peacock."

For a long while she just held Deirdre and let the silence surround them. She needed it for the courage to go on. "Deirdre, I'm going to have to tell the king. What that man did is absolutely forbidden. Faith, when your father hears about it, the man might not live to see the next banquet."

"My father would stop him?"

"Your father would gut him like a fish. And may yet, if the king doesn't take care of him first."

"What if he tries again?"

Orla's smile was terrible. "Slam the door on his hand. Then let me know right away. I'll just pay a little visit to *his* head and he'll never bother anyone again."

She left her little girl with the *bean tighe* that night and attended the banquet, prepared to speak so none could claim ignorance of this outrage. She had only brown to dress in, but she made sure she was groomed and presented like the princess she was. Then, when all were seated, she stalked right up to the king.

"Your grace," she said, her body trembling with fury, her voice cold, her posture rigid as she stopped before the high table. "We women have petitioned you. We have petitioned the council and the court. We have had no response but assurances that we were safe."

The king looked as if he were suffering from indigestion. "And so you are."

"Then tell me, your grace," she said, "how a man managed to invade my daughter's mind this day and suggest he show her the initiation into life-making."

The hall exploded into chaos. There truly could be no greater crime in the land. The women were shouting, the men shouting back. Smaller fairies scrambled for the door or hid in the rafters, screaming their own opinions, for who could possibly believe such a heinous accusation? The king stopped the clamor by banging his goblet on the table.

"These are serious charges, Orla," he said, his expression harsh. "Are you very sure you wish to make them?"

"I would. I do. I beg the king for my daughter's protection."

"Sure, she's looking for attention!" one of the men yelled.

"It's the *Tuatha* bitch," another answered. "Trying to rouse trouble."

Orla turned on them. "Will you say this to Liam the Protector when he returns?" she asked. "Will you dare question *his* word?" Turning back to the king, she held out her hands. "Sadly, I haven't the luxury of waiting for the Protector to return from his king's business. My child is at risk right now."

"Do you have a name?" the king asked.

"A hurler on the griffin team," she said. "With white hair and a deformed ear."

"It's a lie!" came the shout, and goddess, wasn't he stupid enough to gain his feet so that she now knew him?

"Well, I'd say Deirdre described him to a T, your grace," she said, leveling a look on the man that should have left him in cinders. Just to make sure all knew, she pointed to him. "My daughter needs to be kept safe from this man. How can you protect us?"

"Well," the king said, looking around, "it's a grave charge you level, 'tis true, and it carries the most severe penalty. We'll have to investigate it, of course."

She wanted to scream. "That isn't good enough."

The hall went deadly quiet.

"You think to question the *king?*" he demanded, rising slowly to his feet. "You could suffer death for such a thing."

Orla didn't move. "And should I stay silent at the risk of my daughter's innocence? Her peace of mind? Besides which, if she has been approached, have other children? *Children,* your grace. Our most sacred trust."

"You overstep yourself, woman."

And then she knew. He would not help. Not now. Not soon enough. Neither could she wait for Liam, and it cut at her. She'd begun to rely on him so much. But she had no other choice.

Turning again, she faced the hall. "Women of the *Dubhlainn Sidhe!*" she cried, her voice ringing out. "I call you to me now!"

Chairs scraped and women stood. Even Aifric rose at her place at the high table and, glaring at her father-in-law, walked away from her husband to stand behind Orla. There was shouting and protest from the men, but every woman in the room crowded in behind her and faced the king.

And Orla, because she was left with no other option, stood at their front. "We sought your help, your grace," she said. "We sought the protection you guaranteed us. But the men have not only ignored us, they have stepped farther and farther over the line of what is good and right in the world of faerie. Only Liam and some of the men of the *Coimirceoiri* have stood by us, but, sure, they aren't here now. So we must stand for ourselves. We have requests."

She held out her hand, and Aifric offered her the vellum with the list they'd made up. Simple things. Immediate punishment for infractions of violence. A woman on the court to hear complaints. Trustworthy guards in places where women gathered so they weren't harassed. Orla added to them the immediate apprehension of the white-haired fairy.

"Requests?" someone yelled. "You want to take our bollocks!"

The men cheered. Orla faced them. "Faith, you can keep your bollocks. But you've left them with nothing to do, for haven't you forced us into taking the one measure we actually do have power over?"

"What measure could that be?" the king asked, with a bit of arrogance in his voice.

"Until we feel safe again," Orla said, laying the requests before him, "not one woman in the land of the *Dubhlainn Sidhe* will lie with any man."

The king laughed. "Don't be absurd, woman. You can't possible accomplish that."

Orla looked behind her to see every woman standing strong at her back. "Every woman here so swears."

She'd finally accomplished what no one had since she'd been here. She brought absolute silence down on the great hall. Sure, there would be no jolly melee here this night.

"How dare you threaten me, daughter of Danu!" the king grated. "I could have you killed where you stand."

"You could," she said. "I have to trust that you won't. And that, with a bit of time to think in solitude, you'll come to recognize the justice of our mission."

She said not another word, but swung away from the high table and followed the women out the door. It was a good thing there would be no banquet this night. Her hands were shaking so badly, she doubted she could have raised a goblet. The terror of what she'd done lodged in her throat and made her steps wobbly. Ah, goddess, what would Liam do when he found out? Was this what would have him throwing her out? She couldn't bear the thought.

She left chaos in her wake. The men yelled and pounded and began to throw full goblets of wine after the women. One hit her in the back as she walked out behind the other women, but she ignored it. Sure, she had the feeling it wouldn't be the worst thing she suffered before this was over.

She'd followed the other women only halfway to the home of the *bean tighe* when she felt the first attempt at incursion into her mind. And *mallacht,* if it wasn't the white-haired man. She stopped dead in the middle of the lane and turned back. And she let him come.

There in her mind, she saw him sidle toward her, his smile feral. Goddess, she'd never seen such a thing in all the land of faerie. It was turning her stomach, sure. But she let him approach. She even smiled back, the kind of smile she might have given him as *leannan sidhe.* She invited him closer, when she knew he had assumed she would cringe from him.

"I knew you wanted me," he said, and stepped right into her trap.

Or rather, her knee.

She rammed it as hard as she could into his crotch. The scream from the hall was a terrible thing.

"Come near my child again," she whispered into his frantic mind, "and I'll let Liam the Protector have you for carving."

She was still sitting up by the front window of their home in the early hours of the morning when Liam finally passed on his way to the stables. She hadn't changed or bathed or eaten. She was sick with what she'd done this day. But sweet mother Danu, she hadn't known what else to do.

He walked in an hour later with the knowledge on him of what she'd done the night before. His face was taut, his hands wrapped around his saddlebags, as he opened the front door. Orla didn't bother to move. She knew he'd seen her.

"Well, wife," he said very quietly. "It seems I can't return home without hearing of another outrage perpetrated by you."

Orla met his gaze with dry eyes, dry throat, sick heart. Faith, all she wanted was to go to him, to rest her head against his broad chest and drink in the return of him. She wanted to be able to cook him an edible breakfast and laugh over what nonsense Deirdre had been up to while he'd been away. But some things were simply impossible, now, weren't they?

"If it's to be a long talk we're having, Liam," she said, climbing like an old woman to her feet, "you might as well have a seat. I'll fetch us both a bit of mead, shall I?"

"You think I'll need it, do you?"

She closed her eyes for a second against the pain. "Oh, aye. I think you will."

By the time she returned, he'd divested himself of his armor and was sitting in his chair facing the window, his posture rigid with anger. He was still dusty and rumpled, and she could see the weariness of the road on him. She handed him his cup and took her own seat alongside him. It seemed he wasn't about to face her.

"What have you heard, then?" she asked.

He didn't bother drinking. "That you've organized the women into heretofore unimagined heights of folly. There are demands involved, it seems."

"Ah." She nodded. "I see. And you've decided, then, that I fully deserve the clan's denunciation?"

Sighing, he rubbed at the edges of his eyes. "You always have a reason, Orla. You might as well tell me what it is, else I'll never get to bed." He huffed and shook his head. "Alone, it would seem, for crimes I never committed."

"No," she said. "You didn't. That was the most difficult part of this, that you should suffer the punishment meted out for the rest. But I swear on the name of Danu, Liam, we couldn't find another way to open their ears."

"And what was it this time, Orla? Hurlers in the garden? Butchers with a wandering eye? Maybe an especially noisy brawl at the great hall?"

She looked over, daring him to face her when she said it. He did. "It was a man invading the sanctity of your daughter's mind and offering to initiate her into lovemaking."

If she'd thought to shock him, she'd been grossly wrong. Shock was far too mild a word. His features went chalk white. He couldn't seem to breathe. He literally leapt to his feet and stalked the room, back and forth, for what seemed an eon. Then, with a growl of agony, he hurled the cup as hard as he could. The splintering of it was like a bomb going off in the small room.

"You couldn't have been mistaken?"

Orla set her cup on the table un-drunk. "Do you think your daughter could make up something like that?"

"Did he…was he…?"

"No." She jumped to her feet and grasped his hands hard. "Your daughter slammed the door in his face." She grinned a bit. "Then I slammed my knee into his stones."

"And I'll hack them off with a dull blade."

His voice was ragged with agony. He'd shut his eyes and dropped his head, as if the weight of her words had crushed him.

She lifted her hand to his tired face and sighed. "I'm so sorry," she said. "I know things are worse on the borderlands. You're exhausted and anxious with it, and I bring you more burdens."

"*I* should have been the one to protect her." He choked, and Orla thought he was swallowing a sob. "Why couldn't I *protect* her?"

"Because you were protecting us all."

"You don't understand! I thought you were both safe here!"

She reached up to cup a hand around his neck and draw his head to hers. "These are things I can deal with, husband. You have kept the enemies of the other realms from us. And I swear, if it had been anything else, I would have waited for you. But I had to act. No man would stand with us."

He looked stunned. "Even the king?"

Orla shrugged. "He was going to take it under advisement. I imagine he wanted to interview Deirdre himself, just to make sure I wasn't after inventing stories to be heard and all. I could wait no longer. Liam, I'd already brought Binne to him with bruises from her consort."

Liam dropped his head again. "Ah, *no*," he said, holding onto her hands as if afraid of losing her. "I'm that sorry I've dropped such a burden on you, lass. I'm so sorry."

"You dropped nothing on me, Liam. In fact, you're the only one who has sought to ease it."

His smile was too sore for words. "Well," he said, squeezing her hands, "it's off to a lonely bed for me, it seems. Sure, I can't have you standing before your friends when you don't suffer what they do."

Orla was surprised by tears again, welling in her throat. In her eyes. In her heart. "Ah, goddess, I've been given a good husband, so," she said, wrapping her arms around him. "Sure, a girl could fall in love with such an honorable man."

Surprisingly, he bent over her, holding her so close she could barely breathe. "She could, could she?"

She just nodded into his chest, too terrified of the actual words.

"Ah, Orla, sure you deserve a better man than I am, for I can't stay long enough to make a difference, I think. The borders have begun to disintegrate."

She just nodded. "All I ask is your blessing."

His smile was wry. "Well, it seems it's all you'll be getting from me until those demands are granted, now, doesn't it?"

"Requests," she said.

He nodded. "Requests."

There was so much more she wanted to say. She just wanted to hold him there, nestled in their little house where they were all safe. But he was already pulling away from her.

"I hope the king is in the mood for early rising," he said, grabbing his saddlebags. "For doesn't he have a full slate today? Scythies in the far reaches, gremlins in the hills, and women with demands—*requests*—in his hall."

Orla almost smiled. "Ah, so we're on the list with gremlins, are we?"

He almost smiled back. "Sure, you're prettier by far. Would you do me one favor, though, wife? Stay here till I get home. If you have to meet with the women, do it here."

"Liam, I think the king needs to send back the stone."

But Liam shook his head. "No. I've thought on it, and I think we need what power we can if we're to fight. It's going to be a fierce-run thing, Orla."

"And you won't accept the women's help."

"No. I won't."

She sighed, disappointed. "Ah, well, then, there's nothing for it but for you to get a bath before you meet the king."

He sighed again. "Alone, I'm guessing."

"Alone. Will you be back to see Deirdre when she awakes?"

"As soon as I make sure she'll no longer be bothered."

And hefting his bundle over his shoulder, he stalked back out of the house.

His worst nightmare was coming true. While he was out trying to protect his wife and daughter from the evils of the other worlds, he was leaving them exposed to the evils of this one. *Mallacht,* he just couldn't get it right.

And now she said she loved him. How could she, so, when he'd failed her so badly? When he'd left her to the disapprobation of his clan for having the courage to stand up for what was right? Well, she would stand alone no longer.

He should have had the courage to at least admit what he felt for her. He should have told her the truth about how poorly he protected the ones he loved. But he was a coward, and he was paying for it.

At least he could plead her case to the king. At least he could shake some sense into someone. First, though, he had to deliver his own report. For the Ghostlords of the Seventh Realm had allied with berzerkers and scythies, united by the vilest of treaties and ready to prey on the weaker realms. And for the first time, Liam wasn't entirely sure that the armies of the *Dubhlainn Sidhe* would be enough to turn them back. And here in the land of the most honorable of fairies, the women were being preyed upon.

The white-haired fairy was banished into the coldest reaches of the Twelfth Realm, where the beings were pale, silent things and the sun barely shone. He left limping, with a pack of food, a good pair of shoes and a forest of bruises from the beating he'd received from Liam. He was accompanied to the border by a guard of *Coimirceoiri,* led by Faolán, who added a few bruises of his own.

Earlier, little Deirdre had awakened to find her father sitting on the edge of her bed and jumped into his arms. The two spent the morning alone, and came out with reddened eyes and held hands. But Deirdre was smiling and made sure she had a good seat to witness her attacker's ignominious retreat from her world.

As for the women's requests, it seemed that the king resented having women tell him what to do. Women should be submissive, he asserted. A clan should look to the king for guidance, not a transplant from a world of thieves. Liam argued long and hard, sad to see the most reasonable man he knew refusing to see reason. There was nothing else he could do for now, though. He was needed back on the frontier.

Within a day of his leaving again, the women were banned from the Great Hall. Within three they'd set up their own banquet in the field behind Liam's house. Since they were the ones who grew and cooked and served the food, the men were left with half-baked bread and the apples they could gather from the ground. They didn't mind. They still had the mead and whiskey.

That only helped for another four days. Fights broke

out even in the middle of hurling games. Military practice kept the *bean tighe* working overtime. The children were kept completely away to save them hearing the most colorful curses ever uttered in the land of faerie, and surrounded by sacred arrays to keep their minds protected.

The women gathered quietly and followed their stone crafts in the glen where they fed themselves and their children. They welcomed the bard, who had decided that they were a much more appreciative audience, and on his return, Liam, who had argued their case repeatedly before the king and betrayed the effect of the Coilin Stone on him only with his frequent forays to the hurling field, which always ended in the other team being fairly battered.

The women fed those of the *Coimirceoiri* who helped guard their children and the priest who blessed them. And they held an even larger celebration when Eibhear appeared to present Orla with another stone.

"Moonstone for leadership," he said, sliding it onto the third finger of her right hand. "For sure, haven't you gathered an army the likes of which we've never seen and formed them into an effective force?"

The women cheered. Orla wept and ran to her husband, who held her in his arms. Eibhear told her that she had to give a speech.

"Ah, no, Stone Keeper," she said with a watery smile, her beringed hand in her husband's. "Haven't I given enough speeches altogether? I'm just happy to be here with my new clan and my new family."

"Sure I thought moonstone was for the sight?" she asked Eibhear later as he sat with her and her husband. "That wouldn't be me, then. Haven't I spilled the scrying water and shattered the crystals?"

The Stone Keeper fluttered a hand at her, his eyes sly and amused. "Ah, well, I'm thinking you'll be surprised, for isn't there always a bit of the sight in anyone who leads well?"

She shrugged. "I'd argue," she said, "but by the good goddess, you'll not be getting this ring back."

"When do you choose her raiment?" Liam asked.

Eibhear made great show of considering Orla's still-mud-brown dress. "Ah, sad I am to say, for isn't that the sorriest color in nature, but the dress'll take a bit longer."

Orla sighed. "Just as well. I'd only be after staining it with whatever other stone craft I'm mangling."

Liam settled her onto his lap and hugged her. "By the light of Lugh, who needs a woman who knits? Sure, isn't it much more interesting to have one who foments rebellion?"

Orla laughed. "Just what is the stone for a rebellious soul?" she asked.

Liam laughed, as well. "I'd have to say moonstone and iolite, now, wouldn't I?"

The *Coimirceoiri* protected the women when they were there, and when they were gone, the women stood together, but the rest of the men were growing impatient. Then anxious. Then desperate. And Liam could only be with them part of the time, since his skills were so needed on the frontier.

Orla asked again for the chance to help him, to arm the women, to do *anything* to lighten the load on him. Again he refused. So when he wasn't there, she resumed her clandestine lessons in the arts of war. Sure, she had the idea that if they didn't need it for the war to come, they would need it for their own home lives before long.

It was the thirtieth day before the men grew desperate enough to try to invade the women's minds. Because the women stayed together, they were able to protect one another. The incursions worsened. The images grew more and more aggressive, then violent. More than once, a woman came within moments of suffering violation in what should have been the safety of her own mind before a comrade successfully thwarted the attack.

The days grew long and the women tired. The wives grew anxious. The husbands grew angrier and angrier. And then the crisis came. And it came from a direction none of them could ever have anticipated.

Chapter 12

Orla was exhausted. The women had established an official structure for their temporary society, and somehow Orla had become its leader. So she created a shadow government and oversaw its running. She stepped in where needed and advised where requested. She stood her watch when the men approached, and she kept a steady flow of missives headed the king's way. She was sad, she was disheartened and she was frustrated.

"You'd think they could see the obvious," Tullia said to her as they cleaned the dinner linens one afternoon. "They're not getting anything done without us."

"They're not getting anything done because they're so obsessed by the sex they're not getting," Orla said.

"Well, sure, I can't say I'm having a much better time of it myself," her new friend admitted. "My poor Flann keeps looking at me like a whipped pup. And he's been such a stalwart defender." Her hands above a long laundry paddle, Tullia magicked the heavy linens around the huge kettle. "Not that I feel the same way, of course. I'm much too much of a lady to complain."

Orla laughed and leaned close. "You just kind of want to scoot along the ground and howl, though, don't you?"

At least four women broke out laughing.

"We should start a pool," Bevin offered from where she was mixing her sleeplessness remedy. "How long will they hold out?"

"Sure, if Liam doesn't get some relief soon," Orla admitted, "I'm thinking he's going to be after knocking a few heads together himself."

"Snakes and sweetpeas, I wish he would, now." Aifric sighed.

"I don't," Binne admitted. "I hope they forget what those things are for."

Orla exchanged significant glances with the *bean tighe*. "We can add another request to the list if you want," she offered. "Restraint on the procreational apparatus."

"Sure, I could whip up a little something you could slip in his mead," Bevin offered brightly. "A bit of patience, some kindness, and not a little romanticism."

Binne shook her head. "Ah, no. Hasn't Liam had a talking with him? Sure, he's been a perfect gentleman since sporting that lovely black eye. Well, except for screaming at me that he has excess masculinity he has to discharge. I told him I'd see about his discharging when he saw about my safety." She actually grinned. "By the god's light, that man can curse."

"They all can," Orla admitted. "And now so can the wee ones. Not really what you want to pass along, is it?"

"It's all right," Aifric said. "For aren't we also passing along the lesson that a person should stand up for herself?"

Heads nodded across the glen. "We are."

At first Orla thought it was a trick of the light. There, over by the bend in the stream where the willows draped into the water, something moved. Something very oddly shaded.

Her first thought was that the king had probably sent someone to spy on them. Her second was impatience that Liam wasn't there to deal with it. Especially since he was so adamant about her not doing so.

Taking a quick look around to make sure the children were at the far end of the glen learning their flower lore, she gave her laundry paddle a few extra instructions and wiped her hands on her apron.

"We have company," she said quietly.

Nobody moved fast. But they all managed to turn in the direction she was watching. A few began to walk that way.

"Aifric, can I leave the laundry with you?"

"And why not?" Aifric said with a smile. "Sure, I'll slave away on the grass stains while you go off and play fairy avenger."

Orla smiled, but she didn't mean it. Something about that shadow really bothered her. "Everybody ready?"

She got infinitesimal nods. It was time to flush their quarry, then. Taking a breath, she strode toward the tree.

"Sure, you'll not be getting any food that way," she called out. "Besides, we've already eaten all of it."

The willow rustled, and Orla stopped, waiting for whoever it was to slink out from under the tree. She was preparing herself to meet the biggest hurler in the realm of faerie.

What came out from under that tree, though, wasn't a hurler. It was a nightmare.

Faith and the goddess, if she were a screamer, she would be deafening the dryads right now. All about her, women froze in place. Bevin gasped and moaned, "A ghostlord."

Ghostly it was, an indistinct wraith with shifting features and a sinister smell about it. Worse, it had teeth and claws and razor-sharp scales down its back. And yet it looked like a man.

Orla knew the look of him. She'd seen his like once when she'd slipped across into the Seventh Realm on a call for her mother.

So the borders had been breached. Orla went completely still. What did this mean? Where were Liam and his troop? What was she supposed to do? And faith, how did one deal with a ghostlord? Ah, Danu, what she would give for a long sword right about now. She felt slow and stupid and terrified.

"We have the paddles," Aifric whispered behind her.

"Sure, and he'd chew 'em up into toothpicks."

His sharp green teeth had to be the length of her fingers.

"We have several vats of boiling water."

Orla did turn then. "Aye," she said. "We do."

She just didn't know whether that would affect this creature, who stood at the edge of the field sniffing the air like a hound. He had the nostrils for it, big, gaping holes in a dead-white face with sunken, yellow eyes. A mouth, sure, that was curved in a smile of satisfaction.

Obviously it saw a field of prey and no help in sight. And then something made the children laugh behind her, and she saw him turn that way. And the smile grew.

"Bevin," Orla said quietly so as not to reclaim its attention. "Can you run very fast?"

"Away from that? Sure, I'll be a rabbit."

"As soon as his eyes are on me, go get the men. We'll distract him."

"How?" Aifric asked, never looking away from him.

Orla smiled. "Paddles and water. Just pretend the paddles are short swords. Aifric and I will try to draw him closer. The minute he's in range, Tullia, you tip the kettle." She took a couple of calming breaths. "Maeve, when we're making the fuss, you and Binne sneak away and get the children under protection. All right?"

"Yes, ma'am."

"Are we ready?"

A second creature stepped out from beneath the willow. A heavy silence settled over the glen. Orla took a shuddering breath and began to back up.

"He-e-e-e-re, ghosty, ghosty," she crooned, her steps small and careful. Sure, they didn't need to know how badly she was shaking, or that her heart was up in her mouth.

Both creatures stopped and tilted their heads, a curiously feral movement. Orla could see their pupils dilate. They were making an unnerving snuffling sound in the backs of their throats.

"Oh, aye," she urged, smiling her *leannan sidhe* smile at them, although she had no idea if it worked on cannibals. "Here we are, now. All juicy and ripe and ready for the picking."

Beside her, Aifric made a little choking noise. "I'd appreciate it if you didn't make us sound so tasty, altogether."

Stepping to the front of her kettle, Orla pulled the paddle out behind her back. "Do you think they can move fast?"

"Not in daylight." Aifric had a paddle, too, and together they brought them forward, holding them like quarterstaffs.

"Then move left. Take their attention off Bevin."

They cross-stepped to the left. The ghostlords followed. Orla heard Bevin take off like a deer, her steps light, her breathing harsh.

"Come on, now," Orla urged the two beings by her stream. "You know you want to find out how tasty we are. Come a bit closer and all. Tullia, are you ready?" she asked in the exact same tone of voice, as if she were calming a fractious horse.

"Parboiled ghostlord coming up," Tullia whispered. "If it works, sure we can feed them to the men up at the hall."

Orla took another step. Aifric matched her. The ghostlords stood where they were, all but quivering with excitement.

"I fancy the big one with the longer teeth," Aifric said, getting a better grip on her paddle.

"Ah, grand," Orla said with a nod. "I was just about to ask for the squat, smelly one, anyway."

They took another step. Before their feet touched the grass, the creatures attacked.

All Orla seemed to see were those curving, wicked talons, raised to rake out her eyes.

"Go at them low," she ordered, hoping to duck under the danger.

Aifric planted her feet beneath her. "I wonder if they have bollocks."

"One way to find out."

They did not. But they did have vulnerable knees. Orla wound up like Cuchulainn himself and swung with all her might just as the squat ghostlord was reaching for her. The shriek on him would have wakened the dead.

He recoiled from her with hands up, mouth gaping. Aifric brought down the big one.

"Tullia!" Orla yelled. "Your turn!"

Orla and Aifric sprang apart just in time. Boiling water cascaded past them and swept over the two writhing forms in the grass. The creatures screamed, a sound that set Orla's teeth on edge and had the birds shooting from the trees. She lifted her paddle and brought it down on the head of the nearest one. The impact jarred her arm all the way up to her shoulder.

"More water," Aifric demanded.

"To the left!" Tullia screamed.

Two more of the creatures were coming out of the trees at a lumbering run.

"Goddess," Orla gasped, and swung the paddle over her head in an intricate pattern that was usually intimidating enough to at least slow the enemy. The ghostlords might as well not have seen it.

"Where are the men?" Aifric demanded, swirling her own paddle.

"I don't hear them. Draw these two over here by their friends," she said. "Then we need more water."

"I have three more kettles full," Tullia said.

Faith and the goddess, Orla felt as if her heart was simply going to give out. She was sweating so hard that she knew she would lose her grip on the paddle if she weren't careful. She couldn't move. She swore she couldn't. Not again. Not with more of them coming.

"Two more still!" Aifric cried.

Too many. Too many, and she could still hear the children.

"Ready, Tullia?"

"Bring 'em to me, sure, and we'll see who's scariest."

The two were loping up, their arms raised, their eyes flushing red with the killing lust. Orla took a breath. She said a prayer. She swung.

One of them caught her along the arm. The pain almost brought her to her knees. She kept swinging. She screamed at him like a *bean sidhe* and actually got him to hesitate. It was enough to give her the time for a killing stroke.

It didn't kill him, of course. But the boiling water brought him low, all right.

"Horses!" Maeve yelled, running back to them. *"Coimirceoiri!"*

"Liam!" Orla screamed at the top of her lungs as she turned to help Aifric bring her ghostlord down.

"Back away!" she heard, the sweetest words she'd ever heard in her fairy life.

Her husband had come. All would be well.

"To the children!" she called to the other women.

They turned as one and ran down the glen to where the children were racing out of sight. The full troop of *Coimirceoiri* passed them at a gallop, swords raised, war cries echoing through the valley. Orla didn't wait to see them vanquish the ghostlords. She knew she didn't have to. She'd just reached the *bean tighe*'s house, where the children had taken refuge, when she heard the unearthly screams of the dying ghostlords, and she was glad.

Deirdre was standing at the door holding the smaller children back. When she saw Orla, she ran out into her arms, weeping. "I thought you'd be killed!" she cried.

"Ah, no," Orla said, dropping the paddle and crushing her daughter to her chest. "Sure, we just had to hold them back until your da came and finished them off, so."

"How did you know he was going to come?"

Orla leaned back a bit and smiled for the little girl. "Because he promised he'd keep us safe, now, didn't he?"

"He didn't keep my mother safe."

Orla would have chastised her, except the girl wasn't being smart.

"Isn't that something you need to speak to him about, then?" Orla asked gently. "But I don't think it should keep us from thanking him for saving us this time, do you?"

"*You* saved us," Deirdre insisted.

Orla grinned and kissed her on the forehead. "Faith, I was just trying to keep them from making a meal out of me."

"He was closer than you think," Bea said alongside her. "You're bleeding all over my rugs, girl."

Surprised, Orla stepped away from Deirdre. Sure enough, she was bleeding from the slice the ghostlord had taken from her arm. And aye, it was dripping on the floor.

Just the sight of it froze her on the spot. She couldn't seem to think all of a sudden. She couldn't remember if she'd been breathing. She couldn't see.

"Ah, well, she wasn't exaggerating," somebody said far off.

She woke up on the floor.

"Ah, wife, can I never arrive home to find you peacefully knitting in our house?"

Looking up into her husband's frantic eyes, she blinked. "Liam?"

She seemed to be lying in his arms and, ah, goddess, wasn't it sweet?

His grin was brilliant and, goddess, she thought there were tears in his eyes. "Ah, so your brain's still working, then. Can you sit? Bea's already taken care of your battle wound, so. Now we'll have matching scars to show all our generations."

She was a bit dizzy, but she knew it was from the sight of the blood. She was just glad that all she did was faint. She ached as if she'd taken a tumble from her horse. But she was being held in the strongest arms in the land of faerie. Not caring who was there, she wrapped herself around him and held on.

"I knew you'd come," she whispered, and there were tears in her throat.

"Well, you were doing better than I," he said, and his voice was shaky, his face in her hair. "Wasn't I terrified we'd be too late? We were fighting at the border, and a few of them got through."

Orla pulled back to grin up at him. "Aye. We know."

His laugh was weary. "Sure, I've never seen a warrior so braw in all my days, Orla of the *Tuatha*. If it were my gift, sure, I'd craft a statue of you with that fierce laundry paddle raised for a killing stroke."

"Don't forget Aifric," she said. "Her paddle was raised, as well."

"And here we *Coimirceoiri* waste our time with swords and such."

She laid her hand against his cheek, just to feel it. "All we could do was stun them. Sure, you gave the killing blows, for didn't the farthest reaches of the land of faerie hear them?"

He shook his head, and again she thought she saw tears. "No, we were almost too late. We almost…"

She cupped his face in her hands so he couldn't escape her. "I've lived a long time on 'almost,' Liam. It's a particularly unsatisfying word. We stalled them. You stopped them. It's all that matters."

Goddess, his eyes. There was such pain in them that she wanted to weep for him. "What?" she asked. "Is it because you couldn't save your consort before me?"

He stiffened. "Who said?"

"Deirdre, of course. You might want to talk to her about it. But I'm thinking later will suffice. Do you want to talk about it with me, though?"

For a moment, she thought he might. But her warrior wasn't one for sharing his load. Orla wanted to scratch at him until he did.

Instead, he hugged her hard again. "I'm just glad you've come to no worse hurt, lass."

"And so I haven't." Finally she had the chance to realize that they were alone in the little house. "Where are the women?"

He pulled back and smiled. "Outside. Sure, they thought to give you some room and celebrate with the ones they loved."

"The rest of the men?" she asked. "They came?"

He nodded. "And are even now coming to the awful realization of how close they were to losing all they loved because of their own pride."

Orla close her eyes for a moment. The relief was that great. "Then they'll be talking now?"

"About more than just the women's demands—"

She opened an eye. "Requests."

He grinned. "Requests." Then the humor died. "The king said you saw a war coming, Orla."

That got both eyes opened for sure. "It seems I did."

He nodded, and she saw the weight of that news on his shoulders.

"Ah," was all she said.

He nodded. "Ah. You'll come to report with me? All

the clan will be there, for, sure, it's time to work together with no more fuss. We're up against not just the ghost-lords, but the scythies and the gods of the Eleventh Realm."

All responding to the terrible shift of power brought about by the misplacement of the stones, she knew. All ready to take advantage of the weakness of the fair folk.

"Before I come, Liam," she said, holding tight to his hand, "I beg you. Give me leave to travel quickly to my own land and call out our forces. Sure, they're led by a queen, but the most terrible queen the world has seen. And we call elven princes and gremlin besiegers to our side. A combined force could make the difference."

He gazed at her for a long while. Then, with a tiny shake of his head, as if still bemused, he smiled. "It must be the king's word," he said. "But I will stand beside you in this request. For I think we won't prevail without all the forces of faerie."

"I must ask again after the Coilin Stone. I think its theft is what's thrown off the balance of the realms. Send it back, Liam."

He never hesitated, but shook his head. "It must stay with the men now, Orla. Leave it where it can bolster our arms and hearts for this terrible task."

"But if—"

"No! And that's an end to it."

She had no choice, then, did she? At least for now.

"Help me up, then, husband. We have work to do." He did so, holding her even after she was standing. "And one other thing, Liam. You were mistaken a moment ago."

He frowned down at her. "How so?"

Her smile was wholly given. "You called me Orla of the

Tuatha. Haven't you been paying attention to our vows, Protector? Sure, it's Orla of the *Dubhlainn Sidhe,* I am."

Well, then, didn't it seem she'd stolen his words entirely? He held her hard against him and kissed her like a man long gone from home. And she kissed him like the wife who had waited that long while. And then, before they could forget what waited outside and bless the *bean tighe*'s home with their lovemaking, they walked out together to see the king.

In the end, it was ludicrously easy. The king, when he arrived at the hall, was ashen with distress and holding the hand of Aifric, his daughter-in-law, and anxious to address what had happened.

"The Coilin Stone has come to us," he said, standing before them in his full ritual robes and bronze crown, "at a time when he is needed. For sure, the enemy is upon us, and we must rise as faerie lords of the West have done throughout the centuries to stop them. The Coilin Stone will strengthen our arms and our resolve to meet this menace. To that end, I call upon my son and heir to present the crown of the *Dubhlainn Sidhe.*"

It was all Orla could do to keep still. For there it was, that bloody, fiery stone, seated atop the royal crown of the *Dubhlainn Sidhe,* where it had no business being.

The *Tuatha* in her itched to get her hands on it. To grab the crown and run before the king could place it on his head, for sure, the world would tilt completely off its axis then, and sail straight into the sun.

It didn't. There was no sound but the stone's energy humming in her heart, just as it had done all the years she'd coveted the feel of it on her head. The prince settled the crown on his father's head in place of the other, plainer crown, and the king stood to thunderous applause. Orla clapped, because not to would have caused comment. But sure, she was heartsick all the same.

Not this way! she wanted to cry out. *Not at the risk of us all.*

The king turned toward her, and for a moment Orla was afraid he'd heard her. Then he smiled, and she knew he hadn't. "And here is our beloved power stone that will see us through battle," he said. "But sure, haven't we realized of late that along with the power it brings, the mighty stone also saps away our gentler natures? For isn't it our purpose not only to protect our women, children and elderly from the worst of our enemies, but from the worst of ourselves? And I, Cathal, who have reigned almost since the loss of our dear Dearann Stone, should have known this best of all." Turning, he motioned Liam and Orla to join him on the dais. "We call our beloved kinswoman Orla, wife of the Protector, to join those who govern here at the high table, for hasn't she proved herself more worthy even than her king in caring for our women and our children?"

At first Orla wasn't sure what to do. It took Liam nudging her in the back to bring her forward, and the thunderous applause that met her when she reached the high table to bring her to a halt.

And the applause came not just from the women, but from the men. From the sprites and elves and gremlins and brownies and flower fairies.

Again Liam nudged her.

"A true mate of our Lord of the *Coimirceoiri,*" the king pronounced, holding out his other hand to her. "Now scarred in battle, which marks her as a true *Dubhlainn* warrior."

Gingerly Orla stepped forward. She was beet-faced with embarrassment and overwhelmed with the noise. Sure, this was an odd crowd. She wouldn't have merited more than a nod from the queen for her service if she'd been back home.

Ah, well, if it did the women good and all, she would accept it and stay quiet. So she nodded and smiled and took the king's hand, so he could lift hers for a ceremonial kiss. She even kept from flinching at the pulse of power the stone threw off this close.

"Will you sit on my council as is requested in the women's demands?" the king asked.

"Requests."

He actually grinned. "Requests. It is not an easy thing I ask you, Orla."

"You've asked harder things of my husband, your grace. Sure, wouldn't I be unpardonably whiny to do so much less? But I'm thinking there are other women more versed in diplomacy than I."

The king nodded. "But none who has so far had the courage to stand toe-to-toe with their king and call him wrong."

She blushed even harder. "Ah, well, as to that…"

"A simple forfeit of service is required in payment. Sure, you can exchange it for your term at the council seat."

She grinned. "Well, now, since you put it that way…"

All in all, the banquet that night was a rousing success. Not that the men had settled down all that much. Sure, the inevitable fight broke out. But at least this night they waited until the bard had sung his newest tale of the might of the *Dubhlainn Sidhe,* which involved lethal soap paddles and the merits of hot water—and the bravery of women. And wasn't that the best, for even the men had to applaud, the king first of all.

It didn't bring him to call yet for the queen of the *Tuatha* to come to his aid, however. He would think on that for a day or two, he said, since his brave Liam had assured him that they had a bit of time yet. Hadn't he made rash decisions already and regretted them? He had to acknowledge and combat the urge to impulsiveness the Coilin Stone brought with it as he deliberated.

So when Liam and Orla walked back home hand-in-hand, it was with tempered happiness. Sure, the women had made progress, but their way wasn't completely clear. The enemy was coming, and the king hadn't given permission to call a second army in to help.

And, come to think of it, they were alone.

"Do we have to go inside yet?" she asked, her attention drawn to the stream she could hear burbling in the dark.

"What about Deirdre?" he asked, slowing mere feet from the door.

Orla smiled. "Sure, didn't the *bean tighe* invite all the children to her home for a party?"

Liam chuckled. "And isn't that why she's the healer? She had to know they'd get little sleep this night in their own homes, what with the ban lifted."

"But who needs a bedroom?" she asked, and tugged him toward the stream.

Liam gave her a sly grin. "Should I trust you?"

The question she asked in response was much more serious than their banter implied. "Don't you?" she asked.

And he answered just as seriously. "With my life, Orla. More importantly, with my honor and my heart."

It was more than she could ever have dreamed. She knew there were tears on her cheeks, but she was smiling all the same, for there was no more precious charge than honor to hold in one's hands. And Liam, who might never have the words to express his love, had just told her how he felt by putting his honor in her care.

Without another word, she reached out, and he put his hand in hers. They were naked before they even passed the house, entwined by the time they reached the first wildflower, and horizontal the minute they reached what passed for flat ground. They were silent this night, too intent on recovering the time they'd lost with the ban to waste it on talk. Too hungry for the reassurance of health and wholeness. Too deeply moved for mere words to convey their wants and needs and hopes.

They rediscovered familiar landscapes and sought out new possibilities. They tasted and tempted and tormented each other to the point of gasping, and then they teased even more. Alongside them, the stream chuckled in comfortable delight, and they joined it. They made love in the grass. They made love in the water. They made love in the crook of an ancient willow who pillowed them in her arms as if blessing them there. And deep into the night, when the birds were silent and the stars watched alone, they fell asleep in each other's arms, too exhausted to even make it as far as their bed.

"Pssst!"

Orla knew she was dreaming. Sure, she'd exhausted herself so on Liam's body that she couldn't possibly be awake. Besides, the noise was deep inside her mind.

"Psst! Orla, wake up!"

"Go 'way," she snarled, and curled up more tightly.

"Hmm?" Liam mumbled.

She patted him. "Dreaming."

"You are not," the voice said in her head, and suddenly she recognized it.

"Sorcha?"

"Not out loud," Sorcha demanded, and finally Orla saw her, golden-haired and sweet and dear.

"What are you doing here?" Orla asked in her own mind.

"You have to come away," Sorcha said, bending close. "Up by your house. Don't worry. He won't awake. I've taken care of it, altogether." Her sister grinned. "Sure, he's dreaming of you."

Orla scowled. "Well, faith, I should hope so. He shouldn't have the energy to dream of anyone else."

Even so, she opened her eyes to see that he was indeed deeply asleep, a very suggestive smile on his face. As carefully as she could, she untangled herself from him and got to her feet. Her dress lay across the grass, and the air was cool. She bent to pick it up and slip it over her head as she walked to the front of her house. It was there she saw her sister standing by the rose hedge.

Orla didn't care why Sorcha was there. She ran for her and threw her arms around her. "Oh, I'm glad to see you," she said, realizing her voice was full of tears. "You've escaped the mortals, then?"

Sorcha hesitated for a moment before hugging back, as if she wasn't used to this from Orla—which, of course, she wasn't. Orla knew she had a lot to make up for when next she saw her family.

"Aye, after a fashion," Sorcha said.

Orla pulled back to look on her sister and thought her more beautiful than ever. "Faith, you're in love with one of them."

"How did you know?"

"Don't be daft. You're glowing. And *pregnant*." True, her sister's belly was gently rounded. That quickly, her joy died. "Is that what you've come to say? That you're leaving like Nuala for the land of mortals?"

Sorcha gave her another great hug and chuckled. "Ah, can you see me out there with cars and shoes and the like? No, after I leave here, I'm hoping I can talk him into moving to our neighborhood. But I have a task to finish first."

Orla found herself stepping back. For some reason, her heart had just died in her chest.

"What?"

Sorcha pulled a bag from around her waist and held it out. "To bring you this."

Then, as carefully as if she were holding the most fragile child, she opened the deep-green cloth to reveal a large, crystal egg.

Orla immediately went down on her knees. The Dearann Stone. Faith, she had never seen it, but there was no mistaking its power. Sure, it sang to her, a pure sweet note of creation that made her want to sing in return. Suddenly she could smell spring and hear birdsong and see birth. She felt a rush of joy deep in her chest and wanted to call to Liam, so he could share it.

And then the joy died. For she knew what Sorcha wanted before she ever said it.

"You have to sneak into the *Dubhlainn Sidhe* Treasury and steal the Coilin Stone back," Sorcha said, reaching out to place the crystal in Orla's hand. "And you have to replace it with this."

Chapter 13

Orla pulled her hands back just in time.

"No."

Goddess, how had it come to this? How could her sister ask her to do the very thing that would betray her husband's trust? How could she expect Orla to destroy what she'd fought so hard for?

"Orla?" Sorcha looked confused.

But of course Sorcha couldn't realize. All she knew was that she'd succeeded. She'd accomplished what the *Dubhlainn Sidhe* claimed was impossible and found the lost Dearann Stone. And now she had the means to reestablish balance in the joint realms of faerie and mortal. And sure, wasn't Orla here refusing her?

"Ah, goddess," Orla breathed, torn.

Climbing to her feet, she turned aside.

"What has happened?" Sorcha demanded, pulling the stone close as if to protect it from her own sister.

"Faith, they haven't turned you, have they? Have they so soiled your fairy soul that you would turn away your sister, your own chance at saving the earth?"

Orla hiccuped rather than sob. "Don't be daft. There's been no soiling here. Sure, I think you've been listening to the taletellers too much. The *Dubhlainn Sidhe* are faerie the same as we. They simply have a different task, and, faith, don't I think it's the harder?"

"And you would side with them?"

Orla turned on her. "I would not betray my husband!"

Immediately Sorcha's eyes softened. "Ah, no. You've gone and fallen in love, too, haven't you?"

The tears were coursing so fast down Orla's face, all she could do was nod.

Surprisingly, that raised a wry laugh from Sorcha. "Well, now, we knew our quests would be hard, so. But who knew they'd lead us to the loves of our lives?"

They exchanged another hug of sympathy.

"It doesn't change anything, though, does it?" Orla said.

Sorcha wiped Orla's tears away with her fingers. "The trees are still dying. And they will go on dying until balance is restored."

Orla nodded, her face turned to where her husband slept in the deep darkness by the river. "And when I'm exiled for betraying the *Dubhlainn Sidhe,* you'll see that herself takes me back into the clan, will you? I'm afraid the alternative is the Seventh Realm."

Sorcha shuddered. "Why would they call it betrayal? Sure, they've sought the Dearann Stone this age and all."

Orla drew an uneven breath. "Because we go to war, Sorcha."

Sorcha stiffened, but Orla wouldn't allow an objection. "Not with the *Tuatha.* With the lords of the dark realms, who have begun to breach the borders because of the imbalance."

"Breach? But the gates are with us in the land of the *Tuatha*. There's been no breach."

Orla smiled grimly. "Ah, well, that's something else we didn't know about the *Dubhlainn Sidhe*."

So she told her sister of the frontiers and the *Coimirceoiri* and the need for constant vigilance. And how even that wasn't enough anymore.

"And they believe that without the Coilin Stone they won't have the strength and power to triumph," Orla finished.

Sorcha shook her head. "But if the Coilin Stone stays here, the situation on the borders will worsen."

"I *know*. If I were able, I'd ask to lend both stones to the *Dubhlainn Sidhe,* just until this is cleared up. But by the light of the goddess, I think it would destroy us all even faster."

Sorcha held her arm. "Then you know what you have to do."

Orla fought her tears again and looked once more to where her husband slept, dreaming of her.

"I was so happy," she whispered, as if saying good-bye. For she had the very real fear that was just what she was doing.

"Then let's get it over with."

Orla paused for a moment and bent her head. Immediately the Dearann Stone sang to her again, a soft, spring sound that was like rain on her parched soul. It had no power to forgive her what she was about to do, though. So she straightened, and she opened her eyes, and she turned for the great hall.

"It's in the Treasury," she said, walking up the lane.

"I know there are keys, but I don't know where. Evidently the Keeper of the Keys is off visiting somewhere."

"Ah, well," Sorcha said, sounding a bit uncomfortable. "That's something else you'll have to be breaking to the in-laws, I'm afraid."

Orla stopped in her tracks. "Sure, what's worse than stealing their great stone?"

And out of her bag, Sorcha pulled a small ring of ornate keys. "Killing the Keeper of the Keys, I'd have to say. At least we found his backups on him before we had to destroy him."

Orla gaped. "Mab killed the *Dubhlainn Sidhe*'s Keeper of the Treasury Keys?"

"Ah, well, no." Now Sorcha looked beyond uncomfortable. "I did."

Just how many times was she to be surprised this night? Orla wondered. "Because?"

"He was poisoned, I think, so obsessed with getting the Dearann Stone that he threatened to despoil all of faerie before him. He even brought terror to the minds of children."

Orla was completely stunned. "You saw this?"

Sorcha nodded, her eyes clouded. "He tried to destroy us all. Faith, he almost succeeded with me. It's sorry I am to bring you the tidings, Orla, for it's you who must live with the results. But it's not sorry I am I did it, for he had to be stopped, and by the grace of Danu, I don't think there was another way."

Orla couldn't help it. She grabbed hold of her sister again and just held her for a moment. "It makes marriage to a good man not so much of a punishment in comparison, doesn't it? For while I've inflicted a bit of pain, sure, I haven't had to take a life."

Sorcha's answering laugh was a bit strained. Even so, they continued their walk.

"Where are the guards?" Sorcha asked, as they reached the hall.

"On the borders. Sure, the whole land is on alert for invasion, and the enemy would have to make it a far piece to get here first."

Although, hadn't they been close? Even so, she set her mind to searching out any of the guards and came across none. So she settled a dream on the king himself that would prevent him from waking. Which was good, because they would have to walk by him to get to the Treasury.

Orla pulled open the great doors and ushered Sorcha through. Holding up her hand and uttering an incantation, Sorcha lit a light orb and walked in. She made it no more than a few feet.

"Great goddess, what happened here?" she demanded. "Was there a battle already?"

Amused, Orla stepped around her to see the shambles the men had left the place in yet again. "Ah, no," she said walking on. "It's after bein' a bit of after-dinner recreation."

Sorcha stared at her as if she'd gone mad. "I hate to think I have to leave you here."

Orla chuckled. Sure, Sorcha wouldn't have lasted long here. She led her sister on to the back rooms where the food was stored and the plates resupplied, and then beyond, into the royal quarters. They'd just made it into the king's room when Sorcha faltered to a halt again.

"Holy mother of earth," Sorcha gasped.

Orla swung around to see her sister bending over the king, her light right over his face. "What are you doing? Sure, he'll only sleep through so much."

But Sorcha was grinning like a pixie. "This is their king?" When she got a nod, she grinned even more broadly. "I don't suppose there's a myth about him disappearing for a bit quite a long while ago, is there?"

Orla stared hard at her sister. "There was another time of war with the lords of the Seventh Realm. He was among the *Coimirceoiri* then, and found wandering thoughtless in the Seventh Realm after a battle."

Sorcha nodded. "And the Dearann Stone went missing about then?"

"Some say it was taken somewhere for safekeeping and the messenger killed."

"Not killed, I'm thinking. Misplaced for a bit and found wandering in the Seventh Realm."

It was Orla's turn to bend close. "You think Cathal lost it himself?"

"Well, I'll tell you this. He's the spitting image of my Harry, and isn't he a direct descendent of the man who brought the stone to the land of mortals."

It was Orla's turn to giggle. "Ah, faith, I'm not sure I have the courage to bring him another surprise. Do you really think he could completely forget a turn in another realm?"

Sorcha shrugged. "Sure, who knows? But I know one thing. While he was in the land of mortals, he fair loved the woman he took to wife. I think I'm glad he can't remember her loss."

Well, didn't it just figure, now? But that was a story for another day, Orla decided. Thinking that she might soon have to tell the king one truth too many, she stepped away from him and resumed their mission.

Getting the Coilin Stone was no more difficult than getting into the hall. They used the dead keeper's keys to let themselves into the crown vault and pulled out the diadem that now held the Coilin. Orla paused for a moment to see the two stones together, complementary forces that powered all of nature. Sure, she couldn't sing to them, not out loud. But she knelt alongside Sorcha and bowed her head for the joy of the goddess who gave them, and the regeneration the earth could now enjoy at their return.

It was the right thing to do; Orla knew it. Still, she couldn't help but regret that she had to be the one to do it, for she knew perfectly well how her new clan would react.

And so, with the proper prayer and obeisance, she gently detached the great red Coilin Stone from the wrong crown and replaced it with the gentle, living crystal Dearann Stone, and goddess, if she didn't know the minute the stone returned to her proper place, for there was a sigh of completion in the universe at it.

"Now get this back where it belongs," she told Sorcha, handing her the Coilin Stone, "or all our work will have been for nothing."

Sorcha accepted the burden and turned to go.

"One more thing," Orla said. "I have a message for our mother. Ask her to mobilize the army and wait at the border between our lands. The *Tuatha* army is needed here if we are to fight off the abominations of the other realms, but they have to be invited, and I haven't managed to arrange that yet."

And now, after what she'd just done, she wasn't sure she would ever be able to. But they had to be ready to respond if called. Or if the enemies breached their border, too.

Sorcha paused to give Orla a long, tight hug, and Orla felt her sister's tears. "I'll tell her. And I'll tell her she should be proud, all right, of the daughter she sent to her enemies. For sure, don't I think you're going to rout them all?"

Orla hugged back. "I've missed you," was all she could say.

Still, Sorcha knew. "We'll meet again when this is a bit past, then. Stay safe till then, *mo chroí*. I'll see you next with my infantry armor on. And I'll bring your archery gear."

Orla managed a smile. Then, before they were caught, she saw her sister off and returned to the brook, where she woke her husband from his dream and made love to him one more time before inviting him back to their bed.

It was there the king's men found her the next morning.

"Dress," Liam said, doing the same himself. "We've been summoned before the court."

"I know," she said, then braced herself, for her husband deserved the truth before anyone else. "The Coilin Stone has returned to the land of the *Tuatha*."

It was as if he literally turned to stone.

All Orla could do was face him. "My sister—"

"No." Holding up his hand, he held her off. "Dress."

But she saw the betrayal in his eyes. The despair. She couldn't bear it.

I'm sorry. I'm so sorry.

He said not another word. He just turned away. She thought she would die there on the spot, but she didn't. She finished dressing and followed him out the door.

The lanes were filled with fairies making their way toward the great hall. Many of them raised hands in greeting. The women called to her, as they would a friend. Orla didn't know how she would stand it when they turned from her, one by one, just like her husband.

"Do you know the reason for the summons?" Tullia asked, walking arm-in-arm with her consort, Flann.

Orla couldn't speak, and Liam wouldn't. Tullia lifted an eyebrow, but kept her own silence then.

Had it always been so far to the hall? Could she never go there when it wasn't to face destruction? The morning grew around them, the light going from pearl to ruby to citrine. The flower fairies dipped and danced over the fields, and a thousand birds chittered in the trees. Trees that were brighter and fuller than the day before. The stones were back where they belonged, and the decay had stopped. If they could stop the dark lords, all would return to normal.

Orla ached for things to be normal again, though she knew that, for her, they never would.

The king waited for them, bareheaded. He sat alongside his son at the high table, and Orla saw the fury in him. She didn't blame him. She knew her punishment was coming, though the knowledge didn't really touch her. Nothing could be worse than the betrayal in her husband's eyes.

The hall filled with her neighbors, all muttering over the mystery, the pitch of their voices rising as the king kept his silence.

"Orla, daughter of the *Tuatha*," he said, and his voice was terrible in its gentleness.

Orla knew that gentleness. It was her mother's tone of judgment, and all feared it. Orla rose to her feet and approached the dais. Faith, could she never pass time in this place without it being in front of this table?

"I am here, your grace," she said with what dignity she could muster. Her hands were cold, and her stomach rolled. She was facing the end of her life here, and she

knew it. No one else needed to, though. It was the lesson
she'd learned at her mother's knee.

Liam, I swear I'm sorry.

"Where is the Coilin Stone?" the king asked, not even
getting to his feet.

Orla fought an urge to cower. "It has returned to the
crown that keeps it, your grace."

Orla felt a shudder go through the room.

"Where?" And his voice was even quieter.

"In the land of the *Tuatha de Dannan.*"

She'd expected an uproar. She wasn't disappointed.
Goddess, she should have been used to it by now.

She wasn't.

"Turn and face your judgment," the king said.

She turned. She saw the same look of betrayal and
outrage on every face in the room. She heard their judgment in the cries and shouts and accusations. She stood
tall when one of them spat on her.

"You condemn us to destruction!" Tullia cried, her
eyes welling with tears.

"You're a traitor!"

"Didn't we know you were the enemy all along?"

Again and again the accusations flew from the people
crammed beneath the high ceiling. The words and
emotions buffeted her like a hard wind. But it was too
late to hurt her. She couldn't hurt worse than she had
seeing her husband turn away from her.

The king must have held up his hand, because the
noise stopped. "You have condemned us to defeat at the
hands of the dark lords, Orla, daughter of Danu."

Orla faced him. "I have not."

He ignored her. "You are the wife of our greatest Protector. You, of all of us, know how perilous is the fight

to come. And yet you steal away the god's gift that could make the difference."

She said nothing. The king knew full well that another stone rested in his crown. There was no way he could have missed it. She could still feel its sweet song in the marrow of her bones. And the leaves had stopped falling.

"I asked you to make a sacrifice for your people, Liam the Protector," the king said. "I fear I've doomed you to treachery. For am I not thinking your wife has been conspiring?"

"I conspired with no one," she said, anyway, for she had only one chance to make them understand. After that, it would be too late, and they would go to war without the help they so needed.

"You conspired with your clan," the king accused.

She faced him. "My clan is the *Dubhlainn Sidhe*."

That brought the king to his feet. "Indeed. And is this how you protect your clan?"

"This is how I would try to protect all the world of faerie."

The hall erupted in derision, but she waited it out. She had no choice, after all.

"You've stolen the Coilin Stone!" Culley the butcher yelled.

She spun on the room. "And replaced it with the Dearann Stone!"

There was a stricken silence.

"You lie! No one could find the Dearann Stone!"

"My sister did. Open your heart and feel her, for she is near. She is the power of creation, and she sings with joy at returning home to you."

Again the silence fell. A few muttered or laughed, but they were shushed by the others. And still her husband said nothing. Orla closed her eyes and prayed for the words that would turn the people. She prayed for forgiveness from her husband, though she knew she would never see it.

Opening her eyes, she faced her accusers. "I can never apologize enough for betraying your trust," she said, knowing she spoke only to Liam. "If you choose to punish me for my actions, I will accept that punishment gladly." And would carry the punishment in her heart for the rest of her life, she knew. "But please hear me out before you make your judgment."

She looked once again to the king, who glared, but then nodded.

"We face war with the dark lords," she said. "Liam the Protector has said that it will be a close thing. He—all of you—believed that the Coilin Stone would be what makes the difference. And I, too, believe that its power can help us succeed, but only if it rests in its proper place. And I believe the Dearann Stone is also needed. And that it, too, is needed in its proper place, for haven't we seen the effects of its disappearance? Haven't we seen how unbalanced our world is when we rely only on the Coilin? The queen of the *Tuatha* also believes that the only way to repair the distress the earth faces is to set the stones back in their rightful place. Not to take power from the *Dubhlainn Sidhe,* but to grace them with the correct power. The power the first ones chose for them."

"We can't win a war with the power of *birth* in our crown!" someone yelled.

"Aye, we can," she said. "If we call on the *Tuatha* to join us. Not to order us, but to complement us. I agree with the queen. Only together, with *both* our stones in their rightful places, will we have the force, the will and the perseverence to triumph."

"What good will they do?" one of the *Coimirceoiri* demanded. "They're women!"

Orla actually smiled. "Sure, you have a short memory and all, don't you? Were there not women in our last battle? Did they not serve well? And think on it. You've seen me fight, and you know the skills I've taught the women of the *Dubhlainn Sidhe*. I am only one of an incalculable number from the *Tuatha*. And along with us we count elven princes and gremlin besiegers. It is time we stood together again, as Lugh and Danu designed us."

"Why did you change the stones in secrecy?" a voice asked, and her heart skidded.

Liam.

She turned to see his face stoic and cold.

"Why didn't you tell us what you would do?"

Please, she begged. *Believe me.*

"Because you would not have let me."

She held her breath, but he didn't flinch. He reacted not at all.

"And you assume you know better than a king and his advisers?" the king asked.

Goddess, she didn't want to turn away from Liam. She wanted him to understand, even if not one other did.

"No," she said. "I am not wiser. But I'm more familiar with the Coilin Stone. Sure, haven't I spent my life in its light?"

"And that's enough to put an entire world at risk?"

Her instinct would have had her scream at him. *Are arrogance and fear enough to put the world at risk?* She didn't say it. She couldn't. Again she prayed for the right words.

She never had the chance to utter them.

"Yes," a voice came, and it stunned the room to silence.

Orla spun to see her husband rising from his seat.

"Yes," he said again. "It is enough. She's right."

Chapter 14

"Liam?" the king said. "What do you mean?"

Liam didn't bother to look at Orla. He stood tall, so that all would see his position as the Lord of the Protectors, the *Coimirceoiri,* and he faced his king.

"We should be proud of what we have been able to accomplish even without benefit of our great power stone," he said. "For long years we have kept our realm safe from incursion, and that without the light of our stone. Then we acquired the Coilin Stone, and it did bring back some of our lost power. We reclaimed the sense of destiny we'd misplaced so long ago. But I believe my wife is correct. The Coilin Stone does not belong to us. The great power it gives has unbalanced the world, because it is in the wrong crown. It should go back."

"But aren't you the very one brought the stone to us?" the king protested.

Liam nodded. "So I am. I acted out of desperation." Slowly he strode up the aisle. "But Orla is right. It is not enough. Not for what we face. We need help. We need the full force of the world of faerie to stop what comes. And we need both stones in their rightful places."

"She could have kept both stones for us!" someone yelled. "We would have had all the power!"

Liam turned on the voice. "And it would have destroyed us long before the dark lords ever did. I say again, she was right." He faced Orla. "The stones needed exchanging, and we never would have allowed her to do it. And that would have meant the end of us."

The room wasn't just silent, it was breathless. Orla was frozen on the spot, disbelief paralyzing her. She lived. She knew, because her heart suddenly thundered in her head. But it couldn't have been her husband's voice she'd just heard.

"Liam?" the king said. "You believe this?"

But Liam was looking at her, and she swore she heard him not in her head, but in her heart. Her poor heart that couldn't stand another shock. He didn't smile, not really, but she heard it. Oh, goddess, she hoped she did. Could she only be wishing the thing?

She'd already steeled herself to give him up. She couldn't bear to hope again.

"We've thought only of the *Dubhlainn Sidhe*," Liam said to his king. "Now we must think of all life. We have our own stone again, and we need to channel the energy she brings to help us. More, we need to join her to the Coilin Stone where it lies in the crown of the *Tuatha de Dannan*."

"You would have us consort with the enemy?" someone asked.

Liam straightened and looked down on the speaker. "Is my wife the enemy? Has she not brought peace to us, and saved our women from injury and worse? Has she not said her people would help?"

"But they're the *Tuatha*," the objector said.

"And would, at Orla's request, help us defeat the dark lords. Have you any other help to offer?"

There was no answer, of course.

The king looked around the room, his expression grim. "We must take it under advisement."

"We have no time," Liam said gently. "We must act now."

"Your grace," Orla said, stepping forward. "If I may, it might help your people if they saw their stone. She waits for you in your Treasury."

"Aye," the king said with a bit of a scowl. "And that's another thing we're going to have to discuss, just how you entered unwitnessed when our keys were with us."

"Ah, well, that's a story for later," she said, desperate for him to not ask about his keeper. "It is time now to return the lady Dearann to her people."

Orla held her breath. The king looked as if he was about to ask more or maybe refuse outright. But finally he turned to the priest, who had been standing to the side.

"Return our lady to us," he said.

The priest bowed and strode from the room. The assembly, left behind, waited. Orla stayed where she was, too afraid to approach her husband. Too uncertain yet of his welcome. His words might have been only for his people, and, goddess, she was too afraid to walk over to him, take hold of his hand and ask.

She felt the approach of the Dearann Stone in the

deepest reaches of her soul. No new sun shone, and yet the air was brighter. No birds had invaded the hall, but faith, there was birdsong and fairy bells and rushing rivers. She turned, as did everyone, to the archway into the royal chambers and held her breath, because this was the moment she and Sorcha had fought for. This was the future of the world of faerie.

There was a long sigh from the assembly, and suddenly the Dearann Stone was there, nestled high in the golden knot-work crown of the *Dubhlainn Sidhe,* her white light shattering into rainbows, her voice singing through every heart in the realm. The priest held her reverently above his head as he approached, and tears ran down his weathered face.

Orla dropped to her knees and knew every other soul in the room did, too. And when the priest lifted the crown and settled it on the king's head, Cathal shuddered.

"She is home," he whispered, and there were tears in his eyes, too.

For a moment then, just a moment, his eyes widened, and a bittersweet pain the likes of which Orla hoped never to know filled them. "Helen," he whispered, and dropped his head.

And Orla wondered for that moment if he'd remembered, so, how he'd lost that great orb, and what it had cost his heart.

Every other soul in the room met their stone with bent heads and solemn salutes. The harpist bent to set music loose in the hall, and smiles lit all the faces.

Orla felt humbled to have known the two great stones in her life. Kneeling here before the great stone of creation, she understood what the first ones had designed, for with both stones back in their places, all the earth lay poised to settle back into its perfect patterns. Power lay in the two great clans of the fairies, and balance would be restored.

Liam was too afraid to take a step. It wasn't the Dearann Stone that terrified him, for wasn't she the psalm of life? It wasn't the king, who would be swayed in time. It wasn't the others in this hall or the enemy he would soon face. It was his wife.

Lugh, how could he have come to this? How many times would she let him betray her and berate her for his own mistakes? How many times would he have to see that desolation in her spring-green eyes? Hadn't he hurt her enough for all her fairy life?

A man protected his wife. He didn't lead the crowd who would condemn her. Not once. And sure, not time and again, as he had.

He was so afraid. Standing there in the great hall with the beloved Dearann Stone returned to her place in the pantheon of faerie power, surrounded by his friends, his men, his family…even so, he stood completely alone, for hadn't he turned away the only person who really mattered?

Aye, it hurt that she'd acted behind his back. Aye, he wished she had come to him. He wished even more that he'd listened when she'd tried. But when she'd suffered the abuse of his own people in their great hall without even her husband to defend her, hadn't she shown him the worth of her? Hadn't she proved to him the accusation she'd made?

He would never have let her exchange the stones. He would have jealously horded the great red stone, hoping against hope that his theft would save his people.

His theft.

He'd taken the stone for his people. She'd returned it to hers for all of them. And he'd punished her for it.

They had spat at her. He squeezed his eyes shut, his own cowardice stunning in his eyes. They had *spat* on her, and he'd done nothing. Ah, faith, hadn't he challenged her courage time and again, and wasn't she the one who should have challenged his?

The worst of it, the nightmare of it, was that to redeem himself in her eyes, to prove to her that he did love her, he would have to let her do the very thing that would destroy him. He would have to watch her mount her horse and lead an army into battle.

"Liam?"

His breath hitched in his throat. He opened his eyes and almost fell again to his knees, because his wife stood before him, and still she looked so unsure of herself.

"Would you help me speak to the king?" she asked, and her voice trembled.

He still didn't know how to tell her that she held his heart in her hands. That he would understand if she just walked away back to her own clan, where she would be honored. That he would actually prefer it if it would keep her from riding at the front of the *Sidhe* army with naught but armor to protect her.

"Of course I'll speak to the king with you," he said, and gestured to the throne.

He didn't touch her as they walked, because he didn't know how to keep from clutching her to him if he did.

"Your grace," she said with a curtsy to the king. "Will you meet my mother the queen and let the *Tuatha* share in the pleasure of seeing our stones restored to their homes? Sure, wouldn't it embolden every heart to see the great crowns together again, as they were of old?"

The king actually smiled. "So I have to see her crow over her success in finding the Dearann when we couldn't, then, do I?"

Orla's smile was at once gentle and regal. "Sure, she'd never be so crass."

"Liam?" the king said. "What say you? Now that we have our stone returned to us, do we still need the faerie of the *Tuatha?*"

"Aye, lord," he said. "We do. A fight with the dark lords is not a place to take a chance."

Alongside him, Orla stood tall. "I vow in the name of my mother's people that they will stand shoulder to shoulder with you as you face the dark lords, and I with them," she said, then flashed a grin. "Sure, the *Dubhlainn Sidhe* aren't the only ones fond of a bit of a scrap."

No, was all Liam could think. *Not you. You'll stand shoulder to shoulder with no one.*

But the king was nodding, and the stone flashed, the light in it dancing. "Well, it's Lugh's truth they gave us a good run on the field of battle, all right."

Liam couldn't bear to see her fight. But he could let her know of his pride in her. "It might not be a bad thing, either, to express your thanks for the return of our Dearann Stone to us," he said. "My wife suffered much for her part in it."

Orla shot him a look of astonishment. He saw tears well in her eyes and felt worse than before. Lugh, had she really believed he would condemn the bravest act he'd seen? Yet how fast that light would die when he forbade her the fight.

In front of him, the king raised his hands and turned to his subjects. "What say you?" he called out, his voice resonating like a clarion call. "Will we ride to war along-side the *Tuatha de Dannan?*"

For a moment there was silence.

"Who will Orla fight alongside, then?" Bevin called out.

Liam had his mouth open to tell them she would fight beside no one, but be safe home with the women.

"I will fight with my clan," Orla said before he could, and then, to seal his fate, turned proud eyes to him. "I will beg the honor of fighting alongside the Lord of the *Coimirceoiri.*"

For a moment Liam couldn't speak. She asked the impossible. She asked to stand without protection before the nightmares of the other realms in a place where he couldn't save her. She asked too much. Too *much!*

He should tell her, drag her away now. He should show her the risks she could never imagine.

It ripped out his heart, but he faced her. "The Lord of the *Coimirceoiri* would be honored to ride with his wife," he announced, and then smiled. "I hear she has a way with a bow."

She lifted a gleaming face to him, her smile as bright as the power of the Dearann Stone, creation itself. Her green eyes were the light of spring, her sable hair the very earth from which life itself had sprung. Even the uninspired mud of her dress seemed as deep as the trees of the wood. She was *his* life, and he had just consigned her to the deepest region of hell.

Leaping to their feet, the *Dubhlainn Sidhe* filled the hall with a roar of approval. It was their judgment, their commitment, their acceptance of Orla as their own. Stomping, yelling, chanting, they offered their voices in support. And there was nothing Liam could do but join in.

There was music and ale and dancing, for that was the way the *Dubhlainn Sidhe* went to war. Liam joined in, as was expected. He whirled Orla around as he should have at their wedding, and he participated in the famed *Coimirceoiri* sword dance, singing at the top of his voice as he leapt and spun in and around the flashing steel. And as he joined his men in showing his people how ready he was for this battle, his fairy soul shriveled. For even as he vowed to his people that he would welcome Orla's warrior arm in battle, he planned how he could keep her from it.

Orla was drunk on the moment. Her neighbors had pressed ale into her hands and urged her to dance. Her new daughter had hugged her tight when the children came to join the festivities. She'd just seen her husband test his agility to the limit by stepping in and out of four sweeping swords wielded by his own men, who laughed as loudly as he every time he barely missed forfeiting a limb. The stones had been switched and both worlds were in harmony. And soon she would ride into battle alongside her husband at the head of the *Coimirceoiri,* greeting her mother in triumph rather than shame.

"Will you come home with me now?" She heard the words and turned to see her husband standing there, more compelling than deepest night. Ah, faith, couldn't a woman drown in those bottomless eyes? Couldn't she cut herself on the sharp angles of his jaw and nestle into the protection of his arms?

She knew her smile was giddy. "He's time for home, then, isn't it?" she said, holding out her hand to him.

It seemed he hesitated a moment in taking it, but sure, she must have been mistaken, for hadn't he stood before his own people and defended her? Hadn't he called her to fight alongside him, not as a subordinate or even as a wife, but as a compatriot? How could she ask for more than to know she would be able to defend her new home with him?

"Will we leave for the land of the *Tuatha* soon?" she asked. "I can't wait for you to meet Sorcha. She's home, of course, now that she's recovered the stone. And evidently *she's* in love, too."

Had she actually said it? She almost giggled, for the feel of it caught like lightning in her chest. Love. Yes, she loved him. She was *in* love with him.

"And I love you, too," Liam said as if he'd heard her.

She beamed up at him, so full she thought she would burst. "Ah, husband, how did it ever come to this?" she teased. "Sure I'd been positive neither of us was going to give the other the satisfaction."

He smiled back, his fingers entwined with hers as they walked through the darkening lane, the sound of revelry fading behind them. "I'm not sure we should admit it to any others," he said. "Wouldn't they be forever twitting us over it?"

She nodded. "We should at least let Deirdre know we've formed a true commitment. Sure, the girl needs the security of the words. And we need to bid her farewell before we go."

"And who will care for her this time, if her parents fail to come home?"

She looked over at him then, for didn't his voice sound odd? But he wasn't turned to her, and his eyes were lost in the shadows.

"And would your people throw her away for lack of a parent?" she asked, suddenly, inexplicably nervous. "If they wouldn't want her, sure, my people would. They value a woman with a great heart."

Liam was shaking his head. "I'm sure they would, so. But it's not the same. Sure, she's already lost her mother."

Orla stopped in the middle of the lane, forcing him to halt alongside her, his hand still caught in hers. "A familiar tune, Liam," she said, "and one you seem to have grown fond of. Will you tell me of her finally? Why no one speaks of her? Why you seem to remember her with such pain? Faith, all I know is that her name was Aghna."

And that, according to Deirdre, Liam hadn't protected her. That wasn't something to ask about yet, though.

Liam let go of her hand, and Orla felt the disconnection to the core of her. Ah, goddess, what lay at the heart of this grief?

"Aghna. Her name means gentle. And none were named more truly."

And didn't the very sound of it seem to bear down on him?

"Tell me how she died, Liam."

"Died?" he said, and his voice sounded suddenly hard. "What makes you think she died?"

Orla blinked, thrown off balance. "Well, maybe because everyone from the *bean tighe* to your own daughter told me so. Do you have another story?"

"Oh, aye, I do."

"Then for the sake of my sanity, tell me."

She knew he was staring down at her. "If you make me a promise at the end."

Chills snaked down her back. "What promise?"

"That you'll do as I ask."

The words lay heavy in the air between them. Orla suddenly couldn't breathe. She couldn't speak. She wanted so much to just slip into his head and find out the truth. She wanted to demand it, as if it were her right, when it was only his. Only Deirdre's. She fought the terrible conviction that her tiny island of happiness was lost.

"No. I will not stay behind."

He actually closed his eyes, his shoulders slumping a bit. "You must," he grated.

She shivered, the night suddenly cold. "Say it," she said. "Say it now, so there's no more question between us."

And finally he faced her, taking her by the shoulders and glaring down at her as if he were furious, as if he hated her for making him say it, though she knew he didn't hate her.

"You can't fight."

His fingers burned her. His whole mien was agony. And all Orla could think was that once again he'd lured her close and then tossed her aside.

"You promised," she said.

Goddess, did he groan? She couldn't tell, for the wind had suddenly come up, the trees creaking with it. And wasn't her own heart keening its grief?

"You don't understand," he said, holding her shoulders even more tightly.

"Then make me."

Letting her go, he spun away into the darkness, his gaze on the hall, where lights still flickered and the music swirled up into the night sky. "Deirdre's mother is not dead."

"But sure, Deirdre thinks she is."

"Because it's better so."

"But why? Where is she?"

And finally he faced her, and she saw the guilt that raged in his eyes, the utter, bleak despair.

"She's in the Gleann na nGealt."

Orla couldn't breathe. "The Glen of the Madmen? She's—"

"Her mind is gone. She lies curled on the floor all day and night, and she screams."

What could she say? How did she ease the pain that fairly throbbed off him? All she had was a question. "How?"

Even her voice sounded suddenly weak and unsure.

He looked out into the darkness, away from the sounds of celebration to where the deep shadows lay. "You must understand. She was my consort. I had respect for her, but not really love. But she gave me Binne— Deirdre." At least this softened the strain on his features, if only for a bit. "And wasn't she the most fierce-eyed babe the *bean tighe* had ever helped into this world, even tiny and red-faced as she was? But Aghna was not fierce. She was a quiet, placid woman who belonged at home." Orla saw him close his eyes over the memory. "Except for the fact that she swore she wouldn't let me go. That she couldn't bear it if I left her."

"A jealous woman?"

"A needful one. And how could she understand the terrible burdens of the frontiers when I did my best to protect her from them? Sure, I didn't think she needed to worry more than she did."

"I—"

He shook his head. "You'll listen till the end, Orla, or I'll not have the courage. None know but the *bean tighe,* and now you."

Orla fought back the urge to argue, to remind him that she was no gentlewoman who feared the world outside her door. He needed to finish this, if for nothing other than his own peace.

"Aye," she said. "Go on."

He didn't even nod. Just stared into the encroaching night. "I'm not sure why," he said. "I'll never know why. Maybe she thought I was leaving her—for I would have, given much more time. She was wearing with her worries and fears and suspicions. But I was seeing no other woman then, for I was completely taken by the wee bundle of life Aghna had put in my arms." He shrugged. "But I left for the border. I had no choice, sure, for there were holes in it, even then. I left to protect my family, and she came right after me. She carried a spear she'd stolen from a hall guard and clad herself in my exercise armor."

"But she didn't die."

He faced her dead-on, his eyes as bleak as midwinter frost. "She was taken by the scythies."

Orla almost vomited. She squeezed her eyes shut against her own memories. The slimed invasion of that quilled tongue, the feeling of violation and terror that filled her, the paralyzing dread that the venomous tendrils would slip in to burrow into her brain and poison her with insanity.

That was what had happened to Deirdre's mother? Ah, sweet goddess. No wonder he'd stayed away. No wonder he didn't want her to go now. How must it have been for the man who led the *Coimirceoiri*—the Guardians themselves—to have failed to protect his own family?

Orla could think of not a word to say. Sure, what did you say to a man who held himself responsible for that kind of obscenity? She simply walked up to him and wrapped her arms around that rigid back. She bowed her head against his strong, loyal heart and held him.

"And of course you blame yourself."

He turned to enfold her, and Orla could feel the ragged edge of his breathing. "I can barely sleep for the guilt of what I did to her, and I didn't even care for her, Orla. I can't imagine what losing you so would cost me."

He tried to push her away, but she held on. "First of all, Liam, you did nothing to her. She might have been weak and needy, but she was an adult. She was the one who chose to expose herself to such risk."

"She didn't know what—"

"Don't be daft," she said, her voice gentle, her hand stroking that hard, strong chest where his sore heart lived. "A person can't live in this glen more than a day without knowing the risks that surround it. She knew. And she chose to walk into danger without protection, no doubt thinking you'd feel a need to protect her yourself."

Only then did she pull back, so she could take his face in her hands to lift it so he had to meet her eye-to-eye. "Well, I need no protector, Liam of the *Dubhlainn Sidhe*. I learned warcraft at my mother's knee, and there's no fiercer warrior in the twelve realms than Mab. Sure, didn't you see her at the head of her armies, her great sword lifted over her head?"

"I saw a mortal take her to the ground and cover her."

"And she got up and finished the fighting on her feet. Sure, you won't be needing to worry about whether I can fight, Liam. And will you worry less if you have to leave me out of your sight? Will you not wonder if any of the enemy have broken through, with me left behind to fend for myself?"

He had no answer, of course, for when had he thought of it before the day with the soap paddles?

"Well, welcome to the world of women, Liam. You

fear for me out of your sight? Well, I die for you out of mine if there is danger. I stand at the edge of that lane, watching up toward the frontier, wondering when they'll bring your body back to me."

His instinctive response was to scowl. She wouldn't let him. "Don't make me wait, Liam. Don't make me imagine every awful thing that could happen to you without having the chance to stand at your side to help. You would ask no less if you had been married into my army and seen me go to war at the head of my archers."

He was so still. Orla wasn't sure he even breathed. She knew he'd heard her, for she could see the light glint in his eyes, and weren't those tears that threatened? Tears in her brave, strong warrior. It all but brought her to her knees.

Sure, had anyone in her life ever come to tears over fear for her? Did she have the right to ask this of the man she loved more than her own life?

"Ah, Orla," he moaned, and pulled her so tightly to him that she could no longer feel the night around her. "You shame me so with your courage."

"Courage?" she asked, then had to laugh. "Sure, it's nothing of the kind. I'm just not strong enough to do that kind of worrying, Liam."

He bent his head over hers and laid his cheek against her hair. "Princess of the *Tuatha de Dannan*," he whispered, "will you do me the great honor of riding beside me into battle?"

Now it was she who spilled tears. "Ah, sure, Liam the Protector of the *Dubhlainn Sidhe*, will you let me be your left arm?"

"And when I do, girl, who can beat us?"

And finally, finally, Orla felt as if she really belonged here with this warrior and his clan. She just had to make sure she and her warrior survived to enjoy each other.

Chapter 15

They met again at the border between their realms, the great armies of the world of faerie. Brought together in the mist of early morning they came, bridles jangling, fairy bells caroling, the hooves of countless horses, both palest gray and deepest black, thundering over the soft earth. The deep trees of the *Dubhlainn Sidhe* whispered their respect, and the fields of the *Tuatha* hummed with excitement. A thousand pennants curled in the same breeze that wrapped fingers of mist around the horses.

And at the head of each army rode a monarch wearing a gleaming gold crown crafted by the first ones to carry the great stones of faerie, and their combined light warmed the morning air.

As was the tradition of the *Dubhlainn Sidhe,* the Captain of the *Coimirceoiri* rode just behind his king, and he was clad in the sleek leather armor that identified his clan and helmeted with a hard leather helm with its horse-shaped nose-guard. The great battle sword of the *Dubhlainn Sidhe* was strapped across his back. This day the Protector's wife and helpmeet rode alongside him, clad in the shining bronze breastplate of the *Tuatha* and its winged helmet, her short sword at her hip and her bow across her back. None had questioned her for it.

As was the tradition of the *Tuatha de Dannan,* the princesses royals rode alongside their mother, though this day, there was but one, as one of her sisters had been stripped of her fairy strength, and the other now rode with the *Dubhlainn Sidhe.* Sorcha was also clad in the *Tuatha* armor, with the crest of the infantry on her arm, and she smiled as she met her sister and brought her horse to a halt alongside the queen's.

"Well, then, Cathal," Mab said in greeting, "she's home, this great stone of ours." She sat her pale gray horse with comfortable dignity, the great Coilin Stone gleaming crimson above her head. Her hair, that moon-pale silver that seemed all but ghostly in the early sun, flowed behind her like another battle flag. All who saw her felt the urge to bow.

Cathal, who looked younger since the return of his stone, smiled at the queen. "And it's your daughters I must thank, Mab," he said. "Later, when we finish this business, we must meet here for the celebration, and you can tell me how it came to be."

Her smile was slow and satisfied. "Later I would be delighted to. For now, though, I have had speech with my daughter Orla, who is now of your clan, and she has convinced me that for the benefit of us both, the combined armies should be led by your Protector. My people are content with the judgment of their princess, of whom we are proud. She has also said that he will be agreeable to working with my daughters, who lead our own forces, Sorcha the infantry and Orla the cavalry." Again the queen smiled. "I am to understand that a braw young *Coimirceoiri* named Faolán will take Orla's place with her archers. We thank him."

Cathal smiled back, and it seemed that the Dearann gleamed in agreement. "She is persuasive, is our new princess," he said. "The battle tactics have already been worked out. It remains only for us to move forward to the place of our meeting with the dark lords."

"There is one more thing, your worships," came a voice from the core of the *Dubhlainn Sidhe* troop.

All turned to see Eibhear trotting forward on a pale white mare, neither clad in armor of any sort. The Stone Keeper wore his robes of office, though.

"Eibhear?" the king demanded. "Don't you think there could be a better time for this?"

"Ah, well, no, you see, I don't. And as the good Queen Mab's own Stone Keeper can be after tellin' you, we keepers must bestow our stones when the gods tell us, not when we've a whim for it." He'd reached the border where the armies met face-to-face, and he sat at right angles to the monarchs. "And, well, isn't that what's to happen now, before this grand fight of ours?"

The king sighed. "Then be about it."

In that moment, Eibhear became his office, his flighty, fancy bearing disappearing into utmost dignity.

"Orla, daughter of the *Tuatha de Dannan,* sister of the *Dubhlainn Sidhe,* I call you forward!" he cried out.

Orla turned to look up at her husband questioningly. Looking like a god himself with his battle sword strapped to his back, he just shrugged. "I wouldn't keep them all waiting, my girl," he whispered.

She barely had time to settle before her horse headed up on his own, letting her know in no uncertain terms that they didn't have time to waste. Snotty know-it-all, she thought fondly, then forgot her new friend as she came to a stop facing Eibhear beside the rulers, so that the four formed a cross for all the armies to see.

"I am here, Eibhear."

Giving her a glad smile, he lifted his right hand high over his head. "This is the day, then, when you are to be given your last stone, Orla. For haven't we of both fairy realms seen that you deserve it, not only for protecting the personal safety of our beloved women, but the safety of the earth itself and the world of faerie she so loves? Come forth and receive your stone."

Orla kept her gaze on him, no matter how much she wanted to see the stone. The last of who she was to be, bestowed on her by an alien god and his people. By her new, beloved family and the man who guarded them all. She shook with fear and wonder.

"It is the emerald of statecraft, Orla of the Clans," Eibhear said. "For how better to remind you of the fragility of life, of the delicate balance of the earth and her children, of the frailty of the heart of each and every being who relies upon your judgment, your compassion, your wisdom? You have truly led these people, Orla, by tact and by perseverance and by guile and by force when necessary. And we all stand here today, joined as the clans have not been in the years of my life, because you have called us so. Wear the emerald to remind us all that we have a princess to come to when we need guidance and comfort."

Slowly he lowered his hand. The broad valley was

hushed, even the oak dryads watching closely. Orla saw the emerald glint in the sun and froze. Goddess, she already had the iolite and the moonstone. He couldn't really mean to join them with the emerald.

"No, Stone Keeper," she said, cowed by the sight of it. "For these are the stones of a queen. And I am no queen."

She heard the clatter of protest behind her, bless the *Dubhlainn Sidhe* for their loyalty. Eibhear only smiled.

"Stone Keeper of the *Tuatha de Dannan*," he called across to Sorcha, his focus on Orla. "Do you see any sin in this gift of the god Lugh? Will the earth crumble around us for it?"

And, oh, wasn't Sorcha smiling at her? "Sure, hasn't Orla earned this and more like it many times over? And wouldn't she have to be the one who explains it to her own goddess, Danu, if she refuses?"

Orla was shaking now, frightened by the weight of that emerald.

"Daughter," the queen said, and Orla turned to her mother, the queen's last accusations ringing in her memory. For hadn't she been right? She, Orla, had committed treason. She'd torn a nation apart, and brought war and death to her home. How could she be rewarded for redeeming herself?

"Lady, it is wrong."

"Take the stone," her mother said simply, and for the first time ever Orla saw there in the depths of that unearthly green something she had never thought to find. Pride. Her mother the queen truly thought she deserved to wear the same stones.

Orla had never been so shaken in her life. She almost closed her eyes, but knew it would be an insult to all there. Instead, she lifted her left hand, the heart hand, where her most important stone would live. And she extended it to the Stone Keeper.

The emerald-and-gold ring slid onto her third finger as if coming home. Orla immediately felt its warmth and life and light, and she knew that it matched her other rings, her moonstone and her iolite. And she was truly humbled by its presence.

"Well, then," Eibhear said, his sly smile once again firmly in place. "Now that we have a full set of worthy leaders, I'm saying it's time to get on with this war of ours."

Unable to remain where all could focus attention on her, Orla trotted back to her place alongside her smiling husband.

"Ah, well, I'm in trouble now," he said. "For how is a mere Protector to argue with a woman wearing the queen's stones?"

She smiled back, but it was a bit wobbly. "Sure, I don't deserve this, Liam."

He reached out a gauntleted hand and stroked her cheek. "Ah, but you do, Orla. You humble me with what you've accomplished. Were you my queen, I would serve you with joy."

She shook her head, taking hold of his hand and laying it against her heart. "Ah, no, now, there'll be none of that. We two ride side-by-side or not at all."

Leaning over far enough for his saddle to creak in protest and his horse to sidestep a bit, Liam kissed her to again seal their personal pact. Orla was awed by his strength, for didn't she know that he would always fear for her? But he'd given her the great gift of letting her do what she must right beside him, and she would love him for it until the day memory failed the earth.

"Let's make Deirdre proud of her parents, then, shall we?" she asked.

Liam rolled his eyes. "Faith, she'll be impossible to live with after you return with your war victory. She'll be begging for a place in the *Coimirceoiri,* all right."

"And would that be so wrong for her when she grows?"

"Well, I imagine the women will be telling me it will be nothing of the kind. But when she's grown. Not next moon."

The time for conversation was over. The monarchs had turned their horses to ride alongside each other, and the fairy armies fell in behind, a great forest that swept over the land. And Orla, whose first stone gifts had been solitary ones, selfish at best, couldn't help but thrill that she rode just behind the glory of the fairy stones and the combined force of the clans. She couldn't envision fighting anywhere but alongside her husband. She couldn't imagine having a heart more full.

"One more thing," she said as she trotted alongside her husband. "Just so you know."

"You love me?" he asked, grinning.

"Ah, faith, everybody knows that. What they don't know is that I've baked up a great, delicious cake to celebrate when we arrive back home."

"And I love *you,*" he said, then paused in consideration. "A cake," he said, then frowned. "Are you sure that's a good thing?"

It was a great victory. Seduced by the imbalance brought by the loss of the stones, the dark lords had grown greedy, thinking that it wouldn't be a bad thing to have control over other realms. With a crushing setdown, the armies of faerie told them no. The fighting was long and brutal, but in the end, the intruders were pushed back to their dark home.

When the last portal had been forced shut past the bodies of the enemy, and the frontier lay silent and calm once again, the king and queen retreated to their lands to care for their injured and bury their dead. But in the fullness of time, they returned to the border where their armies had joined to celebrate not only the victory, but the marriage that had brought it about.

For Orla's part, she was deliriously happy simply because those she knew had returned home safe, although her husband, never content to lead, had waded into the thickest of the fighting with a war cry that had sent a goodly number of the enemy fleeing and come away with another couple of scars as trophies.

It was a good thing, she thought, watching him recreate one of the fights as he shared a bit of whiskey with his counterparts, that she didn't mind a scar or two. Faith, she should blush at what she'd done with the ones he bore the night after the final battle. Who knew bravery could taste so earthy?

And, well, to be perfectly truthful, Liam had relished hers, collected in the mad cavalry charge that had crushed a line of ghostlords.

But all were safe. The border was secure for the moment, and she was being rewarded with a visit with both her sisters, even Nuala, who had forfeited her life as a fairy for the man she loved.

Upon seeing her, Orla had shrieked and hugged her until both were laughing and crying at once. Then she'd begged her sister's forgiveness for the person she'd been, and they'd fallen to hugging again. It was only the needed introduction of Orla's new niece, Brigid, to Orla's new family that broke it up.

After that she cornered Sorcha and repeated the ritual, and it was even sweeter, for hadn't Sorcha offered to defend her when she'd thought her in danger? Her, who had never had a kind word to say to the sisters she'd thought weak and unworthy of fairy gifts? The sisters she knew now were more precious than stones or armies or realms.

It was only left to meet Sorcha's handsome new husband, Harry, and his funny, white-haired granny, which would happen after Cathal finished his own greeting of the family he'd forgotten. Faith, if that old woman didn't keep laughing out loud and then poking poor Harry, saying, "See? Didn't I tell you?"

And goddess, if Sorcha hadn't been right. Harry looked more like Cathal than Cathal's acknowledged son, Owain. It was all right, though. Owain was as delighted as the rest of them with the turn of events. The horsemaster was particularly pleased, since it seemed that Harry was also freeing him up for the West.

"Can you believe Cathal really had no memory of thirty years in the land of mortal?" Sorcha said with a shake of her head as she saw the king of the *Dubhlainn Sidhe* nose-to-nose with her husband, Harry, and the newest in his line, baby Niall.

"Well, now that you've met the ghostlords, you can understand," Orla said, wine in one hand and cake—not hers, sadly—in the other. "He'd evidently separated from his men to take the stone to safety, then returned to the field of battle in the Seventh Realm. The rest is a mystery."

"I still don't understand how he wasn't missed when he was gone thirty years," her sister Nuala's husband, Zeke, said.

Orla smiled on him. "Ah, faith, you know that fairy time is different from mortal, so. And how's that new baby of yours? Casting spells yet?"

He grinned. Sure, she couldn't think of him without remembering that she'd once tried to seduce him. She'd failed, because he'd been honorable and in love with her sister Nuala. She hadn't understood then. She did now.

"The baby is grand," Nuala herself said, walking up in her peacock fairy dress to put her arm through Zeke's.

Orla still couldn't believe that Mab had allowed Nuala to come home from the land of mortals for the celebration. She just wished it could be a longer visit, and one to be repeated.

"I'm so happy for you, Nuala," she said, wanting to hug her again. She'd done it twenty times at least already. "I can't tell you how glad I am you found what you wanted."

Nuala seemed to have trouble taking her eyes from her husband. "Oh, aye," she said. "I did. I just wish I could have helped back here with the realms. But wasn't I busy having my lovely Brigid?"

Orla looked over, along with her sisters, to see Mab cradling the infant in her arms and looking strangely awed.

"Faith," Nuala said. "I should have brought her one of those years ago. It might have softened her up a bit."

Orla gaped. "Is she actually saying, 'Cootchy cootchy'?"

Then, without having to turn to see him, she knew her husband was approaching. Ah, didn't she feel the heat of him at her back?

"Did you thank Sorcha for bringing a Cherished One to see us?" he asked, wrapping his arms around her. She wrapped her own arms around his and nestled back against him.

"Little Lilly," Sorcha said with a huge smile. "It's such a treat to be able to have her and the other children over from the other side. I think it's that grandmother thing that allowed it. Mab's suddenly mad for all things small."

"Well, sure, Lilly's got her wrapped around her finger," Orla agreed, leaning her head back against her husband's heart. It was a rare treat to have a Cherished One among them, and she and Liam had been enjoying her. Mortals would have said the girl had Down Syndrome. The fairies knew she was blessed with eternal joy. And faith, wasn't she giggling again, giving the new baby a smacking kiss on the forehead? And, of course, she'd had Deirdre and Kieran both by the hand the entire party.

"I'm so glad we're all together," Orla said, tears again in her eyes. Goddess, she'd wasted so much time with her sisters. "If I weren't caught in the fierce trap of my husband's arms, sure, I'd hug you all over again."

"I'm glad, too," Sorcha said, "for don't we have a surprise for you?"

Orla blinked. "For me?"

"Oh, aye. It's time to give you your new dress color."

Dress color? Sweet Danu, she hadn't thought of it. She was still in her wren dress.

"Oh, thank the good goddess," she said, straightening. "I swear, if I have to wear this brown one more day I'll strangle my Stone Keeper. Where is the little man, then?"

"It looks like he's gathering everyone up. Faith, I've never seen a sheepdog dressed in silver before."

Everybody turned to see Eibhear scurrying about, pushing the councils from both clans toward where the great high tables had been set up and still groaned with food and drink.

"Well, come on, then," Sorcha said, heading toward her Harry, who had just turned to look for her.

Orla liked him, too. He was perfect for her quiet, homebody sister, a mortal with more fairy blood than not, who'd finally gotten to come home where his heart lived.

"Well?" Liam asked above her, reminding her where *her* heart lived.

Nuala and Zeke had followed Sorcha. Orla could see the people gathering. Mab handed off her granddaughter and straightened herself, assuming her queen's posture. Kieran, always watching, grinned over at her. Lilly let go of his hand long enough to wave. And suddenly Orla was afraid.

"They're bringing the crowns, Liam."

The Coilin Stone throbbed through the air as the Dearann Stone sang.

"Well, it seems something big's happening," he said. "We might as well get up there so they can get to it. Then you can get your new dress." He sighed. "And here I was just getting used to brown."

"You were not. Goddess, I'm afraid to see—"

He spun her around so she had to look up into his dear deep eyes. He wasn't smiling.

"What?"

"Didn't I just want to look at you a bit before you change all beyond my recognition?"

She huffed. "Don't be daft. It's a dress, not a disguise. I'll be nothing different."

His smile settled deep in her chest where her heart had finally come to life, where it hung on his words and the benediction of his love.

"I love you, *mo mhuirnin*," he said, his eyes soft and sweet.

"Ah, *mo stor,* and don't I love you even more."

Liam answered her with a kiss. A deep, melding kiss that was like nourishment to her, a fierce mating of a kiss, an unbearable sweetness of a kiss, for couldn't she soar on nothing more than the softness of his mouth?

And then, as quickly as he kissed her, he gently set her back. He smiled just for her, then took her hand and led her to where the clans had gathered.

"Let's forget the dress," she said, still a bit breathless. "There's a grand little river down the glen a ways we could christen."

"Ah, no, girl," he said. "Face up to your new self first."

She sighed. Her new self. Ah, well, it was true. She *was* new. She'd changed, just as she'd heard snakes shed their skin, leaving that dead thing back in Gleann Fia. She was a new person, and wasn't it the man next to her who'd helped her discover who she was? Wasn't he the catalyst, the comfort, the endless delight that illuminated her? She didn't really need a new dress to know her true colors.

"Well, it's about time," Eibhear groused as she reached him. "Sure, we have business before the music, and aren't the pipers a bit impatient, now?"

And wasn't Sorcha standing next to him in her own Stone Keeper robes, and both monarchs in their crowns? Ah, so it was a joint ceremony.

"Stone Keeper," Cathal warned.

The great king stood alongside Mab, just as he had when they'd gone into battle, the great stones shining. Orla saw it and felt a frisson up her back.

"We bring you here, Orla of the Clans," Eibhear intoned, "to present you with the color of your robes. And on this day when we celebrate together, sure, your own sister would like to present them."

Orla turned to see tears welling in Sorcha's eyes. *Ah goddess, don't do that,* she thought. She would never get through the thing without sobbing herself, else.

"The color of a person's robes ties the stone colors together and shows the direction of the person's life," Sorcha said in her ritual voice. "Orla of the Clans, you have earned a color that is rare and precious. And I for one know you'll do it justice."

Orla saw the copper-haired Kieran approach through the crowd. She saw that he carried something.

White.

Instinctively Orla reached back for Liam. He took her hand in his.

No. I can't.

Her mother must have heard her, for she approached, her face serene, her eyes bright. She came to stand next to Sorcha. Kieran reached her other side, and finally the gathered fairies saw the color of the gown. A gasp went up, followed by a moment of profound silence.

"Orla," Sorcha said, and her voice was a bit wavery, "each stone you wear is for a different skill, but their powers weave together to show leadership—just as *you* have shown, in the most dire time in our history. It is time to complete the color naming. Come take your robes, Orla, and wear them with pride."

She couldn't move. She held on to Liam as if he were the only thing keeping her upright. She had a suspicion he was.

What do I do? she asked in her head.

She could hear him laughing. *You accept, you daft woman.*

She turned. She saw that, goddess, there were tears in his eyes, too.

"You thought I'd sent you to exile to punish you," Mab said, bringing Orla's attention back again. "Just as Sorcha thought *her* task was punishment, and Nuala thought my challenge to her husband was punishment for *her*." She shot a quick look at Kieran. "Why, didn't even the seer doubt the queen's wisdom? It was in peril, I'll not deny it. But didn't I know that the world was at risk and that only the strongest of us could be leaders? Didn't I know that the test had to be severe?" And finally, unbelievably, she smiled, and it was happy. "And didn't each of my daughters succeed even beyond what I'd hoped?"

"A test?" was all Orla could think to say.

The queen's smile grew sly. "Well, maybe a *little* punishment. But you can't look at your husband and tell me *he* was a punishment. And sure, don't I think he feels the same about you? And as pure benefit for us all, didn't you prove to the entire realm of faerie that you are worthy of being queen?"

Orla couldn't breathe. This couldn't be happening.

Mab spread her arms. "Even better," she said, "my good friend Cathal has agreed to my request that I have my daughter back."

There was a rustling among the *Dubhlainn Sidhe*. "To keep the balance we fought so hard to find," Cathal said, "we need a strong queen of the *Tuatha de Dannan*. Come get your robes, girl."

Orla still wouldn't have moved if Liam hadn't pushed her.

But there were Sorcha and Nuala ready to help her change right there on the border where she'd lost her last colors so long ago, it seemed. And here with her this time was her Liam, who'd helped her gain these.

"I go to the West as soon as I introduce my daughter Orla to her new office," the queen said. "It is my time. And a time now for a new Mab. I name Orla of the Clans to be queen after me."

For a second the silence held. Orla kept her gaze locked with Liam's. It was too much. She wasn't sure anymore that she even wanted it.

But there in his eyes was the answer. *He* believed she could do it. He would support her and protect her and let her stand alone as she needed.

The robes slipped over her head as if they'd only been gone a bit. She looked down and was dazzled by them, a silvery sheen to the white that caught the eye in the late-afternoon sun. She brushed her hands over the silken material, and her rings flashed green, blue and that wonderful milky white. And then, taking a deep, steadying breath, she stepped away from her sisters.

The fairies all waited. Even the trees waited, and the winds from the mountains. Orla straightened. She turned to her mother.

"If it is your will, my lady, I will accept." The crowd readied itself to celebrate. "But on one condition."

Even Mab was slack-jawed. "A condition, is it?"

Orla smiled at her mother. "Well, aren't you the one who sent me to learn the lessons of statecraft with another clan, then?"

The queen wasn't nearly as amused as Orla. "And the lesson you brought back demands a condition?"

"Balance," Orla said. "Sure, haven't we all seen the cost of imbalance, be it in our realm or in our clan? Haven't we suffered too much from it already? Well, just as I'd want my husband to consider me his equal in all things, so do I consider him *my* equal. I will not rule the *Tuatha de Dannan* if Liam the Protector does not rule alongside me. Equally. And I sincerely hope that when my lord Cathal follows you to the West, his son will have Aifric stand at his side as he guides the *Dubh-lainn Sidhe*."

She heard Liam draw a surprised breath behind her, but she ignored him. He had no choice, really. She would tell him why when they were alone. For now, she just held on to his hand with her suddenly damp one.

Mab looked at Cathal. Cathal looked at Owain. Aifric just looked stunned. Finally Mab shook her head, looking pleased. "Well, didn't you learn more over there than even I'd anticipated? The throne is yours to do with as you want, girl. I wouldn't have handed it over if I didn't trust you to care well for it. And as my gift to you, I've left your sisters who can help, for won't Sorcha act as adviser and Nuala as plenipotentiary to the realm of mortals, who we might just need, as well?"

Orla's head was spinning. "You'll let Nuala go back and forth? Is it possible?"

The queen gave her a dry smile. "Sure, don't we have a seer who's doing it already?"

Orla turned to Cathal. "And the amity between the two clans is restored? We both can come and go as we please?" She looked back at Liam, then at Aifric and Tullia, and at all the women she'd met and grown to love in her husband's world. "Sure, there's too much to learn from each other to stay apart, don't you think?"

Cathal, still a bit distracted, nodded. "I do. We welcome the *Tuatha* and hope they do the same for us."

Orla was smiling at Aifric now. "They will. You can be sure of it."

And that was it. She was to be queen. She was to be

the Mab, her lifelong dream. Her obsession. But what she had once thought she would feel at this moment was missing. There was no pride. No triumph. But sure, wasn't she surprised at how many times a person could feel humbled and not resent it? And, she guessed, that was probably a good thing, especially for a queen.

Goddess. A *queen!*

She didn't even notice when the cheering started, for she'd already turned back to Liam to step into his arms. His smile was as big as those mountains he'd patrolled as he returned the favor.

"Will you come with me into my world, Liam?" she asked.

He laughed. "Ah sure, *now* you ask. What if I'm wanting to wander those lonely mountains with Faolán and the lads?"

She tilted her head. "As long as you come back to me. I can't do this alone, Liam. I can't do it without you."

"But why as equals?" he asked, and Orla saw that he was sincerely perplexed. "The office is yours, and haven't you earned it?"

And it was because he was perplexed that she knew her decision was right. Faith, how could you not love a man who seemed confused by your thinking he was the best man in two realms?

So she reached up her ring-bedecked hands and cupped his dear, harshly crafted face between them. And while the rest of the fairy realm began the celebration they'd really come here for, she had eyes only for him.

"Because I love you," she said.

"That's not enough, and you know it, *mo stor.*"

"And because I trust you," she answered, knowing her heart was in her eyes. "I trust you with my life. More important, *mo chuisla,* with my honor and my heart. And with my people."

Never had she seen such a light in a man's eyes. At once glad and overwhelmed and awed. Never had she thought she would see that light turned on her. Tears filled her own eyes and slid down her cheeks even as she smiled, as he laid his hands against her own to hold her to him. As he slowly, never looking away, enfolded her once again in his powerful arms and held her gently, as a good man did. As he tried three times to get the words out.

"Ah, well, I guess we're going to be after moving soon." He sighed, and she heard the wicked amusement. "And we'd just gotten the place decorated."

Orla couldn't help it. She laughed. "Sure, we'll just bring it all along with us. Besides, Deirdre's begun working on her own stone gifts, and trust me, husband, they're no better than mine."

"She wants to be horsemaster."

"She'll be mother to the next *Dubhlainn* king."

Liam pulled back. "What?"

And Orla smiled, certain. "Ah, well, I must have the gift of the sight, after all. For can't I see her directing everyone in that great hall with her children smiling on?"

Liam shook his head. "Well, that's a worry for another day. Today, it's time to acknowledge your colors, for they were well earned, girl, and you deserve a celebration."

Orla peeked around Liam's shoulder to see the population of both clans spinning in a mad dance to the sound of the pipes and fiddles and whistles. Whiskey flowed, and children clustered around the *bean tighe,* who was telling them stories. There was laughter and joy and the satisfaction of a peace hard won.

Aye, she would join them, for it was her triumph, too. But later. For now, she had only one person she wanted to celebrate with.

Turning back to her husband, she smiled. He smiled back.

"The river?" he asked.

Her smile was pure seduction. "The river."

That night, in the world of mortals, strange music was heard in the glens near Lisdoonvarna. Lights flitted along old fairy paths, and startled animals wandered over to the noise. The trees whispered among themselves, and a couple who wandered down by the river swore later they heard giggling and splashing. But there was nothing for the mortals to see, so they shook their heads, went inside and closed their doors.

In the land of faerie, the celebration went on through the night and many more to come. A queen had been crowned. An old one stepped through the portal to the seas to the West, and a new generation was welcomed. The realms had been once again secured, and the great creator stones returned. The life of faerie went on. And out along the sharp spines of the MacGillicuddy Reeks, men of the *Coimirceoiri* stood their watch alongside *Tuatha* warriors, for that was the price paid for the endless fairy dance.

* * * * *

Chapter 1

October
New York City

Nicole Masters was sitting cross-legged on her sofa while a cold autumn rain peppered the windows of her fourth-floor apartment. She was poking at the ice cream in her bowl and trying not to be in a mood.

Six weeks ago, a simple trip to her neighborhood pharmacy had turned into a nightmare. She'd walked into the middle of a robbery. She never even saw the man who shot her in the head and left her for dead. She'd survived, but some of her senses had not. She was dealing with short-term memory loss and a tendency to stagger. Even though she'd been told the problems were most likely temporary, she waged a daily battle with depression.

Her parents had been killed in a car wreck when she was

twenty-one. And except for a few friends—and most recently her boyfriend, Dominic Tucci, who lived in the apartment right above hers, she was alone. Her doctor kept reminding her that she should be grateful to be alive, and on one level she knew he was right. But he wasn't living in her shoes.

If she'd been anywhere else but at that pharmacy when the robbery happened, she wouldn't have died twice on the way to the hospital. Instead of being grateful that she'd survived, she couldn't stop thinking of what she'd lost.

But that wasn't the end of her troubles. On top of everything else, something strange was happening inside her head. She'd begun to hear odd things: sounds, not voices—at least, she didn't think it was voices. It was more like the distant noise of rapids—a rush of wind and water inside her head that, when it came, blocked out everything around her. It didn't happen often, but when it did, it was frightening, and it was driving her crazy.

The blank moments, which is what she called them, even had a rhythm. First there came that sound, then a cold sweat, then panic with no reason. Part of her feared it was the beginning of an emotional breakdown. And part of her feared it wasn't—that it was going to turn out to be a permanent souvenir of her resurrection.

Frustrated with herself and the situation as it stood, she upped the sound on the TV remote. But instead of *Wheel of Fortune,* an announcer broke in with a special bulletin.

"This just in. Police are on the scene of a kidnapping that occurred only hours ago at The Dakota. Molly Dane, the six-year-old daughter of one of Hollywood's blockbuster stars, Lyla Dane, was taken by force from the family apartment. At this time they have yet to receive a ransom demand. The house-keeper was seriously injured during the abduction, and is, at the present time, in surgery. Police are hoping to be able to talk to her once she regains con-sciousness. In the meantime, we are going now to a press conference with Lyla Dane."

Horrified, Nicole stilled as the cameras went live to where the actress was speaking before a bank of micro-phones. The shock and terror in Lyla Dane's voice were physically painful to watch. But even though Nicole kept upping the volume, the sound continued to fade.

Just when she was beginning to think something was wrong with her set, the broadcast suddenly switched from the Dane press conference to what appeared to be footage of the kidnapping, beginning with footage from inside the apartment.

When the front door suddenly flew back against the wall and four men rushed in, Nicole gasped. Horrified, she quickly realized that this must have been caught on a security camera inside the Dane apartment.

As Nicole continued to watch, a small Asian woman, who she guessed was the maid, rushed forward in an effort to keep them out. When one of the men hit her in the face with his gun, Nicole moaned. The violence was too remi-niscent of what she'd lived through. Sick to her stomach, she fisted her hands against her belly, wishing it was over, but unable to tear her gaze away.

When the maid dropped to the carpet, the same man followed with a vicious kick to the little woman's midsec-tion that lifted her off the floor.

"Oh, my God," Nicole said. When blood began to pool beneath the maid's head, she started to cry.

As the tape played on, the four men split up in different directions. The camera caught one running down a
long marble hallway, then disappearing into a room.
Moments later he reappeared, carrying a little girl, who
Nicole assumed was Molly Dane. The child was wearing
a pair of red pants and a white turtleneck sweater, and her
hair was partially blocking her abductor's face as he carried
her down the hall. She was kicking and screaming in his
arms, and when he slapped her, it elicited an agonized
scream that brought the other three running. Nicole
watched in horror as one of them ran up and put his hand
over Molly's face. Seconds later, she went limp.

One moment they were in the foyer, then they were gone.

Nicole jumped to her feet, then staggered drunkenly.
The bowl of ice cream she'd absentmindedly placed in her
lap shattered at her feet, splattering glass and melting ice
cream everywhere.

The picture on the screen abruptly switched from the kidnapping to what Nicole assumed was a rerun of Lyla Dane's
plea for her daughter's safe return, but she was numb.

Before she could think what to do next, the doorbell
rang. Startled by the unexpected sound, she shakily swiped
at the tears and took a step forward. She didn't feel the glass
shards piercing her feet until she took the second step. At
that point, sharp pains shot through her foot. She gasped,
then looked down in confusion. Her legs looked as if she'd
been running through mud, and she was standing in broken
glass and ice cream, while a thin ribbon of blood seeped
out from beneath her toes.

"Oh, no," Nicole mumbled, then stifled a second
moan of pain.

The doorbell rang again. She shivered, then clutched her
head in confusion.

"Just a minute!" she yelled, then tried to sidestep the rest of the debris as she hobbled to the door.

When she looked through the peephole in the door, she didn't know whether to be relieved or regretful.

It was Dominic, and as usual, she was a mess.

Nicole smiled a little self-consciously as she opened the door to let him in. "I just don't know what's happening to me. I think I'm losing my mind."

"Hey, don't talk about my woman like that."

Nicole rode the surge of delight his words brought. "So I'm still your woman?"

Dominic lowered his head.

Their lips met.

The kiss proceeded.

Slowly.

Thoroughly.

* * * * *

Be sure to look for the **AFTERSHOCK** *anthology next month, as well as other exciting paranormal stories from Silhouette Nocturne.*
Available in October wherever books are sold.

nocturne™

NEW YORK TIMES BESTSELLING AUTHOR

SHARON SALA

JANIS REAMES HUDSON
DEBRA COWAN

AFTERSHOCK

Three women are brought to the brink of death...
only to discover the aftershock of their trauma has
left them with unexpected and unwelcome gifts of
paranormal powers. Now each woman must learn to
accept her newfound abilities while fighting for life,
love and second chances....

Available October wherever books are sold.

www.eHarlequin.com
www.paranormalromanceblog.wordpress.com   SN61796

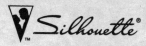

Silhouette®

ROMANTIC SUSPENSE

Sparked by Danger, Fueled by Passion.

USA TODAY bestselling author

Merline Lovelace

Undercover Wife

CODENAME: DANGER

Secret agent Mike Callahan, code name Hawkeye,
objects when he's paired with sophisticated
Gillian Ridgeway on a dangerous spy mission
to Hong Kong. Gillian has secretly been in love
with him for years, but Hawk is an overprotective
man with a wounded past that threatens to
resurface. Now the two must put their lives—
and hearts—at risk for each other.

Available October wherever books are sold.

SRS27601

REQUEST YOUR
FREE BOOKS!

2 FREE NOVELS PLUS 2 FREE GIFTS!

Silhouette®

nocturne™

Dramatic and Sensual Tales of Paranormal Romance.

YES! Please send me 2 FREE Silhouette® Nocturne™ novels and my 2 FREE gifts (gifts are worth about $10). After receiving them, if I don't wish to receive any more books, I can return the shipping statement marked "cancel." If I don't cancel, I will receive 4 brand-new novels every other month and be billed just $4.47 per book in the U.S. or $4.99 per book in Canada, plus 25¢ shipping and handling per book plus applicable taxes, if any*. That's a savings of about 15% off the cover price! I understand that accepting the 2 free books and gifts places me under no obligation to buy anything. I can always return a shipment and cancel at any time. Even if I never buy another book from Silhouette, the two free books and gifts are mine to keep forever.

238 SDN ELS4 338 SDN ELXG

Name	(PLEASE PRINT)
Address	Apt. #
City	State/Prov.	Zip/Postal Code

Signature (if under 18, a parent or guardian must sign)

Mail to the **Silhouette Reader Service:**
IN U.S.A.: P.O. Box 1867, Buffalo, NY 14240-1867
IN CANADA: P.O. Box 609, Fort Erie, Ontario L2A 5X3

Not valid to current subscribers of Silhouette Nocturne books.

Want to try two free books from another line?
Call 1-800-873-8635 or visit www.morefreebooks.com.

* Terms and prices subject to change without notice. N.Y. residents add applicable sales tax. Canadian residents will be charged applicable provincial taxes and GST. Offer not valid in Quebec. This offer is limited to one order per household. All orders subject to approval. Credit or debit balances in a customer's account(s) may be offset by any other outstanding balance owed by or to the customer. Please allow 4 to 6 weeks for delivery. Offer available while quantities last.

Your Privacy: Silhouette is committed to protecting your privacy. Our Privacy Policy is available online at www.eHarlequin.com or upon request from the Reader Service. From time to time we make our lists of customers available to reputable third parties who may have a product or service of interest to you. If you would prefer we not share your name and address, please check here. ☐

SN08R

nocturne™

COMING NEXT MONTH

#49 AFTERSHOCK • Sharon Sala, Janis Reams Hudson, Debra Cowan

Don't miss these captivating tales of how life-threatening accidents vest three ordinary women with extraordinary powers. In "Penance," a gunshot wound provides Nicole Masters with the unusual ability to tune in to people in jeopardy. Now she and her boyfriend, Detective Dominic Tucci, team up to rescue an innocent child before time runs out.

In "After the Lightning," Hailey Cameron starts hearing voices in her head after being struck by lightning. Can former police detective Aaron Trent now help her channel this ability to stop an underground child- smuggling ring?

And in "Seeing Red," a near-death experience has firefighter Cass Holister witnessing fires before they happen. But it's proving harder to deal with Ben Wyrick, who is investigating the blazes, than it is to handle her new talent....

#50 VEILED TRUTH • Vivi Anna
The Valorian Chronicles

Not even her skills as a witch can help one of Necropolis's best crime-scene investigators, Lyra Magice, solve a series of gruesome and bizarre murders. Who is behind these horrific crimes, and why? Then Lyra discovers an ancient text owned by dark witch Theron Lenoir. Lyra has every reason to distrust Theron. But with the threat of a gateway to hell opening, it's imperative that the two find a common ground....

SNCNM0908